PRAISE
PERFECT LITTLE

T0247076

"Fast-paced, dark, with a twist that satisfied my evil side, He's debut is a showstopper!"

—Jesse Q. Sutanto, bestselling author of
The Obsession and *The New Girl*

"This tense and twisty thriller will keep readers looking over their shoulder."

—Natalie D. Richards, *New York Times* bestselling
author of *Five Total Strangers*

"*Perfect Little Monsters* is a viciously shocking examination of bullying with an ending that will leave you floored. A riveting debut you won't want to miss!"

—Chelsea Ichaso, author of *Dead Girls Can't
Tell Secrets* and *They're Watching You*

"With characters you'll love to hate and a twist that you won't see coming, Cindy R. X. He's debut thriller *Perfect Little Monsters* is a book that will keep readers up all night. He deftly weaves the past with the present to create questions you'll only think you know the answer to. A shocking delight."

—Jessie Weaver, author of *Live Your Best Lie*

"*Perfect Little Monsters* is a heart-pounding, harrowing, and twisty tale about the legacy of bullying and cruelty and its devastating consequences. An extraordinary debut from an extraordinary talent."

—Alex Finlay, author of *Every Last Fear*
and *The Night Shift*

"A dark, voicey, and inventive debut from an explosive new talent. Prepare to be captivated from start to pulse-pounding finish, and blown away by the many twists and turns. *Perfect Little Monsters* is at once a fast-paced thriller and a thoughtful, incisive look at the impact of bullying."

—Laurie Elizabeth Flynn, author of *The Girls Are All So Nice Here* and *All Eyes on Her*

Perfect Little Monsters

CINDY R. X. HE

sourcebooks fire

For the misfits:
you are beautiful,
you are loved.

Published by Sourcebooks Fire, an imprint of Sourcebooks
P.O. Box 4410, Naperville, Illinois 60567–4410
(630) 961-3900
sourcebooks.com

Cataloging-in-Publication Data is on file with the Library of Congress.

Printed and bound in the United States of America.
LSC 10 9 8 7 6 5 4 3 2 1

HIDE AND SEEK

NOW

The soft, tuneless whistling drifts over to where she's hiding, as she crouches in the dark closet, peeking through the slats.

She hadn't known how loud simply breathing was. Surely the person hunting her can hear her panicked, shallow breaths—and her too-loud heartbeat, thumping against her ribs like a frantic trapped bird. To make things worse, it's so dusty that she's going to sneeze. She pinches her nose, fights the deadly urge. Sweat trickles down her back, like the faint caress of ghostly fingers.

Her eyelids droop closed…but she snaps them open again. She focuses her eyes on the narrow line of light pooling under the closed bedroom door. She must not fall asleep. Absolutely cannot sink into the darkness that is threatening to engulf her. But she can feel how heavy her limbs are, heavy and clumsy with the drug slushing through her bloodstream. She pinches her left arm hard, twists the tender skin to keep herself awake.

A nightmare. That's what this is. Even so, she can't quite believe that this is happening, that someone is trying to *kill* her. Surely, she'll wake up soon in her queen-sized bed with its eight-hundred-thread-count Egyptian cotton sheets. The muscle in her right calf seizes in a painful cramp from crouching for so long, and she stifles another sob.

It's so unfair. She doesn't deserve this, no matter what she did. The punishment is too harsh! She could cry from the injustice of it. A sob bubbles up from her chest to her throat, and she clamps her shaking hands over her mouth to keep it from escaping. Her mind is shrieking, but she mustn't make a peep because the smallest sound would give away her hiding place in a second. And then this game of hide-and-seek would be over. *The end. You lose. Time to die.*

Soft, deliberate footsteps now, in the corridor. That insane, tuneless whistling. The footsteps grow louder…and louder…until they stop just outside. There is a shadow under the door. She watches through the slats as the knob turns slowly…

But she's locked the door from the inside! The knob stops turning, and she's almost giddy with relief. She starts to smile…

But then there's the unmistakable *scritch scratch* of a key entering the keyhole. The bedroom door swings open, and that horrible whistling starts up again. She tears herself away from the slats, scrambles backward into the darkness at the back of the closet. Shrinks into a small ball, her knees pressed against her chin. *Nonono, I can't die like this can't die like this can't—*

The closet doors open. She looks up at the person standing over her trembling body. The whistling stops.

"Found you."

Those empty eyes.

That awful smile.

The dull gleam of the carving knife.

She opens her mouth and screams.

DAWN

TWO MONTHS AGO

The bell for the first class is going to ring soon. But I'm still sitting on the closed lid of the toilet in a stall in the girls' restroom on the second floor of Sierton High. I can't seem to make myself get up. My head is lowered almost to my knees as I try not to hyperventilate.

I'm still safe for now in here, where no one can see me. But once I step out…who knows what might happen? Not for the first time, the feeling that my being here is a mistake rears its head… but I push it away quickly. *I'm a new person. Nobody knows me here.* I try to focus on what my mom told me—her warm brown eyes crinkling in the corners like they always do when she smiles— before I left the house with Aunt Maddy this morning: *Everything will be fine, you'll see. I know you'll do us proud.*

I try to take slow, even breaths. Okay, I think I'm okay now. I get up, unlatch the door.

I've just taken a step toward the sinks when the door swings open and hits the wall with a loud *bang*. Three girls enter: one with hair so blond it has to be very expensive and high maintenance, her waist-high shorts showing off her long coltish legs; the second a pretty Latina girl with long-lashed dark eyes and black hair flat-ironed to shiny perfection, in a trendy cropped top and lululemon leggings; and then possibly the prettiest one of them, half-Caucasian, half-Asian, with caramel doe eyes and impossibly perfect glowing skin, in an expensive-looking minidress and cashmere cardigan. I recognize them. I know them because I'm like them.

They stare at me, and my heart starts beating triple time as I walk self-consciously past them to the sink and start washing my hands. I can see them checking me out in the mirror out of the corner of my eyes. Their eyes travel over my appearance too, taking in my hair, my face, my clothes, my bag. They're curious because I look like them, like I could be part of their clique. I could be their friend…or a possible rival.

Thing is: I might look like them, and once upon a time, stuff like being popular or being part of this friend group was important to me too. But not anymore.

Luckily, they soon lose interest in me. The Latina turns her attention back to the girl with the white-blond hair. "What's wrong with my leggings?" It sounds like a continuation of whatever conversation they were having before they entered the bathroom.

"Oh, nothing." The blond girl smirks. "It's just that color makes your legs look *thick*. But if you like them, that's what matters, I suppose." She turns to the mirror, inspects her flawless makeup.

"Oh come on, Ella," interjects the third girl, rolling her eyes. "Don't listen to her, Lucy. *I* think they look great on you."

The door swings open again, and another girl enters the increasingly claustrophobic space. She flinches as the three girls check *her* out, then she disappears quickly into a stall.

Ella reaches in her bag, pulls out a mascara wand. The other two fuss with their hair, their clothes. I head over as unobtrusively as I can to the paper towel dispenser, grab a sheet, and start drying my hands. Throw the used paper towel into the bin. Slink toward the door.

I've almost succeeded in making my escape when one of them says, "Are you new here? You don't look like a freshman."

I guess the problem with a small town like Sierton, Wisconsin, is people notice when you're new. Reluctantly, I turn around to face her, and nod. "I'm a senior. I just transferred here."

Ella pulls something else out of her bag and starts to touch up her lip gloss. I'm shifting my weight from foot to foot, not sure if the conversation is over and I can leave, or if they want to say anything else to me, when the girl in the stall comes back out.

The vibe in the bathroom is weird now. Lucy snickers, then Ella says, "Stop staring at me."

The fourth girl's brown skin flushes. "I'm not—"

"You totally are. Look, I'm not interested, okay?" says the blond girl, rolling her eyes. Then she sashays out, followed closely by her two friends, who mutter *lesbo* before the bathroom door slams shut behind them.

The girl walks to the sink, turns on the tap with a slightly trembling hand.

"Are you okay?" I say.

"I'm fine," she says curtly, not looking at me, but she's still trembling. "Those girls…Ella Moore, Naomi Chen, and Luciana Aguilar…let's just say you don't want to get on their bad side."

"I sensed that," I say. "I'm Dawn."

She finally turns to me and smiles shyly, revealing turquoise braces on her teeth. It's like the sun breaking through storm clouds. But she still doesn't make eye contact with me. "I'm Raquel. You don't sound like you're from around here. I mean, you have a slight accent. Where did you transfer from?"

"Oh, California. Santa Cruz."

"I'm a senior too. Wow, transferring to a new school senior year sucks."

"Yeah." I don't tell her *why* I transferred here. I don't tell her because I can't bear to see the pity that will inevitably pass over her face, a look that I've seen too often recently.

Raquel is staring at me. Maybe my expression changed, and she noticed. Luckily, she doesn't ask any more questions.

A bell rings somewhere very loudly.

"Guess we'd better get to class." says Raquel, moving toward the door.

"Hey, um…could you tell me where class 2B is?"

CINDY R. X. HE

"Oh, you're taking American Lit? Me too!" Raquel nods. "Follow me."

I think I might have made my first friend here.

———

The cafeteria is easy to find at lunch; I just follow the laughter and chatter of hundreds of voices. The smells of onion and burnt bologna hit me as soon as I step through the double swinging doors.

I line up and grab a greasy-looking slice of pepperoni pizza—which I have no intention of eating—an apple, and orange juice. I scan the room, my stomach queasy with nerves. Where to sit? Then I spot Raquel sitting alone at a table in the far corner. Is she waiting for some friends, or does she normally sit alone?

"Hi again." I nod at the empty seat across from her. "Is it okay if I join you?"

"Oh, um. Yeah, sure." She seems surprised but pleased.

She must be as bad at small talk as me, because we eat in awkward silence for a while until she clears her throat. "So...why did you transfer here?"

I look down, stare at a small stain on the table. It looks like a kidney bean. "Um. I moved in with my aunt. She lives here," I mumble. "My parents...they lost their jobs. We had to sell our apartment." All because of the car accident. We also don't have a car anymore because my parents' car was totaled. Good thing Aunt

Maddy chauffeurs me to school every day, because I now have panic attacks if I try to drive.

After a few minutes, Raquel breaks the silence. "Sorry, I tend to be too direct. It's the autism."

I muster a smile. "Don't apologize! It's okay."

"I've never been to California. What's Santa Cruz like?"

Grateful for the change of subject, I answer quickly. "Sunny. I guess it'll take me a while to get used to how much colder it is here."

She takes in my dark blond sun-streaked hair, blue-green eyes, and tanned skin. "So do you, like, surf and everything?"

"A little, but I'm not very good at it."

She peppers me with friendly questions and tells me more about herself too. I learn that she's biracial, Black and Chinese, and that her favorite class is Computer Science.

While Raquel chatters on about the merits of living in Wisconsin versus California (apparently while Wisconsin's low cost of living is a plus, Cali is the most diverse state with a diversity score of 70.75), my gaze wanders around the rest of the cafeteria...landing on a long table in the middle of the large room and the fifteen or so people sitting there. They are ostensibly better looking than the rest of us. The guys are more muscled; some of them are wearing the same navy blue and orange letter jackets. They must be on the football team. And the girls are all white teeth, shiny hair, and muscular long limbs.

The three scary girls from this morning are among them. The one with white-blond hair—Ella—is sitting beside a tall, athletic-looking boy with dark blond hair and deep blue eyes. She's feeding her boyfriend a fry, teasing him afterward by licking her fingers.

Nobody from that table is looking over at us, so I'm free to observe them all I like.

Every once in a while, Ella glances over at another table in the corner—the briefest glance—before looking away. And every time, the strangest expression floats over her face—anger...mixed with something else?—before she composes herself again as she turns away. Maybe she isn't even aware that she's doing it. Or maybe she is but she can't help herself, even if she doesn't want to be caught looking.

Curious, I check out the table that she seems so interested in. There are three people sitting there: a girl dressed all in black, her face decorated with several piercings and pimples; a guy with green spiky hair, who is talking and gesticulating wildly; and a pale lanky boy, who is scowling at his food. His messy dark brown hair looks like it needs a good cut, and his clothes are ill fitting, his jeans ending too high over his ankles, like he suddenly grew several inches over the summer but didn't bother to get new clothes. A surprising tattoo on his neck peeks out just above the collar of his worn-looking jacket, jarringly incongruous with how the rest of him looks.

"Who are they?" I ask, jerking my head over at their table.

Raquel peers at them. "I don't really know the girl or the guy with the green hair, but the other guy is Isaac Caldwell. They always sit only with each other. I used to have a class with Isaac. He's always been quiet, but even more so after…" Her voice trails off.

"After what?"

"After what happened two years ago," she says in a hushed voice.

"What happened?"

"Wow, he's really grown over the summer," says Raquel, either not hearing me, or choosing not to answer my question. She squints at the poor boy who is completely unaware that he's being discussed. "He looks a bit different. Not as skinny."

Interesting. Is Ella sneaking looks at *him*? Curious, I look back at her to see if she'll do it again.

Raquel sees where I'm looking and sighs. "It's such a cliché, isn't it? It's like living in every Hollywood high school movie. At least the cheerleaders from previous years were alright. Pity they've graduated. These ones are so *bitchy*. It's Ella, you know. She brings out the worst in everyone. Anyway, who cares? Five years from now, none of this will matter." She pops a fry in her mouth. "What are you going to choose for your extracurricular?"

I mumble something, and she shakes her head. "What's that? I didn't catch what you said."

"Cheerleading," I mumble again, a little louder.

Raquel stops chewing. My face starts getting hot as she stares at me, and the words "I was a cheerleader back in Santa Cruz" stumble reluctantly out of my mouth.

"Oh, I might have guessed," she finally says.

"Why?"

"Well, I mean, you already look like them."

I don't know what to reply to that, so I keep quiet.

Raquel casts me a sideways look. Her face is flushed now. "Maybe forget what I said about those three earlier this morning."

"I'm not going to tell them what you said," I say quickly. "Besides, I might not get on the squad anyway."

Awkward silence as we finish our food, each carefully not looking at the other. Until Raquel blurts out, "Why did you first join cheerleading? Not being snarky. I'm genuinely curious."

"My mom was a cheerleader, and it made her happy that I was one too."

"That makes sense." Her brown skin flushes again. "Sorry for my earlier reaction."

"Don't worry about it," I say hastily.

I know that I don't *have* to join cheerleading again. But I want to make squad. I want to because it would make my mom happy.

And I would do anything for them to be happy again after the accident.

The accident that left my dad hideously scarred, and my mom never able to walk again.

DAWN

After my last class, I head to the gym to sign up for cheer tryouts. All the other girls trying out look to be freshman; I'm the only one who isn't, which makes sense. My stomach sinks when I realize that one of the "mean" girls from this morning is the person in charge of registrations.

I brace myself as she focuses her eyes on me. "Dawn Foster… the new transfer student, right?"

"Um…yeah." My palms are starting to sweat, something that happens every time I'm anxious. *Don't panic.* I wipe them as discreetly as I can on the side of my jeans.

"I'm Naomi." She takes an even closer look at me. "Why do you want to join the squad?"

"I was a cheerleader at Harbor Valley High in Santa Cruz before transferring here."

Naomi does a double take that's almost funny, and suddenly her tone is warmer. "Oh! The routine should be easy for you then."

I don't really know how to reply other than "I just hope I'll make the team."

"If you've already been cheering, I don't see why you shouldn't. Good luck!"

"Thanks." My hand is shaking slightly as I fill out the registration form while Naomi looks on. Then she hands me a tryout pack, and I hurry away as she turns her attention to the next person.

Over the next two days, I learn the basic cheer routine by heart, practice it over and over. Once, I would have been confident of nailing it, but I'm not as good as I used to be before the accident.

Wednesday in American Lit, Raquel nudges my foot with hers. "Hey, relax. You'll make it."

My anxiety about tryouts later must be showing. I make myself stop fidgeting and smile back at her. "I wish I were as confident as you are of me, but thanks."

"And forget what I said on Monday," she continues. "I can see cheerleading is important to you. So I hope you make it."

Raquel comes with me to the bulletin board the next day, her steadying presence by my side as I peer at the list posted there, sweaty palms clutching my elbows. There are only eight names on it; I scan it quickly and locate mine almost immediately, third from the top.

HETTY BROWN.

RITA DAVIS.

DAWN FOSTER.

I made it.

"Guess you're going to stop being friends with me now."

Raquel's delivery makes it hard for me to tell if she's joking or serious, and I bite my lip. "Don't be silly. Of course we're still going to be friends."

"Oh yeah?" Her eyes don't leave my face. "So you're still going to sit with me at lunch?"

"Of course," I say.

But as soon as we step into the cafeteria, the cheerleaders wave at me, beckon me over to their table. I turn to look at Raquel. She stares back at me. *What are you going to do?* her eyes seem to say.

"Hey, Foster," Naomi calls, tilting her head. "Saved you a seat."

Beside her, the other cheerleaders and football players are staring at me now. I can't help it; I take a step toward their table almost unconsciously. Behind me, Raquel whispers *It's okay, go* and gives me a little shove, and my feet keep moving until I'm at their table. The table where Sierton High's social elite reign, and where I'm probably going to be eaten alive.

"Hey!" Lucy chirps as I place my tray at the end of the table and sit down. "I'm Lucy! Dawn, right? I saw you at tryouts yesterday. You were really good!"

"Thank you," I say.

"Naomi told us you were a cheerleader at your old school, I forget which one," says Ella.

"Yeah, at Harbor Valley High. Santa Cruz."

She continues staring at me, frowning a little, and my palms start sweating again.

"Have I seen you before? You look a bit familiar," she says.

"She does!" pipes Lucy, also staring at me. "You're very pretty. Are you a YouTuber or something? Or a TikToker?"

Everyone is acting so nice, it's alarming. I laugh nervously and shake my head. "No way. I mean, I have accounts, but just for watching videos."

"You *are* very pretty." Ella smiles at me with all her teeth showing, like a shark. They're so white. She must have them bleached regularly, like her hair. "I love your hair. It's so golden. And shiny."

"Um…thank you. I love *your* hair," I say.

The other two girls are watching this exchange with interest, their heads swiveling back and forth between us like spectators watching two tennis players battle it out on the court. I realize with dismay that I'm fidgeting, jittering my right foot and picking at the cuticle on my left thumb, and I make myself stop. I'm starting to sweat all over, especially under my arms, despite the deodorant I swiped on in the morning.

"It's great that you were a cheerleader at your old school. But you should know that some things may be different here." Ella continues, a little bit softer this time. The sweetness of her voice barely masks the sharp warning in her words. *I'm number one here; keep that in mind if you want to fit in.*

"Yes, of course, I understand," I say hastily, lowering my eyes. *No problem, I know my place.* I don't blame her. Every school has that girl, and of course she wants to make sure the newcomer she welcomes graciously into the fold knows it. Satisfied, she turns her attention back to the guy beside her, who I soon learn is named Scott.

Lucy nudges me. "I should have known as soon as I first saw you that you cheered."

"Oh? Why?"

"You've got the look. How do you do that?" She eyes the fries on my tray.

"Do what?"

"Eat like that and stay thin. Seriously though, are you going to eat all that? Can I steal some?"

"Oh, of course," I say, and she takes a few fries and puts them in her mouth.

"Anyway, you should have told us earlier. Then you could have sat with us instead of with that reject." She points her chin at the table where Raquel is sitting and shudders, prompting a round of giggles from several people around us.

Annoyance prickles my throat, and the words tumble out before I can stop them. "I didn't mind sitting with her. She's nice."

Lucy frowns. *Wrong reply.* "You know she's obsessed with Ella, right?" She tilts her head to one side as she stares at me.

I stare back at her. "I don't think—"

"And she's so weird." She takes some more of my fries.

I can feel the back of my neck heating up. "She's not weird. She's autistic."

"She's *so* weird." Naomi giggles. "The other day in Calculus, someone asked her how she was, you know, like offhandedly, and she actually launched into a five-minute speech about how she was, as if anyone was really interested."

Lucy snorts, and she and Naomi start gossiping to each other, ignoring me now. I glance over to the table where Raquel is sitting and looking at me. She gives me a little thumbs-up. I resolve never to let her know what Lucy and Naomi just said.

"Oh my god," Lucy mutters suddenly, a horrified look on her face, breaking me out of my thoughts. "Why did I eat so many?" She shoots me a glare as if it's my fault, then she jumps up and walks out of the cafeteria so quickly she's almost running.

"Is something wrong?" I ask Naomi.

"She, uh, has a complicated relationship with food," says Naomi. "She's a bit insecure about her weight."

"She thinks it's the only way she can stay thin enough. And maybe it is." Ella shrugs. "Just pretend like you don't notice."

When Ella turns away again, I whisper to Naomi, "Why doesn't Lucy think she's thin enough?"

Naomi sneaks a look at Ella before replying, "She was a bit chubby when we were in grade school, and Ella has never really let her forget it."

When the bell rings and I've cleared my tray, I look around for Raquel, but she's already left the cafeteria. I text her when I'm at my locker:

I'm sorry

I wouldn't blame her if she doesn't reply or speak to me again. But my phone beeps a few minutes later:

It's fine. Wanna study together in the library after school?

Yes

I reply immediately, my heart lifting.

———

Practice is every day after school except Wednesdays. On nice days it's held on the side of the football field, not too far from where the guys are having football practice. The guys enjoy looking at us practice, and the girls enjoy the extra attention.

When it's raining like today, we practice in the dance studio—a large, brightly lit room with a padded floor and a wall of mirrors on one side—which we share with the dance team.

Ella is cheer captain, which I'd kind of guessed—even though she's not the best among the seniors. Naomi's motions are just a little neater, her tumbles more perfect than Ella's. Of course, the cheer captain is picked based on more than that—it also depends on who the coach thinks is the best girl for the position, and a team vote. This is where popularity comes in. Because of the team vote, it's usually the most popular girl who gets voted into becoming captain.

Surprisingly, even though Ella is captain, she doesn't seem to be the most popular girl on the team. I watch as Lucy and two other seniors gravitate to Naomi, gossiping and giggling with her, as Ella, her face stiff, pretends not to notice at first. After a few more minutes though, she faces them, her perfectly manicured right hand on her hip.

"Something funny you want to share with everyone, Naomi?" says Ella.

Naomi stops smiling immediately. "No, sorry," she says quietly, her skin turning slightly pink.

"What about the rest of you?"

The girls shake their heads quickly, looking like little children being chastised.

Ella smiles sweetly. "Then maybe we should work on the new routine like Coach said?"

When Ella turns her back, Naomi and Lucy exchange a quick look, which I pretend not to see.

After dinner, I'm just finishing my homework when there's a soft knock on my door. My parents enter my room, my dad wheeling my mom in her wheelchair slowly, with obvious effort. I resist the urge to jump up and help because they'd hate that.

The room I'm sleeping in used to be my dad's old room when he was a kid. My dad moved out after college when he found a job in sales—he's never going to sell anything again, not with his face disfigured from the accident—while Aunt Maddy never moved out, which makes sense since the accounting firm where she works is located in an office block just a fifteen-minute drive away. It's nice of her to let us move in now, when we have nowhere else to go.

The room hasn't changed much; the twin bed is the same one he used to sleep in, only with new white sheets; the walls are still navy with white shelves along one wall. Against another, a small study table in laminate wood painted a cheery yellow.

"How are things going at school? Everything okay?" asks my dad in a low voice. Aunt Maddy goes to bed early recently. She's been working long hours ever since someone in her department quit and she got saddled with that person's work too. From what I understand, her boss is an asshole. So at night, we keep our voices down so as not to disturb Maddy's rest.

"Everything's fine, Dad." I know they're worried after what happened. I wish they wouldn't be. Everything is going to be fine.

Dad looks around the room. "It's so much smaller than I remember." He furrows his brows. Only the right side of his face has an eyebrow now; the other side never grew back. "I'm sorry you had to move into my old room. It won't be for long, we promise."

"I know."

"I'm so proud of you for getting back in cheerleading. We both are," says my mom. She's going prematurely gray, her once luscious brown hair now streaked with white. "We know you're doing your best. And what happened wasn't your fault, remember that."

———

A week later, we're changing in the locker room after practice when Ella makes her announcement.

"Okay listen up, bitches, because my parents will be out of town this weekend. You know what that means."

"Another party? Aren't you worried your parents are going to catch you one day?" says Naomi.

"They won't, and even if they do, I don't care. What are they going to do? Ground me? I'm eighteen." says Ella.

"They might cut off your credit card," says Naomi, and Ella shoots her a glare.

"When?" asks Lucy.

"This Saturday. But I can't have my house messed up like the last time so it'll be a small one this time. So Lucy, Naomi, you two are invited. You too, Olivia, Cece, Nora. Not you, Gretchen, because I haven't forgotten how you and that guy you brought left that stain on my parents' bedsheets the last time."

Gretchen mutters something like *It was an accident* and slinks away as Ella tilts her head at me. "You can come too if you want, Dawn. Bring your bikini; it's going to be a pool party."

"Oh! Yes, okay!" I flush. It's great that I'm invited. My parents will be happy, and Aunt Maddy too. This'll help dispel some of their anxiety about whether I'm fitting in here.

"By the way, what's up with all those scars on your legs?" asks Ella.

I flinch slightly. "I…I was in a car accident. Had to have a few operations."

"Wow. Amazing that you can still cheer." Her eyes travel over the ugly raised ridges running from my hips down the sides of my thighs, and my heart sinks. I really don't want to talk about the accident. *Please don't ask about it*, I pray internally.

Ella starts to say something else, but luckily Naomi cuts in. "A pool party? It's October. Won't it be too cold for that?"

"It'll still be warm like today. I checked the weather forecast. Come anytime after seven. My parents won't be home till Sunday night, so you can all even stay over."

"Just us? What about the guys?" Lucy asks.

"Scott and some of the guys from the football team will be coming, so there'll be someone for you to hook up with, Lucy."

Lucy looks away, her face turning slightly pink.

Ella turns back to me. "I don't suppose you have a boyfriend, since you just moved here."

"No, you're right. I mean, there was this guy back in Santa Cruz, but—"

"Yeah, okay," she cuts me off, already bored. "So you're coming alone. I'll text you my address."

After saying goodbye to everyone, I head to the parking lot to wait for Aunt Maddy. But she doesn't show. After twenty minutes I check my phone. Ugh. I forgot I'd switched it off just before practice started. I switch it back on. My phone beeps immediately, and I open the text she sent me an hour ago.

Kid I'm so so sorry but I'm going to be held up at work today. Is there anyone else there who can give you a ride home?

Damn it. All the other girls have already left, and I'm not sure which bus to take to get home. I sigh, plonk down on the sidewalk, and open Google Maps.

"Problem?"

I startle, snap my head up. A tall lanky boy with a pale serious face is staring at me. It's the guy I saw that first day in the cafeteria. Isaac. He's standing beside a beat-up, ancient-looking green sedan, presumably his. His pale face flushes slightly as I stare back at him, and he breaks eye contact and looks away.

I scramble back up to my feet. "Umm…no. Why?"

He gestures to the parking lot. "Because there are no other cars left, and you were sighing repeatedly, so I assumed your ride bailed on you."

"My aunt didn't bail on me. She just got held up at work."

"Okay." He pats the back of his head, as if debating something internally. Then he looks up at the sky for another few more seconds, as if this exchange wasn't awkward enough already. Just as I'm trying to think of an excuse to extricate myself from our strange conversation, he says, "Do you need a ride home?"

I stare at him. "I don't want to bother you."

He shrugs. "You seem stranded, and I don't have anywhere I need to rush off to today."

"I…then…yes. I'd appreciate a ride." Wait, what am I doing? I don't even know this guy. Plus, he's now frowning as if he's already regretting his offer to help me.

"Get in, then." He yanks the door open and gets in the driver's seat, actually inserts a key and turns it physically to start the engine. This car must be *ancient*. As if to agree, the car's engine starts coughing and sputtering. I hurry over to the passenger side and get in, and it's too late to back out now no matter what reservations I might have.

For some reason, I'm struggling with the seat belt, which is absolutely just *refusing* to cooperate, and he reaches out to help me. This close, I notice that his eyes are a startling shade of green, framed with thick dark brown lashes, and that he smells like soap and a citrusy shampoo.

"So. Where do you live?" he asks as he fastens his own seat belt. His legs are too long for such a small car; they're bunched up awkwardly in front of him, his knees jutting into the bottom of the dashboard.

"Number thirty-two Vermont Avenue. That's—"

"Okay, I think I know where it is."

As he puts the car in reverse and starts pulling out of the parking lot, I peek at him out of the corner of my eyes. The tattoo on his neck is a pair of angel wings. Why does he have a tattoo like that? It looks like something only leather-clad bikers would have, not a pale lanky high school boy who looks like he enjoys doing math and would volunteer to help mow your lawn. I can't help but wonder what's the story behind it.

Thankfully, he doesn't speak the entire drive, sparing us from having to make small talk and making this any more awkward than it already is. Fifteen minutes later we come to a stop in the driveway of Aunt Maddy's house, a small detached. With Isaac here, I see it through fresh eyes. It used to look better. One of the wooden shutters is broken, and the house itself could use a fresh coat of paint. Little chores that my dad would have helped with, except he's too busy taking care of Mom now.

Isaac turns off the engine, and the car gives a final shaking sputter before going still. I grab my bag and turn to open the door, but he says, "Did you just transfer to Sierton?"

"Um. How did you know?"

"You're new to the cheerleading squad, right? But you don't seem like a freshman."

"Oh. Right. Yeah, I just moved here. From Santa Cruz. I'm Dawn," I say, sticking out my hand. Why am I trying to shake his hand, like I'm some kind of salesman? His awkwardness must be catching.

He looks at my hand for a second as I consider dropping it and pretending I never did that. Then he holds out his hand and shakes mine solemnly. I can't tell if he's being serious or ironic. "Hi, Dawn from Santa Cruz. I'm Isaac."

"Do the wings on your neck mean something?" I blurt out. He stiffens and turn his head back to the front. I bite the inside of my bottom lip. "Sorry, it's none of my business." He still doesn't reply, and I can feel my face start getting hot as I open the passenger door and get out of his car, walk self-consciously up to the house, unlock the front door, and close it behind me.

It's only afterward that I realize I didn't thank him for the ride home.

"Hey. Did you hear what I said?" Ella's voice jerks my attention back to her. She's frowning, irritated that I haven't been paying full attention to whatever she was talking about.

"Sorry. What were you saying?"

She keeps looking at me for a second, then turns her head in the direction that I've been staring—the table where Isaac normally sits, only he's not there today—then turns back around to me. "Why are you staring at them?"

Her sharp tone catches the attention of everyone at the table, and their heads swivel toward us, like sharks scenting blood. I feel like a deer caught in headlights, about to be run over but frozen to the spot, unable to move. "I—I'm not. I was just wondering why someone isn't here today."

"Why are you looking for Isaac Caldwell?"

Why does she seem so pissed? "He gave me a ride home after practice. I just want to thank him. I forgot to yesterday."

Lucy sits up straighter, suddenly interested. "Isaac Caldwell gave you a ride home? Why?"

"Because my aunt was supposed to come get me, but she couldn't make it and I was stuck at school. He saw me sitting in the parking lot all alone, looking at Google Maps on my phone."

"Wow, a knight in shining armor," says Naomi. She's smiling slyly, as if she's enjoying this.

Ella is also smiling, but in a thin-lipped kind of way.

I clear my throat. "Did I do something wrong?"

"Something wrong, babe?" says Scott, looking at his girlfriend, who is still staring at me.

"Nothing's wrong," says Ella, "I'm just worried for Dawn, that's all. She got a ride home yesterday from Isaac Caldwell."

She frowns when Scott starts laughing and says, "Isaac Caldwell doesn't seem particularly dangerous to me." Then he trains his dark blue eyes on me, still looking bemused. "But you're lucky you got home. I'm surprised that piece of junk still runs." Next to him, his friends snicker in a particularly annoying way, and I have to resist the urge to roll my eyes.

"I just thought I should thank him, that's all," I repeat.

"You should stay away from him," says Ella.

"Why?"

"Because he's such a loser," she pronounces. "He looks like someone who hangs around in basements, playing those weird make-believe games. *RPGs*. It's for your own good. We care about you, Dawn."

I don't know what to say to that, so I keep quiet. But for some reason, I don't quite believe her.

If Isaac's the one she'd been sneaking looks at, maybe I can find out why during the party tomorrow.

DAWN

We pull into Ella's driveway at half past eight. That's when I realize just how rich her family must be because her house is *huge*. Aunt Maddy must be thinking the same because she peers at the three-story glass and stone mansion and whistles. "Jesus, how big is that house? It must have at least a dozen rooms."

"Her dad's an orthodontist," I reply. "I guess they make good money."

She turns off the engine and turns to face me, her eyebrows knitting together, fingers tapping at the steering wheel, brown eyes full of worry. "Are you sure you're going to be okay? I mean, I'm glad that these girls are being nice to you, but—"

"I'll be fine. Don't worry. School's going great. Cheerleading's going great. This is my chance to fit in," I say, impatient to get out of her car. Mom and Dad didn't have a problem with me coming to this party, so I don't get why Maddy is acting like this.

"Kid, wait. I know I haven't been around much since you moved here." She sighs and rubs her face tiredly. "I've just been so busy with work. But I've been meaning to talk to you. You know that it wasn't your fault, right? It wasn't your fault. And I know your parents would never blame you either—"

"I know it wasn't." I keep my voice light so that she doesn't have to worry about me. So that we don't have to talk about this.

Maddy sighs. I can see she wants to say more, but thankfully, she drops it for now. "Okay, kid. Text me when you want me to come get you."

"I will. Thanks, Maddy. And I'm sorry for the trouble. I know you're tired—"

"It's no trouble. I don't have work tomorrow, and it's not like I've got anything on tonight anyway, since Liam put a rain check on our date."

Liam's her on-again, off-again boyfriend. "Oh no, again?"

"Yeah. I guess it's another evening of binging a murder show on Netflix for me. Just as well, I'm too tired to go out. Okay, get out and have fun. But not too much fun!" She waggles her eyebrows at me, trying to make things light again, and I laugh obligingly.

I get out of her Toyota Camry and wave as she drives away, her headlights illuminating the long gravel driveway. Ella's weather forecast had been right; it has been a warm day for October in Wisconsin, and the evening is not only still hot; the air is heavy, unmoving. Almost stifling. I swing the strap of my little Ralph Lauren knapsack—where I have my swimsuit and phone—on one shoulder and look around me. Light spills from the large windows of the house, but from the sounds of loud throbbing music and laughter coming from just around the side of the house, that's where the party is at.

I wade through the treacly darkness, following the music until I find myself by a large kidney-shaped pool lit up with floating pool lights. The pulsing music is coming from a laptop set up with speakers on one end of a long table. On the table are also a heap of red plastic cups, about a dozen or so bottles of soft drinks, and an alarming number of bottles of beer and other alcohol.

Scott and the rest of the guys are there, mixing drinks, their board shorts hanging low on their hips. Lucy and a few of the other girls are beside them, giggling at their antics. Naomi is in the pool beside Ella, who is lounging in the middle on a giant inflatable swan. Ella's in a glamorous striped bandeau bikini top and tiny matching bottom, one hand holding a cup, other hand gesturing furiously as she talks. She sees me and waves. "Dawn! Finally!"

As I wave back, one of the guys chooses that moment to do a cannonball into the pool, rocking Ella's swan and splashing her with water. She rolls her eyes and continues shouting to me, ignoring him. "You can go get changed in the pool house over there." She gestures to the small wood and glass structure at the end of the garden, and I go and change into my swimsuit, a turquoise one-piece.

Heading back to the rest of them by the pool, I wander over to the drinks table so that I have something to do. They've all known each other for years. I try not to let my awkwardness show. Scott is talking in a low voice with Brett—also on the football team and seemingly one of his best friends—as I approach, their heads bent close to each other. I think Scott says something like *The bitch thinks I don't know* before he sees me and breaks off. He stalks away and I find myself beside Brett, whose eyes light up when he sees me. He flashes a crooked grin and raises a bottle of vodka. "What's your poison?"

I eye the table. "Oh, a rum and Coke please." He starts mixing the drink, eager to please.

"I love how your swimsuit is the same color as your eyes," says one girl beside me.

"Thanks! I love the color of yours," I say.

Lucy snickers. "I love how *retro* it is."

By *retro*, I suppose she means how I'm the only one wearing a one-piece instead of a bikini like the rest of them.

"Seriously though," she continues, "that swimsuit could be my mom's. Are you, like, a prude or something? A Mormon?"

The other girl giggles. "Stop it, Lucy. Dawn doesn't have to wear tiny bikinis like you if she doesn't want to."

"Yeah," drawls Brett. "I think she looks great."

"Oh yeah?" says Lucy. "What about me?"

"You look *sensational*," says Brett, giving her an over-the-top leer, and Lucy laughs and swats him, even though she's now smiling widely.

CINDY R. X. HE

"Scott? Aren't you coming back with my drink?" Ella calls, and Scott obediently takes two cups and heads into the pool to join her. Lucy stops smiling, her eyes following him there.

I want to ask Lucy if she's okay, but Brett hands me my drink and starts asking me questions about me. His eyes linger all over my body as he asks me about what it was like living in Santa Cruz, making me glad I'm wearing a one-piece. I make up some story about how I enjoyed surfing sometimes after school, even though I didn't really surf that much. In return, he tells me about how he's caught the eyes of several football scouts. I know that most girls would think he's cute, but he's standing too near, and his breath already smells like alcohol.

Finally, I jump in the pool to get away from him. Naomi must have been watching us, because she's laughing as she whispers to me when I'm beside her in the pool, "I think Brett is into you. Don't you like him?"

"I…" I'm flustered, but she laughs again.

"I'm just teasing. High school boys are so boring, ugh. I'm not dating until I'm in college. Bet Harvard boys won't be as lame."

"You'll have to get in Harvard first though, won't you?" Ella says with a smirk, and Naomi's smile slides off her face.

The party really gets underway as everyone consumes more and more alcohol. I don't enjoy the feeling of being drunk so I don't drink as much, but the others don't seem to share the same sentiment. Ella reigns on the inflatable in the pool as everyone takes turns bringing her drinks. Naomi, especially, snaps to attention when Ella snaps her fingers. After the third time (yeah, I'm counting) she brings Ella a drink, I can't help but ask her *why*. Naomi shrugs her creamy slender shoulders and drawls, "We're just her minions." But even though she's smiling, as if to give the impression that she's joking, her voice drips with something. Annoyance? Disdain?

Somebody cranks up the thumping, pulsating music, and we dance. The air is so warm and heavy I'm starting to sweat, and I jump in the pool again to cool down. A few people jump in after me, and Scott picks up Ella and throws her screeching in the pool, then does a cannonball, splashing all of us.

"God, it's such a relief that they're gone for the weekend," says Ella, floating on her back.

"Who? Your parents?" I ask.

"Yeah. When they're around they just pick on me nonstop. Especially my mom, she's such a *bitch*." Her words are slurring slightly. She's still floating, staring up at the sky, and I'm not sure, but her eyes are shiny as if they're wet with tears. "Nothing I ever do is good enough for her. Everything I do is wrong. Screw her. As if she's so great, when all she knows how to do is spend my dad's money." She turns her head, stares at me fiercely. "Well, I'm better than she ever was, aren't I?" Then her lips curve up in a sly smile. "You're not afraid of me?"

My mouth is suddenly dry. "Why should I be afraid of you?"

"I don't know. The other girls are." Ella laughs, an ugly sound completely devoid of humor. "It's the only way I keep them in line, you know. They're all terrified of me."

I feel uncomfortable, as if I'm peering in someone's secret diary, but I don't know how to extricate myself from her drunken rambling. Luckily, Scott swims up to her and she latches on to him, wrapping her long legs around his waist, and I make my escape.

I climb out of the pool and go back to the drinks table, pour myself a cup of soda. Lucy, who didn't join everyone in the pool, sips from her cup as she watches Ella and Scott. There's a strange expression on her face.

I nudge her with my elbow. "Hey. Everything alright?"

"Yeah, just fine," she mutters, in a voice so miserable it's obvious she's anything but. She takes a long swallow, draining the remainder of her cup. Suddenly, she blurts, "She doesn't deserve him."

"Who?" I ask, startled.

She throws me an irritated look. "*Ella*, duh."

"Oh." I cast around for a reply that won't piss her off. "Because she's sometimes a bit…"

"Mean?" She laughs softly, but the sound is sour. "You noticed, huh?"

I can't help it; I have to know. The question tumbles out before I can stop it. "Then why are you still friends with her?"

Lucy grimaces. "You don't understand. It's better to be friends with her than to be her enemy. You don't know what she can do to you." She puts the cup to her mouth for a moment, remembers that it's empty, and flings it onto the grass. She's swaying slightly. "Yup, better to be besties. Even if sometimes I *hate* her." As the words leave her mouth, her eyes widen and her right hand reaches up to cover her mouth, as if she immediately regrets spilling her thoughts to me. "Don't tell her I said that," she says.

"I won't," I say hastily.

Lucy stares at her empty cup. "Why did I drink so much? Do you have any idea how many calories are in these drinks? Shit! I gotta get it all out." She takes a step toward the pool house, but Ella's drunk voice pierces the air.

"Lucy, babe, could you get me another vodka cranberry? I don't know where I put my towel!"

"Coming," Lucy mutters as she starts mixing Ella's drink, her shoulders slumped.

Someone taps me on my shoulder. "Hey," says Olivia, another girl on the squad. "Have you seen Naomi?"

"No, why?"

"I want to ask her if she needs a ride home with me and my boyfriend, but I can't find her anywhere."

"Maybe she's just in the bathroom or something. How long has she been gone?" I ask.

"Uh, about fifteen minutes, maybe?"

An image of Naomi passed out in a room somewhere flits across my mind. "Maybe I can help look for her. Why don't you keep looking around here, and I'll go look for her in the house?"

"Yeah, good idea."

Olivia heads toward the pool house, and I walk back to the front door of the house. It isn't locked, so I go in.

I find myself in the front hall. Right off it on the right is an absolutely massive living room, with designer-looking furniture and what looks like an actual crystal chandelier. Where to start looking? At the end of the hall is a big staircase going up, but I don't want to start poking around what's most likely bedrooms and whatnot. I peer around the open doorway on my left into the kitchen with its marble countertops. Nobody's there, so I head further down the hall, stopping just before the two doors, one on each side of the hall. One of them is closed, the other slightly open with the light on inside. It's probably a bathroom, so I push the door open. "Naomi? Are you there?"

Naomi is indeed inside, checking her phone. At my voice, she jumps and spins around to face me—the hand holding the phone flying behind her back—her face pale. "What is it?" she snaps.

I take a step back. "Nothing—I was just checking to see if you're alright. Olivia's looking for you."

She relaxes slightly. "I came to use the bathroom here because the one in the pool house was occupied. Come on, let's head back."

She pushes past me, holding the phone close against her body, but I catch a glimpse of the pink phone case. *Ella's* phone, not Naomi's, which has a sky-blue case.

What was Naomi doing with Ella's phone? Curiosity burns inside my belly. But she obviously didn't want me to see her with it, so I pretend not to notice.

We head back to the pool. It's only because I'm watching Naomi closely that I see her casually drop Ella's phone on the table as she walks past, before joining Olivia, who asks if she wants a ride.

"Thanks for the offer, but I'm probably going to crash here," says Naomi.

Ella's voice cuts through my reverie. "Dawn, be a dear and make me a vodka cranberry," she slurs, throwing her empty cup in my direction. It falls short and lands in the water with a tiny splash.

I mix her drink and bring it to her dutifully. "How much have you had to drink? Maybe you shouldn't have any more," I say.

She glares at me and defiantly takes a big swallow. "Who are you, my mom? Don't tell me what to do," she says, her words slurring so much it comes out more as *Dun del me wa do do*.

I sigh and back away, wade to the side of the pool, and climb out. The heat of the day is all gone now, and I shiver as the chilly night air raises goose bumps on my skin. Scott emerges from the pool house, lurching wildly. Some guy is now fully passed out on the lounge chair, a girl beside him nudging him to wake up.

They leave, and the only people left by the pool are Ella, Scott, Naomi, and me. Naomi is stumbling back toward the house, probably to find a room to crash in. Beyond the garish pool lights, everywhere around us is in shadows, the dark seeming to swallow us up.

"Hey, can I help you?" calls Scott. I turn to where he's staring, just in time to see a figure just beyond the pool lights at the far end of the pool slip into the shadows.

"Who is it?" I ask.

"I don't know. That was weird. They were just standing there.

Like they were watching us." Scott frowns. "Did you see the way they ran away when I called to them?"

"Maybe it was just someone checking to see if they left anything behind before leaving," I say, shivering again.

"Did you make out who it was?"

I shake my head. All I saw was a figure wearing what seemed to be a dark-colored hoodie that covered their head. All of a sudden I feel exposed, my skin crawling with the strange sensation of being watched, and I just want to go home.

Shivering uncontrollably now, I take my dress out of my bag and throw it on over my swimsuit, then text Maddy to pick me up.

———

An insistent knocking drags me awake, even though I throw my pillow over my head in an attempt to ignore it and go back to sleep. I was having a strange but pleasant dream where I was floating on a warm sea of stars, and a boy with green eyes was on a pink inflatable boat nearby, trying to persuade me to get on board. Maybe if I manage to fall back asleep quickly, I can somehow get back into the dream. But then Maddy calls my name. There's a tense note in her voice, so I sigh and give up.

"I'm up," I say, dragging myself into a sitting position as she opens the door. The stressed, stricken look on her face gets me fully awake. She's picking at her cuticle, something she only does when she's really upset. "What is it? What's wrong?" I ask, pushing the rising panic down. *Have Mom and Dad taken a turn for the worse?*

"The police are here," she says. "It's about the party last night. At your friend's house. They want to speak with you."

Cold fingers creep down my spine. "What? Why?"

"I don't know; they wouldn't tell me. But I'd guess that something went wrong."

We stare wordlessly at each other for a moment before I reply, "I'll be right down."

She disappears back out of the room, probably to wake my parents. I pull on a hoodie and sweatpants, pop my contacts in, run my fingers quickly through my hair, and head down too.

Maddy is already talking in a low voice to the two people standing in the hallway as I make my way down the stairs. "Can't you tell me what's happened? She's been through a lot. My brother and his wife—her parents—there was an accident and..." She breaks off as I appear, arms wrapped around myself tightly.

"Miss Dawn Foster?" says the man on the left, a man who looks to be in his forties with pouches under his eyes, saggy jowls like a bulldog, and thinning brown hair, in a white shirt, a navy blazer, and slacks.

"Yes, that's me," I say. "Is something wrong?"

"I'm Detective Doyle, and this is Detective Mulchaney," he says, gesturing to the person by his side, a severe-looking woman with black eyes and brown hair tied up in a tight knot at her nape, and who is also dressed similarly, in a white shirt, a brown camel blazer, and slacks. "You were at Ella Moore's house at number two Mulholland Drive yesterday evening, is that correct?"

The fear intensifies, cold fingers squeezing my throat. "Is—is this about the alcohol? I didn't have any. I don't even like drinking." At least the second part is true.

My parents appear just then behind me. "What's this about?" asks Dad in a sleepy voice as Mom reaches up to put her arm on my back. I glance quickly at the two detectives to see if they react to my parents'—especially my dad's—appearance. But they don't even blink an eye, they're so focused on me.

Maddy pipes up again, "Officers, surely it can't be that serious. Teenagers will be teenagers, and—"

"It's not about that," Mulchaney cuts in. "We'd like you to come down to the station and provide a statement. Today, if possible."

"I don't understand…" My voice fades off as Doyle glares at me.

"Ella Moore was found dead this morning."

HANNAH
THREE YEARS AGO

Hannah Smith slips inside Sierton High's gym, a stealthy little mouse, panting slightly. There are already a few dozen girls there; she's probably the last to arrive. Luckily, for now everyone seems to be just milling around waiting.

Standing in a corner and doing her best imitation of a potted plant, she looks around her. The gym is large, the ceiling high overhead, the dozens of fluorescent lights—so glaringly bright there's nowhere for anyone to hide—reflecting sharply off the shiny wood floor. Sierton High is newer, better equipped than the only other high school in small town Sierton. Even so, the gym still smells faintly of old sweat.

The other girls are all enviably long thin limbs, glossy hair, and flashing white teeth, wearing their confidence like armor. Hannah marvels at how poised and cool they look even though the gym is slightly too warm for comfort; she herself is sweating like a pig in a slaughterhouse. A couple of them glance curiously at her, then giggle and whisper to each other. Their words drift over:

Look at her.

She can't think she'll make the squad?

Hannah cringes and hides behind her hair as these beautiful creatures stare at her: at her limp hair, neither blond nor brown, just a mousy noncolor; her thick glasses, giving her muddy-brown eyes a bug-eyed, bewildered look; her hooked, too-big nose and weak, receding chin; all the things that cemented her friendless fate all through elementary and middle school, where even the other unpopular kids didn't want to be her friend. It was like they sensed her desperation to be accepted, to be liked, and instinctively veered away.

She pushes the memories away. High school will be different, starting from right now. The key to being happy is having friends and fitting in. Hannah knows this because she has always been friendless and unhappy. And also because her parents keep telling her that.

But today is the day she's going to change everything. That's what she has to focus on. Not at these girls staring at her, not on the anxiety fizzling in her gut.

She watched others in middle school fawn over the cheerleaders and athletes. High school will be the same, if not even more pronounced. And since none of these popular girls will want to be friends with her—a lesson she learned very well in elementary and middle school—the only solution is to *become* one of them herself. Then everyone will want to be friends with her. Then her parents will stop nagging her. (She knows they think there's something wrong with her, even though they haven't actually come right out and said it. Yet.)

So most of these girls were probably already cheering in middle school, or did gymnastics. But she spent all of summer watching basic cheerleading motions, jumps, splits, and tumbles on YouTube and practicing them by herself at home. She pulled more than one muscle, and sprained a wrist and ankle, but she kept at it; and now she can actually do a decent toe-touch jump, or a forward roll, or a cartwheel.

For now, she tries to look confident, look like a normal girl doing normal things. Like texting a friend, because she has many friends like normal girls do. She scrabbles for her phone. Okay, it's surprisingly hard to pretend to be texting when you're not really. Hmm… maybe there's a Pokémon in this gym. She opens *Pokémon GO*, scans the room discreetly. She loves Pokémon, loves collecting the different monsters. The game is her guilty secret. Her parents took away her Nintendo Switch because they didn't understand why she preferred to spend her time playing games rather than "getting out there and making real friends." She didn't know how to tell them it was because she had no friends, didn't understand how to make them. Besides, collecting Pokémon is so fun, so relaxing. Unlike other people, the little monsters didn't judge her or laugh at her. And look! There's one right now in the room, a Nidorino, which she doesn't have yet—

"Hey," someone calls out, making her jump and hurriedly close the app. It's a pretty girl with dark blond hair pulled back in a perky ponytail, staring at Hannah with a small smile.

Hannah looks around her for a moment. There's nobody else standing near her, so the girl is definitely talking to her. Maybe this person will be her first friend. She smiles tentatively back. "Um. Hi."

"Are you lost?" says the blond, tilting her head. Beside her, two equally pretty girls giggle and nudge each other. The blond girl smiles wider and continues, "Because this is cheerleading tryouts. Are you looking for the cafeteria?"

Heat floods Hannah's face. "No, I'm here to try out too."

"Oh." The girl's eyebrows shoot up on her forehead—then her smile widens. "Good luck." She turns and whispers to her friends, *She'll need it*, and the trio bursts into peals of laughter.

Hannah's resolve, tentatively built up over the summer, cracks and dissolves in an instant. Why did she think this was a good idea? She doesn't belong here. She whirls around to leave, but a loud whistle stops her in her tracks.

"Hello, girls! I'm Coach Davis, and welcome to Sierton High's 2021 cheerleading tryouts!" a cheery voice announces, and Hannah has no choice but to turn back around. A lean woman with freckles and short curly ginger hair stands with her hands on her hips, smiling at all of them. "First off: go ahead and register at that table over there, and collect your tryout packet. Then gather back here, where we'll teach you some jumps, kicks, and the cheer that you'll be trying out with on Wednesday. Go on now!"

Hannah stays where she is. Register, or leave while she still can? She takes a step toward the exit…stops. She can already imagine her parents' usual disappointed expressions when they find out that she'd chickened out after all. As she hesitates, Coach Davis's gaze slides over to her, and the woman frowns slightly. Hannah bites her lower lip…and shuffles over to the table to join the line forming there.

It's her first year of high school, her chance at a new beginning. She has to be brave. Whether or not it's a good idea, it's too late to back out now. She can only do her best and cross her fingers that it will be enough.

DAWN

I'm sitting in a small sparse room that smells of stale coffee, the only furniture a table and three chairs. It's cold in here even with my hoodie, and I shiver. Maddy is standing diagonally behind me, her hand on my shoulder gripping me a little too tightly. Sitting across the table from me are Detectives Doyle and Mulchaney, both of them staring at me; Doyle with his arms crossed in front of him, Mulchaney with her mouth pressed into a grim, thin line. *Oh god, this is an interrogation room.* Panic surges inside me, from my stomach up into my throat, into my dry mouth. Thank god I managed to convince my parents not to come too. The trip down would have taken too much of a toll on them, especially my mom—this room would have freaked the hell out of them.

"Is this an interrogation?" says Maddy, her voice thin. "Because

Dawn is a minor, and I don't think she has to speak with you unless she has a lawyer—"

"No," says Doyle, holding his hands up with his palms toward us. "We would just like Miss Foster to give a witness account of everything that transpired yesterday evening."

"Are—" I croak, my throat too dry to speak. "Are you sure she's dead?"

"Yes," says Mulchaney.

"But…I don't understand…"

"Yes, I think you need to tell us what's happened first," says Maddy.

Nobody speaks for a few seconds, then Doyle nods. "Ella Moore was discovered dead this morning by Mr. Scott Russell."

I stare at him. "Oh my god. What—"

"I'm not at liberty to disclose more information until we have a better understanding of what happened. So we'd appreciate it if you can help us fill in the blanks."

I swallow. "Of course. What do you want to know?"

"Start from the beginning. When did you arrive? Who was there?"

"I arrived at Ella's house at around half past eight, I think." I look to Maddy, who nods in confirmation. "Maddy—my aunt— gave me a ride there. Um, everyone who Ella had invited was already there."

I give an account of everything that happened, or at least, everything that I can remember. When I finish speaking, my throat is even drier from talking so much, and I start coughing.

Mulchaney gets me a paper cup of water. I'm sipping the water gratefully when Doyle asks, "What about drugs? Anybody doing them last night?"

"Drugs? No!"

"You sure?"

"At least…I don't think so? I didn't see anyone doing drugs." I bite my lower lip. "She was still alive when I left! I can't believe she's dead."

"What time did you leave?" asks Mulchaney.

"Umm…just before midnight, I think. Oh, hang on, I texted Maddy to ask her to pick me up. Let me check—" I pull out my phone and check the time stamp on my text. "I sent the text at eleven thirty-eight."

"I was there around ten to midnight," says Maddy. "Dawn was in the driveway, waiting for me."

"And you're certain that Miss Moore was still alive then?" asks Mulchaney.

"Yes. I mean, she was still in the pool, on her pool float. I spoke to her just a few minutes before I left. Oh god. She was so drunk! They all were. I should have gotten her out of that pool before I left! Did she drown?"

"We'll know the cause of death for sure when the autopsy report comes back," says Doyle. "Thank you for coming in to speak with us, Miss Foster."

"Of course. Can I—can I leave now?"

Doyle cocks his head at me, his sharp eyes seeming to take in everything. "Yes. But it will be best if you don't leave town for a while. Just in case we have any more questions."

———————

As soon as we step outside the station, Maddy shoves a cigarette in her mouth. "I can't believe she's dead! How horrible! And why can't those detectives tell us how she died? Do you think they're speaking to all the others who were there last night?"

"I think so," I murmur, only half-paying attention to her because I see someone else in the parking lot, just getting out of his old rusty-looking car. "It's somebody else from school. Sorry, can I have a minute? I'd like to speak with him…"

"Who is it?" She exhales a puff of smoke and cranes her neck to see who I'm looking at. "Was he there at the party last night too?"

"He wasn't." So why is he here at the police station? "I don't really know him," I add hastily, "but he was nice enough to give me a ride home the other day when you couldn't make it to come get me."

Maddy looks at him again—obviously also wondering what he's doing here—then back at me. Finally, she sighs. "Okay, I'll wait for you in the car."

"Thanks, Maddy."

Maddy walks off, and I go up to Isaac. He's leaning against his car, his shoulders drooped, staring at the entrance of the station as if psyching himself up to go in. "Hi," I say.

He jumps slightly, focuses his eyes on me. "Hey."

"What are you...? Do you know? That..."

He glances away, doesn't reply.

"You do know that Ella is dead," I state. "How?"

Isaac's eyes don't quite meet mine. "They told me when they said they wanted me to come down to *answer a few questions.*"

"But—why do they want to speak with you? You weren't even there last night."

There's an uncomfortable stretch of silence at first, then he says, "I don't know."

I stare at him skeptically until he sighs and runs a hand through his messy, too-long hair irritably. "Could be the texts," he mumbles.

I'm utterly confused. "What texts?"

Another long silence, then he snaps, "What's with all the questions?"

I can feel my face turning hot. "Sorry, it's none of my business."

He glares at me. "You're right, it isn't."

"Sorry," I say again, irritation and curiosity wrestling each other for dominance in me. So that's why Ella was looking at him like that. He'd been texting her, even though she had a boyfriend. Maybe she was angry with him because he wouldn't leave her alone. Or...maybe she was afraid of him.

Although I have trouble believing anyone would be afraid of him. He looks so ordinary. Harmless. In fact, right now he looks downright miserable as he says, "I can't believe she's dead. How did she die?"

"I don't know. They wouldn't tell me. She was still alive when I left last night."

Maddy taps her horn, making me jump. "I gotta go," I say reluctantly.

"Yeah…I guess I should go in too."

He starts toward the entrance, but then I remember. "Thank you," I call out.

He turns around. "For what?"

"For giving me a ride home the other day. I forgot to thank you then."

"Oh…no problem." He turns back, pushes the door open, and disappears into the station as I hurry back to Maddy's car.

———

Back at the house, my parents and Maddy keep taking turns coming into my room, but I manage to convince them that all I really want is to be left alone right now. Finally, they stop trying to talk to me, and I start on my school assignments.

Half an hour later, I give up. Who am I kidding? As if I can pretend like nothing happened.

Everybody must be so horribly shocked. I want to talk to Lucy or Naomi. But I hesitate. Should I call them? I'm new, but these girls have been friends with her forever. I'm staring at my phone screen when it rings. *Naomi.* I answer immediately. "Hey."

"Hey," Naomi replies in a hushed, thin voice. "You know about Ella?"

"Yeah. I just came back half an hour ago from the police station. They wanted me to give my statement."

"I was there this morning too. I slept at her place last night. *God.* I wanted to go home first, but they literally dragged me down to the station directly from her house. I can't believe she's *dead.*" Her voice rises on the last word, almost hysterically.

"Me too."

We're both silent for a while before Naomi speaks again. "We don't even know *how* she died, for god's sake."

"Those two officers told me that Scott was the one who discovered her…body…" My voice trails off.

"Yeah." Frustratingly, she doesn't elaborate.

"But…where did he…? Was it this morning? So she died sometime in the night or this morning? What *happened*, Naomi?" I can't help asking.

"I don't know. I was still sleeping when she… I woke up because Scott was screaming."

"And then?"

"He kept on screaming, so I ran over to her room. He was standing by the bed. And she was *blue.*" She sounds distraught, like she's on the verge of tears. But…how much of her distress is actually for Ella, and how much of it is for herself at still being there when a dead body was found? What was she doing with Ella's phone last night?

I shake my head, try to shake away that thought. So she hadn't died in the pool. "She died in her sleep?"

"I don't know. Maybe? Although that wasn't my first thought." Her voice drops to a hush. "At first, I thought he'd strangled her."

"*What?*"

"I mean, it did look a lot like it. I told you, she was *blue*."

"Maybe that's normal if she'd been dead for a few hours…"

"Yeah. Maybe," she says reluctantly.

"I guess the police will investigate. I can't imagine how horrible that must have been for him. And for you too."

"It was *so* horrible. You were smart to leave early. I wish I'd left too instead of sleeping over there." Naomi breaks off, and I hear a woman's voice in her background. Then she says, "I gotta go. See you in school tomorrow."

"Yeah, see you." I hang up, get back to my assignment. But I can't stop thinking of Ella, of when I last saw her. Lying on that giant pink swan, completely wasted.

———

On Monday we're all gathered in our usual seats at our table in the cafeteria. With the exception of Ella, of course.

Ella will never sit at this table again.

Nobody is doing much eating. Scott's eyes are bloodshot, and he looks like he's having one hell of a hangover.

This morning during assembly, Principal King announced the news of Ella's death to the school, as well as informed us that grief counseling will be provided all day for anyone who needs it. With the news out, the other students in the cafeteria are now all staring at us—some discreetly, others openly—and whispering among themselves. I pretend not to notice all the eyes on us, even though their stares are like ants crawling on my skin. Even Raquel is staring in our direction. My phone *dings*, a text from her:

> You have to tell me what happened, like, EVERYTHING 😮

Everything? Fine. I reply:

> Wednesday

Ever since getting on to the squad, Wednesday is the only day I get to hang out with Raquel after school, usually at the library or her house, since it's the only weekday there isn't cheer practice.

My eyes drift over to Isaac, sitting with his two friends as usual. He's wearing a green sweater today, the same color as his eyes. Nobody else must know that the police asked him down to the station too, since nobody else is looking at him. He looks up and catches me staring, and I look away.

With Ella gone, Lucy is now sitting beside Scott. She places a tentative hand on his. I try not to stare as his head jerks toward her, and they lock eyes before he slides his hand away. Her face is pink as her own hand snakes back to the side of her body.

It's a relief when Naomi finally speaks, breaking the silence. "I can't believe she's dead."

"Right?" says Lucy, her eyes wide. "I didn't know people could really die like that. I'm *never* drinking that much again."

"What do you mean?" I ask.

"I mean, that's why she died, right? Alcohol intoxication?"

"I don't know," says Brett. "Did she really drink that much?"

"She did drink a lot," says Lucy.

"But enough to die?" He frowns. "I don't know."

"What are you saying? How else do you think she died?" says Lucy, looking confused.

"I guess we'll know soon. There's going to be an autopsy," says Scott, his voice low and flat. "Her parents told me. They're blaming me, of course."

"What! Why?" Lucy says, putting her hand on Scott's again. "It's not your fault she drank so much!"

"No, it's not," he says, shaking her hand off. "Everyone was bringing her drinks yesterday."

"I didn't," says Naomi quickly.

"Shut up," says Lucy. "I saw you bringing her a drink."

"Only because she ordered me to!" says Naomi, her fair skin flushing pink. "What about you? You brought her so many. You were totally trying to get her drunk on purpose!"

"I only brought her two drinks!" says Lucy.

Naomi laughs sourly. "More like four or five, you liar."

They glare at each other.

"I tried telling her she shouldn't drink anymore, but she told me not to tell her what to do," I say in a subdued voice.

"Nobody could ever tell her what to do. She'd bite your head off if you tried." Naomi shakes her head. "She's always liked partying, but last night was the drunkest I'd seen her in a long time."

Scott frowns. "She's been drinking a lot more recently. It's just…she's been so angry."

"Yeah, and taking it out on us," Lucy mumbles.

"Angry about what?" I ask.

"I think she was just feeling more insecure than usual," says Naomi.

I stare at her, surprised. "Insecure? Her?"

"Yeah, her tough act?" Naomi rolls her eyes. "It's all a façade. She's really insecure, always has been. It's her mom. It's why she always felt like she had to be the best."

We all stare at each other. I feel the hair on my skin rise, and I suppress a shiver as one by one, their eyes land on me. "You know," says Naomi, "nothing like this ever happened before we let you in our group."

"What?" I say.

"Yeah. We've had so many parties before, and nothing bad ever happened. You arrive, and someone dies," says Lucy.

Their accusations are so ludicrous, I struggle for a few seconds to even come up with a reply. "Are you saying that I had something to do with…with what happened?"

"I don't know. Did you?" says Naomi.

"That's ridiculous! Of course not." My heart thuds hard in my chest. "I was one of the first to leave the party. My aunt came to get me just before midnight. She was still alive *then*. Where were all of *you*?"

Scott's face turns red, and Lucy and Naomi shift in their seat as one by one, everyone else who was at the party chimes in to declare how they also left early.

"I only crashed at her place because I was too tired to head home," mumbles Naomi.

"I had to wait for my sister to come get me," says Lucy, her face pink.

"Well, I stayed because someone had to look after Ella," says Scott hotly. Someone mumbles, *Yeah, you sure took good care of her*, and Scott shoots him a withering glare. "I brought Ella into the house after you all left," says Scott. "She had fallen asleep on that inflatable thing. I was pretty drunk too, but I managed to carry her into the house and put her in bed."

Lucy is biting her perfectly manicured nails. "My sister came to get me at around one. That's when Scott brought Ella into the house," she says.

I eye her. I didn't see her anywhere just before I left. Where was she, and what was she doing between midnight and one, while she was supposedly waiting for her sister? Lucy catches me looking at her, and she looks away quickly.

Scott takes a swig from his bottle of water and swallows, his Adam's apple bobbing up and down in his throat. "I was so drunk that after I put her in bed, I collapsed beside her and fell asleep almost immediately myself." His face is pale, and his voice has started shaking. He rubs his mouth with the back of his hand. "I woke up in the morning with the worst headache," he continues in a flat voice. "I turned around and hugged her before I realized… she was cold. Stiff. Dead."

I eye him too. He hadn't seemed that drunk to me that night.

"Christ," Brett swears under his breath. "When do you think she died?"

"I don't know," Scott snaps, looking sick. "I'm trying not to think about it. Trying not to think about possibly sleeping next to a dead body for half the night."

Naomi and I lock eyes for a second, and her words drift back to me: *At first, I thought he'd strangled her.*

As everyone falls silent again, I can't help but wonder if anyone is going to grief counseling. Because nobody seems to be too torn up about Ella dying. There's shock and horror—but there doesn't seem to be a lot of grief. Kind of what I'm feeling too, but at least I've only known her for a few weeks.

These people have been her friends for years.

Any lingering feeling of guilt I might have dissipates when Naomi speaks again. "I wonder who Coach will choose as the new squad captain."

"Oh! She'll choose you for sure!" pipes Lucy, and Naomi rewards her with a brilliant smile.

HANNAH

After signing up for tryouts, the next forty-eight hours pass in a blur, and all too soon, she's back in the gym. As she faces Coach Davis—alongside two other girls also trying out whose names she can't recall—she wipes her sweaty palms on her shorts. Her heart is beating way too fast, and she feels light-headed and sick. It doesn't help that she spent half of last night awake, stressing about today.

Then Coach Davis says *Go*, and Hannah's mind goes blank as she pastes a huge smile on her face and launches herself into the set routine that she's learned by heart.

Afterward, sweating and breathing heavily, she squints at the coach. Without her glasses, she can't really be sure of the woman's expression, but it looks like she's frowning slightly. What does that mean? Hannah's chest squeezes slightly.

"Alright, thank you, girls. Next group, please," says Coach Davis.

Hannah files out of the room with the others. As one girl hurries away, the other one whips out her cell phone and soon starts gushing to whomever she's talking to about how great tryouts went for her. Then she stops and frowns at Hannah. "Can I help you?"

"Sorry, I..." Her face burning, Hannah looks away stiffly. She must have been staring at the other girl. Why is she always so awkward? And how is everyone else not? She fumbles for her phone in her bag, starts texting her mom to let her know she's done.

"Stop freaking out, Ella. Why are you so nervous?"

Hannah looks up. It's the three pretty girls she met the other day—they must be up next.

Ella is pale, her lips pressed into a grim line, nervous energy crackling off her. "You don't understand, Naomi," she snaps at her friend. "I have to make squad. I need to show *her*." She turns suddenly and glares at Hannah. "Can I help you?"

Hannah shrinks slightly. "Um, good luck."

"Yeah, okay, thanks." Ella turns back to face her friends, and Hannah slinks away down the corridor.

"So? How did it go?" The question bursts out of her mom as Hannah climbs into the Suburban's passenger seat.

"I...I don't know, Mom. They'll announce it tomorrow morning."

"I know you don't know yet," her mom presses on insistently, "but how do you *think* it went? Did you get all the moves right? Did you remember to smile? How did the coach look?"

"Um. I couldn't really see her expression without my glasses. I think I did...okay?"

Her mother's face falls a little, then she smiles again. "Well, at least you tried. It's important to have friends. You know that, right? You know, I was pretty popular when I was your age—"

"I know, Mom, you've told me before."

"And I know you have it in you too. After all, you're my daughter, right? I know you'll definitely make it! We should already celebrate. I'll call your dad, tell him to buy some ice cream—" Her voice trails off as she casts a critical eye over her daughter. "Actually, you don't need ice cream. I'll tell him to get sushi..."

Hannah deflates a little. Her mom knows she hates sushi, knows how she always gags on the cold slimy pieces of raw fish when she tries to force herself to eat them. She wonders if she'll ever be thin enough for her mother. She turns her face to the window, crosses her arms to hug herself, blocks out her mother's voice. If she doesn't get in, her parents will be so disappointed in her again. It's only when her arms start to hurt that she realizes she's digging her nails into her skin, hard enough to draw blood.

———

"I made it!" Ella's shriek is so loud, everyone turns to look at her. In front of the bulletin board in the hallway, she, Lucy, and Naomi are holding on to each other's arms, jumping up and down.

"Of course you did," says Lucy. "Duh."

"I mean, I never had any doubt, of course," says Ella.

Hannah finally musters up the bravery to go up to the board, makes herself look at the thick piece of paper pinned to it.

Holy crap. Her name is there—third from the bottom on the short list—on the notice congratulating the girls who have passed tryouts and made squad.

She made it. *She made squad.* The hard ball of anxiety that's been gnawing away on her insides for the past three days unknots and fades away, leaving her light-headed and slightly dazed— and Hannah realizes that up until that moment, she never truly believed that she would actually make squad. She's smiling so wide her cheeks are starting to hurt. She must remember to tell her mom she'll need contact lenses now. No more practicing with the world as a big fuzzy blur. She pulls out her phone, almost dropping it in her excitement.

I MADE IT

she types, hits send.

You did???? YES!!!! That's my girl!!!

Her mom replies almost immediately, and a bubble of happiness balloons in her chest, filling her up with golden warmth. She can't remember the last time her parents were proud of her. She finally did something right.

"Wait, *you* made squad too?" It's Ella, staring at her with incredulous eyes.

Hannah shoves her phone back into her back pocket and blinks at Ella, too surprised to say anything, until Naomi drawls, "She *did* do well during tryouts yesterday."

Hannah gapes. "You…you were watching?"

"Yeah, you went just before us."

"She did do surprisingly well, didn't she?" Ella turns back to Hannah. "How do you know to do all the jumps and kicks? Did you cheer in middle school?"

"Um…no…"

"Then how?"

"YouTube," Hannah mumbles, feeling her face grow hot again.

Ella stares at her. "YouTube." Then she bursts out laughing, and her two friends with her. "Guess we're going to be teammates, YouTube Girl. I'm Ella."

Hannah smiles, hope creeping up her chest. "I'm Hannah."

Ella just continues staring at her with that small smile on her lips as Lucy purses her lips and says, "Will there be uniforms that'll fit her, though?"

"Lucy, don't be rude. I'm sure there are bigger sizes too," says Ella, still smiling. "Well, see you at practice, YouTube Girl."

Hannah smiles at their backs as the three girls stroll off. She's one of them now. She can barely believe it. One of the pack. Already, she feels more confident. She glances around at the other girls still milling around the notice, catches the eye of a tall freckly-faced girl who shoots her a glare and stomps off. Oops. Maybe that one didn't make squad.

Hannah shoulders her backpack a little higher and heads down the hall, lighter than she's ever felt before. No more sad, friendless little mouse. The new Hannah is going to be popular. Everything is going to change. She can feel it.

DAWN

Raquel shoos her two younger sisters out of her room, ignoring their outraged cries of protest. "I don't get why you two like to be in here so much. Go play in your own room."

"But your bed is bouncier!" says Imani, trying to duck under Raquel's arm, but Raquel catches her, pushes her firmly back outside, and closes the door on her and Shanice.

"Aww, they're so cute. Maybe we can let them stay." I plop myself on the edge of Raquel's bed.

"And listen to how a girl died?" Raquel rolls her eyes. "Sure, if you want them to have nightmares and not sleep tonight." She sits cross-legged on the thick rainbow wool rug beside her bed. "So what happened? Tell me everything!"

"I don't really know much. When I left, she was still fine. Well...very drunk, but still alive." I recount the events of the evening, picking at the bedspread with my fingers and not realizing I was doing so until Raquel puts her hand gently on mine to stop me. Her sudden touch makes me jump, pulls me out of the memory of that night.

"That's so horrible," she breathes. "So she basically died in her sleep, from alcohol poisoning, right? This is why I don't touch alcohol. What a horrible way to go. Almost as horrible as that suicide."

I stare at her. "Suicide?"

"Yeah. Three years ago, a freshman at Sierton High tried to kill herself." Raquel's voice is hushed, solemn. "Isaac's sister."

Ice trickles down my spine, pooling in my insides. "Isaac has a sister?"

Raquel nods. "I think she was bullied. Isaac used to be friendly with everyone, but after that…he's never been the same ever since."

"What happened to her? Where is she now?" I ask, but before Raquel can answer, the door bursts open, and her sisters tumble in giggling and shrieking, making it impossible for us to continue our dark conversation.

But her words repeat in a loop in my head for the rest of the afternoon. *Tried to kill herself… She was bullied… He's never been the same ever since.*

The amazing thing about teenagers is their ability to recover. Especially if they're beautiful, with a lot to live for, like the girls on the cheerleading squad or the guys on the football team. Even if one of their friends has just died.

Even if everybody in school looks at us with suspicion. Hell, even if we *all* look at each other with suspicion now.

Even if the whispers don't really stop, about how *suspicious* Ella's death is, how *unlikely* it is that she died from alcohol intoxication.

With Ella gone, Naomi quickly becomes the new queen at Sierton High. Coach also selects her to be our new captain, much to her delight.

Lucy doubles her effort to win Scott over, and he succumbs quickly enough.

Everyone gets what they've always wanted...except Ella, of course.

———

Ella's funeral was delayed for two weeks due to the autopsy and tox report.

I'm obligated to attend the service on Sunday morning at St. Anthony's, the local church, since I'm part of the cheer squad. And also because I was at the now-infamous party, of course. Even though I really, really don't want to be here. I hate funerals; they make me feel panicky, claustrophobic.

I'm sitting in one of the pews near the back, Maddy on my left. She insisted on coming, even though I told her she didn't need to. Mom and Dad are staying home, probably because they didn't want people staring at them, and at me because of how they look.

The other cheerleaders are sitting near the front, behind a couple sitting stiffly in the first row. They must be Ella's parents. Ella's words (*she's such a bitch*) float into my head. I couldn't bring myself to sit so far up front. Scott, Lucy, and Naomi are dry eyed; their faces pale and grim as they turn around, looking. Maybe they're looking for me, wondering why I'm not sitting with them. Lucy and Naomi manage to look glamorous in what I'm sure are designer dresses, their makeup done in appropriately discreet, somber shades. I'm not wearing any. I'm wearing an old black dress and jacket that I found shoved at the back of my closet.

Lots of people from school are also here, if only to gawk at us, Ella's friends—or at least, the people who were at the party. I think this is the first funeral I've been to where no one is crying.

Isaac Caldwell slides onto the bench beside me on my right, five minutes before the service starts. I sneak a look at him sideways; he looks ill at ease as usual, in a black jacket that's not fitting him properly, a faded black Nirvana T-shirt, and black jeans. All that black is making his pale skin look even paler than usual.

His warm proximity to me is distracting, but it's a distraction that I welcome. I find myself wanting to say something to him. "I didn't think you'd come," I say in a low voice. Maddy turns to see who I'm talking to, and she frowns when she sees Isaac.

"I almost didn't," Isaac replies equally softly, then he sighs. "But I'd feel like an ass if I didn't."

PERFECT LITTLE MONSTERS

"I hate funerals," I blurt, and he casts me a startled look. Heat floods my face. I guess I should elaborate, explain why. But I can't. There's just something about funerals that make me feel really uncomfortable, like an itch in my head. Like something that I've forgotten, but don't want to remember or examine too closely.

"I hate funerals too." His voice is rough and low.

The service starts. The pastor goes on about how life doesn't end with death, how death doesn't have the final word.

The itch in my head gets worse. There's a rising tightness in my chest, making me tremble. I can't breathe. I can't stay for this entire thing. I stand up unsteadily. People are staring, but I don't have it in me to care.

"Kid—" Maddy tries to take my left hand, but I shake her off.

Isaac stands up too and takes my right hand. His hand is large and surprisingly warm. "Let's get out of here," he says, and I nod and let him lead me out of the church.

Just before I step out, I turn back one last time. Naomi, Lucy, Scott, and Ella's parents are staring at me, and they do *not* look happy.

———

I'm in Isaac's car, the window rolled down a little—I had to hand crank it down—for some air because the air-conditioning isn't working. We keep going until we're out of town, the houses by the side of the road appearing less and less frequently until they're completely replaced by foliage.

"Where are you taking me?" I ask.

"You'll see. We'll be there soon."

I don't ask again. I find that even though I have no idea where he's taking me, I don't care. He's taking me away from that awful funeral, which is exactly what I want.

He slows down, and I see a small road turning off into the trees, which he takes. It's not even a road—it's just a dirt path, really—and he slows down even more, his car groaning as it bumps along. After about five minutes of this, we come to a complete stop in the forest, and he turns the engine off.

He gets out and I do the same. We're surrounded by pine trees, their sweet smell on the crisp air tickling my nose. I can hear birds singing and also a faint lapping sound. I look around, and sure enough, further in front is the wide blue expanse of a lake.

"Where are we?" I ask.

"Lake Michigan. Come on."

Isaac starts walking, and I follow until we stop just by the water. He sits down on the stony bank, crossing his long legs, and I sit too.

The Indian summer that we've been having is truly over, and fall is here in all its chilly glory. It's a lot colder here this time of year than in Santa Cruz, and I'm underdressed for the weather in my thin wool jacket. The icy breeze blowing in from the lake bites through the fabric of my clothes to my bones, and I shiver.

We stare at the shimmering blue water for a long moment, neither of us saying a word. It's peaceful; there's nobody here but us, and the only sounds are the soft, rhythmic lapping of the water on the lakeshore and the occasional bird singing. Slowly, the tightness in my chest loosens until I can breathe again.

I glance over at him, and he turns to meet my eyes. "What was that, some kind of panic attack?" he asks.

"Told you I didn't like funerals," I mutter.

"You weren't kidding. Feeling better now?"

I nod, cast around for something to say to change the subject. "This is a nice spot."

He shrugs. "Yeah, I guess. I come here sometimes when I want to be alone. It's a big lake and a small path. Hardly anybody ever comes here. A fisherman or two, sometimes. The other kids prefer a different spot, where they can swim, sunbathe, and have barbecues. There are too many trees here for that."

We sit in silence again for a while, until I can't help myself anymore. "I heard about your sister. I'm…I'm sorry." Isaac doesn't reply, just continues staring off into the distance. But I can't help it; I have to know more. "What happened? If you don't mind telling me."

He sighs, looks suddenly terribly sad. "She's my twin." He pauses for the longest time before continuing. "She was being bullied in school. We only found out afterward, when we came across the comments on her social media." His voice is flat, seemingly emotionless.

"Is she…is she okay now?" I can't help asking. Both he and Raquel talk about his sister in the present tense, so her suicide attempt mustn't have been fatal…but why haven't I seen her in school with him?

Isaac throws me a guarded look. "Her attempt wasn't fatal, but it left her with a brain injury. She was in a coma for two weeks. When she finally regained consciousness, she was unable to speak. Or eat." He looks away. His fists are tightly clenched. "Or basically do anything. She was in a rehab facility for six months. She's back home now, but...the damage was too severe. She'll never lead a normal life again."

"I'm so sorry," I say again.

He nods stiffly. "I should have realized she wasn't alright, but I didn't. I was too caught up in my own stuff. Stupid stuff. Fuck, I don't even remember now what they were." He laughs, but it's an angry sound.

"Do you know who was bullying her?"

He turns his face away. "No." Something in his tone is off though, makes me feel like that isn't the truth. But then my gaze is drawn to the tattoo on his neck. He must guess my question because he says, "She was only born two minutes before me, but she always acted like my older sister. She was always looking out for me. We joked that she was my guardian angel." He reaches back with his right hand, touches the tattoo. "I guess I got this as a reminder of how she was always there for me." He drops his hand. "I make sure that I'm there for her now. I just wish that I was there for her before. Hey, are you alright? You're shaking."

"I...I'm just cold. Isaac...I'm so sorry."

He shrugs and looks down, chooses a small rock, turns it over in his fingers. Throws it at the water with a deft flick of his wrist. It skips on the surface of the shimmering water—three times— before sinking.

"I've always sucked at that," I say.

I pick out a round flat rock. It feels smooth and cool against the skin on my fingers. I try skipping it, flicking my wrist the way he did. It hits the water with a small *ploof*—and sinks immediately.

"That did suck," he says, his mouth quirking up at the side as if he's trying not to smile.

"I suck at many things," I agree.

"Do you? You seem pretty perfect. Like your friends."

I turn my face away so that he can't see my expression.

"Sorry, did I say something wrong?" he asks.

I throw another rock into the water. It sinks with an angry *plop*. "Do you mean the other cheerleaders? You say that like you don't like them. But you were texting Ella."

Isaac stiffens as we lock eyes. "That's not exactly right."

"You said that the police wanted to speak with you because of some texts—"

"She was the one who got hold of my number and was texting me."

"Wait. What?" I shake my head. I don't quite manage to keep the incredulity out of my tone. "Why was Ella texting you?"

He flushes slightly, turns his face away toward the lake. "We hooked up once. At some dumb party. She's been texting me ever since."

I gape at him. He flushes slightly. "Oh," I say. "Did you know that she was dating Scott?"

Isaac doesn't reply immediately, takes his time to choose another rock. "That was Scott's problem, wasn't it?" He whips the rock across the water. It skips five times before sinking. "I didn't know that she would get all hung up on me."

But again, something about the way he says it makes me think that that's not quite true. "Does Scott know?" I ask.

"Nah. Nobody saw us together at the party, and I don't think she let anyone know. Probably too ashamed of what other people might think of her if they knew she was into someone like me."

I look at him. He's actually cute, but not like Scott. His movements are awkward, like he grew too fast and hasn't yet figured out what to do with those long limbs yet. He's pale, he *really* needs a haircut, and his nose is a bit too big. But his mouth is beautiful—his lips wide and expressive—and long lashes frame those stunning eyes. The little smile lines at the edges tell me that he smiles a lot, and easily. Or used to anyway.

My head spins from everything that he's just told me. So he wasn't hounding Ella. *She* had a secret thing for *him*. Was texting him nonstop. The police wanted to talk to him because they'd probably gone through her phone and seen all her text messages to him.

Oh shit, that reminds me. I fish my phone out of my dress pocket. I switched it off before the funeral. There are five missed calls and a dozen texts—all from Maddy.

> Where r u?

> U ok?

And the last one:

> Young lady, you are this close to being grounded!

> I'm ok. On my way home now

I text back before she really loses it.

"It's Maddy. She's worried about me. I should probably go." A thought occurs to me, and I cover my mouth with my hand. "I can't believe I left her all alone at the service, oh my god." Isaac and I lock eyes again, and when I start to giggle, Isaac grins, the smile lighting up his entire face and transforming it. It's the first time he really smiles at me, and I discover that he has the cutest dimples. I was wrong. He isn't just cute; he's beautiful. I tear my eyes away, back to the lake.

"Then let's get you home," he says.

———

Maddy's silver Toyota Camry is parked in the driveway when we arrive.

"See you in school," I say.

"See you," says Isaac.

He drives away, and I stare at his car until I can't see it anymore, then shake my head. What am I doing? I only just met him. I can't possibly be… I'm much too much of a mess to start falling for someone right now. My life is too complicated without me complicating it further.

I'm just going to have to try to avoid him.

I open the door. Maddy is sitting on the couch in the living room, pretending to leaf through a magazine instead of totally watching us through the window just a moment ago. Thankfully, I don't see Mom and Dad, so I guess she hasn't told them how I just walked out of the service. They're probably taking their usual afternoon nap. She puts the magazine down on the coffee table, and I brace myself because I know she's going to want to talk about what just happened.

I totally called it because she says, "What happened, kid?" without wasting any time.

"I'm sorry I left like that. I just…I couldn't handle being in there anymore."

She sighs and pats the spot on the couch beside her, so I walk over reluctantly and sit down. "Is everything going okay at school?"

"Yeah." I mean, I guess, considering someone just died.

Maddy shoots me a doubtful look. "You know you can tell me anything, right?"

"I know, Maddy."

"Listen, I know you've said before that you don't need it," she continues, taking a deep breath, "but you should really reconsider if therapy might be something you want to try. Like, a trained professional might—"

"I'm fine. Really." I try to push the annoyance down. Why would I need therapy?

She gives me a look, but she drops it. Instead she says, "Where did you go with that boy just now?"

"We just drove around a bit," I say. "We ended up by the lake and talked for a while."

"The lake, huh? He's cute, I'll admit it."

"Maddy!"

"What's his name?"

"It's Isaac, and there's nothing between us." I start heading up the stairs, and luckily, she doesn't try to follow me.

———

That night after dinner, Isaac and his sister occupy my thoughts as I lie in bed.

Who had been bullying her, so much that she felt she had no choice but to try to take her own life? And does Isaac really not know who her online bullies were? It's true they must have hidden behind fake usernames. But...could he have found out who they were nonetheless and is lying about that for some reason?

There's a soft knock on my door, and I sit up as my parents come in.

"So, Isaac, huh?" says my dad. "Tell us about him."

Ugh, I knew Maddy would tell on me. "There's nothing to tell, Dad. He's just someone from school."

My mom arches an eyebrow. "Someone from school who gave you a ride home, after you walked out of your friend's funeral service and ran off with him to the lake?"

"It's not like that," I say lamely.

Dad sighs. "I just don't think getting involved with a boy is the best timing right now, kid."

"I know, Dad. You have nothing to worry about."

———

The next day at lunch, Isaac is already sitting at his customary table with his friends when I walk into the cafeteria. It's like he's some kind of magnet, I'm that aware of his presence. He's wearing a lumpy green sweater today, the kind that looks like some overly enthusiastic grandmother knitted it, and I have to resist the urge to giggle. As I walk past his table, he sees me and straightens up. "Hi," he says, and my heart actually *lurches* this time.

"Um. Hi," I say. Meanwhile, his friends are both staring at me, like I'm a Chihuahua that has suddenly started talking. The girl even has her fork halfway to her pierced lips, as if frozen in surprise.

A giggle rises in my chest, and Isaac grins at me. He gestures to the empty seat beside him.

I stare at him. Is he *challenging* me? "I don't think that's a good idea," I hear myself say.

"Oh." His smile slides off his face. "I should have known you'd care what your friends think."

"I don't care what people in school think," I say. And I don't. Not anymore.

He cocks his head. "Bullshit."

Suddenly furious, I plop down beside him and smile at his friends. "Hi."

"Uh. Hi," says the guy with green hair.

The girl finally realizes that she's still holding the fork halfway to her mouth, and puts it down. "Hi?"

I turn to look at my friends' table. Everyone there is staring at us. No, scratch that. Almost the *entire cafeteria* is staring at us.

"You're a rebel," says Isaac.

"I hate labels," I say.

He grins at me, flashing his dimples, and I can't help but smile back at him.

"Wow. Get a room," says the guy with green hair.

"Mind your own business, Jagger," says Isaac.

The girl is smirking and Jagger is raising his hands in mock surrender when the PA system comes alive and Principal King's voice floats into the cafeteria.

"The following students will please come to my office

immediately. Scott Russell. Naomi Chen. Luciana Aguilar. And Dawn Foster." Principal King repeats our names one more time, then ends the PA announcement.

Isaac is frowning as he stares at me. I stand up on shaky legs, looking over at the others. They also stand, their faces pale and worried. Everyone in the cafeteria is staring at the four of us. The room is suddenly too hot, too bright. The hushed whispering starts even before we're outside.

"Why does King want us in his office?" whispers Lucy to me as we're walking to Principal King's office.

"It has to be related to Ella's party," says Naomi.

Principal King nods to us as we file in. The room is too small for all of us, the space claustrophobic. I try to quell the rising sense of unease, ignore the crawling sensation on my skin.

Then I see who else is in his office, and my heart starts to race. It's Detectives Doyle and Mulchaney. They smile at us, but something about their smiles puts me even more on edge.

"What's this about, sir?" asks Scott, looking from the police officers to Principal King.

Principal King grimaces. "The detectives inform me that they have more questions for all of you."

Doyle nods. "We're going to need a moment of your time."

"Right now? But—why? What about our classes?" says Naomi.

"We just have a few follow-up questions. You do want to assist us in the case, don't you?" says Mulchaney.

"I don't understand," says Lucy, clutching Scott's hand. "What case? Isn't the investigation closed yet?"

The two detectives exchange glances. Doyle is the one who finally replies.

"Ella Moore died from strychnine poisoning. We're now looking at a possible homicide."

HANNAH

Hannah clutches her tray tightly, looking at the long table in the cafeteria where the other cheerleaders are all sitting. The three girls she'd met yesterday, Ella, Naomi, and Lucy, are already there. That should mean that she can sit there too, with the rest of the cheer team. Right?

But what if she tries, and they laugh at her?

Should she, or shouldn't she?

Someone bumps into her from the back, and she stumbles, almost dropping her tray.

"Could you, like, not stand in the middle of the room like that?" the boy snaps at her.

"Sorry," she mumbles automatically.

Maybe she should just find an empty seat somewhere in the corner of the room, like she's been doing since school started. Like that table over there. She starts walking, but as she passes the long table, Ella looks up. "Hey, it's YouTube Girl."

The other cheerleaders, all fifteen of them or so, look up too. They're *all* looking at her. It's the most attention she has ever gotten from her peers in school, and Hannah freezes like a deer caught in headlights.

"YouTube Girl?" asks an older-looking girl with glossy chestnut hair done up in French braids.

"Yeah. She said she learned her cheerleading moves from YouTube," says Ella. Everyone laughs, and Hannah is so mortified, she wishes she'd never told them that.

"Awesome," says the girl with French braids. "Did you make squad?"

"Y-yes," says Hannah.

"Then sit," French Braids says. "Make some room for her, girls."

They all start shifting, and Hannah seats herself at the end of the table, too stunned to say anything.

"I'm Katie," says French Braids. "What's your name? Or do we have to keep calling you YouTube Girl?"

"I'm H-hannah," she stutters.

"Katie is captain of the squad," says the girl sitting on Katie's right. "And I'm Nell. We're seniors. Welcome to the squad, Hannah."

"It's cool that you learned moves on your own like that," says Katie. "Who did you watch?"

Hannah feels like she's in a dream. Everyone is looking at her, smiling at her, like they're really interested in what she has to say. Or almost everyone. Ella is frowning, glancing first at her, then at Katie, then back at her. But everyone else is still waiting for her to answer. "Oh, um…*The Cheer Twins*, and, uh, *Cheerleading for Beginners*…"

"Cool," repeats Katie, nodding. "I watch cheer vids on YouTube too."

Ella's mouth gapes open. Then she seems to catch herself and say, "Which are your favorite channels, Katie?"

"I like *Cheer Champions*. They do some crazy stunting, really impressive."

"Oh, that's my favorite too," says Ella.

The cheerleaders start talking about various cheerleading channels on YouTube, and Hannah wishes that her family were there, that they could see her with all her new friends.

———

When her mom picks her up after school and asks the same question she always does, "So, made any new friends today?" Hannah can't keep her pride out of her voice as she finally gets to reply for the first time, "Yes, Mom, I made friends with all the other cheerleaders."

"You did? That's great!" Her mother turns and beams at her, and the Suburban swerves a little to the left, crossing slightly into the oncoming lane.

"Mom!"

An angry driver honks at them, and her mom corrects the car back into their lane. "Sorry, was just so excited! Look at you, making friends even before the first practice! What are their names? Tell me about them! Hey, you should invite them over to our house after practice—"

"For what?" Hannah goggles at her mother.

"To hang out, silly. That's what teen girls do."

"Oh. I…I don't know. I don't think they'd want to. Especially the seniors." She feels deeply doubtful, but her mother just laughs.

"Then ask the other freshmen. You can all practice in the yard. Your dad and I'll be cool parents and order pizza or something. Come on, Hannah, just try."

"I… Okay. I'll ask them if they want to hang out." They probably wouldn't be interested, but her mom isn't taking no for an answer. A pang of anxiety hits her chest.

But maybe her mom is right. Maybe she should ask them.

Maybe they'd say yes.

DAWN

There is a moment of complete, utter silence. then Lucy exclaims, "Oh my god! Ella was poisoned?"

"What's strychnine?" I ask.

"I know what it is," says Scott. "It's rat poison, isn't it? I've seen it on the label."

Lucy jumps at that, and I turn to look at her, but everyone else is still staring at Scott, whose face has turned sickly pale. "Wait," he says. "Are you saying that one of us *killed* her?"

"I think it's best if we talk to all of you again one by one," says Mulchaney. "Principal King has helpfully agreed that in light of the seriousness of the case, you all do not have to return to your classes until we are done speaking with you."

"You want us to go down to the station with you right now?" says Naomi, her voice rising toward the end of her question until the *now* comes out as an almost-hysterical squeak.

Mulchaney smiles. "That won't be necessary. Principal King has also helpfully agreed to let us have the use of the two counseling rooms right here in school."

We follow the detectives to the waiting room just outside the counseling rooms, like livestock being led to slaughter.

"This shouldn't take too long. Why don't we start with you, Scott?" says Doyle, gesturing to one of the rooms.

"Wait, is this because I know about rat poison? I knew I should have kept my mouth shut about that," mutters Scott as he follows Doyle into the room.

"Luciana, let's use the other room," says Mulchaney, standing in the doorway of the other counseling room.

As soon as the door closes behind them, Naomi says, "Do you think this is, like, an interrogation?"

"I think so," I say in a hushed voice. "I think we're, like, *suspects* now."

"They can't really think that one of us killed her!" says Naomi.

We stare at each other. It's clear we're thinking the same thing. *Is it true? Is one of us a murderer?* It seems impossible, and yet, that's exactly what the detectives are implying.

Naomi pulls out her phone. "God, thank god they called Lucy and Scott in first. I'm calling my parents. I'm not answering any questions until I have a lawyer."

I take my phone out too, but I hesitate, staring at the screen. I should probably call my parents, but I immediately drop the idea. I can't possibly make them worry after what they've been through. Are still going through. I can't call Maddy either because she'll definitely tell my parents.

I put my phone back in my bag. I should be fine. After all, I was one of the ones who left the party first, when Ella was still alive. But then… Cold trickles down my spine. Why have they called me here when they haven't called the others who also left early?

Scott comes out after around twenty minutes, his face pale. He grabs his bag and leaves without saying anything to the rest of us.

I guess it didn't go too well in there for him.

"Your turn, Naomi," says Doyle, standing in the doorway.

Naomi hugs her arms around herself, her lower lip trembling. "I'm not answering any questions until my parents get here. With my lawyer."

Doyle frowns. "You're not under arrest, Naomi. And this isn't an interrogation. We just need to know more clearly what happened that night. You want to help us find out what happened, don't you?"

"I—"

"Unless you have something to hide? It's up to you, but not cooperating with our investigation won't help the way you look."

Naomi visibly blanches, her mouth dropping open for a few seconds, then clamping shut. She stands and shuffles into the room without another word.

They've ambushed us.

Lucy comes out a few minutes later, a blubbery mess. Like Scott, she grabs her bag and runs out of the waiting room without saying anything to the rest of us.

Mulchaney fixes her black eyes on me and flashes me that smile that doesn't reach her eyes. "Your turn, Dawn."

It's my first time in the counseling room. The wall is painted a pale cream, and the armchairs are a cheery canary yellow, decorated with blue cushions. There's a framed picture of a white sailboat, clear blue skies, a shimmering calm sea. The entire room is done up to be as warm and comforting as possible—which is funny now that it's been turned into an interrogation room. I stifle the hysterical urge to giggle.

"Have a seat," Mulchaney says, settling into one armchair. I nod stiffly and sit in the chair across from her as she opens her laptop on the small table between us. She taps at it for a while, then says, "I just want to emphasize again that you're not under arrest, and this isn't an interrogation. You're not a suspect, okay? We just need to really understand what happened that night. So try to relax and recount everything to me again. From the beginning, when you first arrived at Ella's house."

I clear my throat and repeat everything that I told them before.

"Who gave Ella drinks?" she asks.

"Um, everyone at some point, I think?"

"Why didn't she get her own drinks?"

"I don't know," I say, but I do. Ella did it to exercise her power over us. To make it clear that we had to do what she told us to do.

"She stayed in that pool inflatable the entire evening?" asks Mulchaney, raising an eyebrow.

"No, she got out of the pool a few times. To use the bathroom in the pool house. She also danced with us for a while. And she was in the water with Scott for a while too. They were making out."

Mulchaney makes a few more notes, then she fixes those black eyes on me again. "Some of the others mentioned that you just moved to Sierton not long ago."

"Yes…?" How is that relevant to this? Annoyance prickles my chest, and the memory of how they all suddenly turned on me in the cafeteria rose in my mind. *We've had so many parties before, and nothing bad ever happened. You arrive, and someone dies.* It was Lucy who said that. Was she the one telling the detectives now about me, trying to make me look like a possible suspect?

Maybe I can reason with her. "Look, I didn't even know Ella that well. Maybe you should be trying to find out who didn't like her."

"Are there people who didn't like her?"

"Yup, lots. Some of them, her supposed friends."

The memory of Scott saying something at the party flashes across my mind. *The bitch thinks I don't know.* Who was he talking about? Doesn't think he knows about what?

Lucy saying to me, *She doesn't deserve him... Sometimes I hate her.* She clearly wanted Scott for herself. And where was she anyway, just before I left?

Naomi sneaking off with Ella's phone, doing who knows what with it.

Mulchaney is staring at me the entire time as if she's trying to read my thoughts. "Her friends didn't like her? Why don't you tell me why you think so?"

I open my mouth...close it again. What if I was wrong? The *bitch* Scott was talking about could have been anyone. And even if Lucy really had a thing for Scott, it didn't mean she would have killed Ella for him. As for what Naomi was doing with Ella's phone, maybe Ella had asked her to reorganize her aesthetics or something. Thing is, I didn't know enough to say anything for certain. If I told all that to the police, they'd just dismiss it all.

So I keep quiet.

"Is it true that you were the last person who gave her a drink before she died?" says Mulchaney, casually dropping a bomb.

"What? I don't know..." My heart starts beating a hard staccato against my ribs. "Who said that I was the last one to give her a drink?"

Mulchaney doesn't reply, just continues staring at me. Maybe she's just making it up, to see how I would react. Or maybe someone did say that, to try to make me look guilty. Damn it, they really are out to paint me as the one who killed Ella. The world seems to darken around the edges of my vision as I struggle to keep my breathing even. I take a deep breath, try to calm down. Try to reason with the detective. "Look, when she *ordered* me to bring her that drink, I asked her to stop drinking, and she basically told me to butt out of her business. And when I left, she was still alive. She was still *fine*."

"Hmm, that may be the case. But apparently she became unconscious shortly after you left, and according to another witness, you were the last one seen talking to her."

I knew it. I'm a suspect. "Obviously, I can't say if anyone else talked to her or gave her another drink after I left. But it seems unlikely to me that *nobody* talked to her after I left, since the three of them were still there," I say, but her face remains impassive. Too late, I realize that I should have called my parents just now. "I…I'm not answering any more questions without a lawyer. If you want to keep questioning me, you'll have to give me time to get one."

Mulchaney's black eyes pin me down. "I'm done asking questions for now. Just remember my advice from before: Don't leave town."

———

I walk out of school instead of to my next class, ignoring all the curious eyes on me. I'm trembling all over, panic clutching its fingers around my throat. But there's something else besides panic. There's also rage. I can't believe that one of them told the detectives that I was the one who gave Ella her last drink.

Calm down, I order myself. *Think*. From the way Mulchaney spoke to me, the way they spoke to the others, it doesn't look like anyone's officially a suspect yet. They're still gathering information, asking us any questions they can think of that might throw the real killer off guard enough to reveal themselves. They definitely haven't started looking into any of us in particular yet, because if they had, they would have already found out what happened in Santa Cruz.

My mouth goes dry as I realize that if they do a real background check on me, they'll find out what I did in Santa Cruz.

Don't panic. I think over everything that I've seen and heard.

Naomi with Ella's phone.

The bitch thinks I don't know.

Sometimes I hate her.

It's fair enough that Scott, Lucy, and Naomi have their secrets. We all have secrets. But I can't have the police looking into me. I need to do something to clear myself. I need to act fast, find out what the others are hiding—who might have killed Ella—on my own.

HANNAH

The first cheerleading practice is beyond anything Hannah has dared to imagine. For the first time in her life, she feels like she actually belongs. When Coach's whistle rings out, she sinks down to sit on the padded floor, muscles aching but happy.

"Good work, girls. Especially Hannah and Naomi," says Coach, and Hannah feels like she's going to burst with happiness. "Ella, practice your tumbling. It's too messy. Look at Hannah's; it's perfect. You need to practice until you get it right like that."

"Yes, Coach," says Ella in a flat voice, turning to look at her with a strange expression, like Hannah is a toad that suddenly sprouted wings and started flying.

"If tomorrow is sunny like the forecast says, practice will be out on the field. Alright, today's practice is over."

In the locker room, Lucy, Naomi, and Ella are giggling in the corner as they change. Hannah dumps her sweaty clothes in her bag and zips it up, summons up her courage. "Umm, do you guys want to…want to come over to my place?"

They turn to look at her, looking surprised.

"To hang out," Hannah blurts out. "Maybe we could practice in the yard. My parents say they'll order pizza."

Ella exchanges looks with the other girls, then smiles at Hannah. "Sounds fun. Maybe you can help me with my tumbling, since you're *so* good at it."

"Yeah, of course! No problem!"

"Oh! You know what. You go on first. I just need to get some stuff from my locker," says Ella as Naomi and Lucy exchange looks.

"Oh okay, sure! Come on, Naomi, Lucy—"

"Oh, I need Naomi's and Lucy's help too," says Ella.

"With what?" says Lucy.

But Ella ignores her and continues, "Give us your address, and we'll head over right after."

"It's forty-seven North Carline Avenue," says Hannah. "See you all soon!"

"Yeah, see you soon," says Ella.

"Are you sure your friends are coming?" asks her mother, glancing again at the clock on the living room wall. "It's already eight thirty."

"I don't understand. Ella said they were coming right after she got some stuff from her locker." Hannah picks at the bed of her right thumbnail, more and more confused and dejected as the hours pass and the three girls have still not shown.

"Maybe they got lost or couldn't find our address," says her mom. "What's their numbers? Why don't you call them?"

"I...I don't have their numbers."

Her dad sighs and picks up his phone. "Well, I'm hungry, so I'm going to order the pizzas now."

"Something probably came up, and they couldn't make it," says her mom. "I'm sure they'll have a good explanation tomorrow."

———

When Hannah sits down at the long table beside Ella, Lucy, and Naomi at lunch the next day, they don't seem to notice her.

"French manicures are boring," says Ella.

"I think you mean they're classy," says Naomi, admiring her own French manicure.

"I like scarlet nails," says Lucy.

"That's because you're a whore," says Ella, which makes a few other girls laugh.

"Hey! So, um...what happened yesterday?" asks Hannah.

"What?" says Ella.

"I was waiting for you at my place. You were supposed to come over."

"Oh, I guess I forgot," says Ella, smiling with a little shrug of her slim shoulders.

Hannah looks at Naomi, who's staring at her fries, then at Lucy, who shrugs, slightly red in the face. "Did you two forget too?"

"Look, I had a family emergency, and they were with me, and we all forgot, okay?" says Ella.

"Oh! What—"

But Ella has already looked away, as if the conversation was over. "I like Katie's nails. That color's so fresh. What is it?"

"Thanks. It's Mint Dream by Pardon My French," says Katie.

"Oh my god, do you mind if I get it too? I *love* it," says Ella.

"No, course not," says Katie, smiling.

Hannah bites her tongue and picks at her food as the others continue talking.

Nobody ever mentions that day again.

DAWN

I shouldn't be surprised that word gets out quickly in school that Ella's death wasn't an unfortunate accident. Soon, nobody is talking about anything other than her murder.

In the hallway, I try to pretend I don't notice heads swiveling to stare at me as I make my way to my locker. Try to pretend I don't hear the whispering—*I heard that all four of them planned together to kill her!* Try not to panic when I see Detectives Doyle and Mulchaney. Even though they've left the four of us alone since the last time they ambushed us—with the exception of me, all the others have lawyered up—they must be here to question the teachers and other students.

I'm opening my locker when Raquel finds me.

"Is it true that someone gave her rat poison?" she asks, her eyes big in her face. "Or that Scott slept beside her dead body the entire night?"

I glance quickly around us to make sure that nobody is listening in, then nod reluctantly.

Her eyes widen. "So she *was* murdered! Who—"

"I don't know, but apparently I'm also a suspect because someone told them that I was the last to speak with Ella, to give her a drink," I say bitterly.

Raquel gapes at me. "That's ridiculous! But seriously, who do you think might have done it?"

"I have no idea, but I'm going to find out."

———

"Do you have *any* idea how difficult it was to sit through all my classes waiting for school to end today?" says Raquel when I'm finally in her room that evening. I'm seated at her study desk, but she's bouncing up and down on her toes in the middle of her room, full of pent-up energy. "And then to wait further for you to finish practice and come over? Well? Tell me what you mean by you're *going to find out!*"

"I'm going to do my own investigation on what exactly happened that night. But first…whatever I tell you from now on, please don't talk about it outside of this room, okay?"

She stops bouncing. "What? Why not?"

"So that I can find out what I need to know without the killer getting tipped off about it. Do you promise?"

She nods quickly. "Of course. But only if I can help."

"Okay!" I reach for my bag, pull out a blank notebook. "I need to approach this methodically. Maybe I can start by making a timeline of that night's events."

She pulls up a vegan-fur stool and plops herself beside me. "Like where everybody was, what they were doing, that kind of thing?"

"Exactly like that."

Thinking back furiously to that evening, I get to work as Raquel looks on:

8:30–9

- I arrived; everyone else was already there
- overheard Scott saying to Brett, "The bitch thinks I don't know" (??)

9–11:15?

- Everybody brought Ella a drink at some point (I think)
- Ella told me that everyone else was afraid of her
- Lucy said she hated Ella and that she didn't deserve Scott, then she brought Ella another drink

11:15–11:30?

- Found Naomi in one of the bathrooms with Ella's phone (!!!) we came back to the pool, Naomi put Ella's phone back on the table

11:30?

- Ella asked me to get her another drink. She seemed very drunk.

11:35?

- Others start going home, leaving only me, Scott, and Naomi
- Didn't see Lucy, where was she??
- Naomi went in the house
- Scott came out of the pool house

I stare at my notes. Writing all that down has jarred a memory loose. It was after Scott came out of the pool house…

"What is it?" says Raquel.

"There was someone else at the party."

"What? What do you—"

I look up at her. "There was someone else. Scott and I both saw someone lurking at the pool, at the far end. In the shadows. When Scott called out to them, they disappeared without replying."

"What? Who?"

I shake my head. "I don't know. They were too far away, and it was too dark." I shiver, remembering the way the person slunk into the shadows as soon as we saw them. As if they didn't want to be seen.

Raquel frowns. "You just remembered this? You haven't told the police about this person?"

"Yeah. It was only a couple of seconds, and…I guess I didn't think too much of it at the time. We thought she died from alcohol intoxication at first, remember? But maybe Scott did tell the police

CINDY R. X. HE

about it. Regardless, I should go update my statement." I pick up the pen again:

> NOTE: Tell the police about the person we saw at the pool!!!
> 11:45?
> • went to wait for Maddy in the driveway. She arrived
>   5 mins later and we left.

Raquel pulls my notebook closer to her and goes over my notes. "*The bitch thinks I don't know* sounds juicy. What's that about?"

"I have no idea. He stopped talking as soon as he saw me."

"And what was Naomi doing with Ella's phone?" says Raquel, and I turn my palms up and shrug. *Who knows?*

"Okay, so Scott, Lucy, and Naomi were still around after you'd left."

I nod. "Scott was by the pool, and Naomi went in the house to sleep."

Raquel frowns. "And you have no idea where Lucy was."

"No idea, but I know she was still there because she told us that she only left later, when Scott brought Ella into the house at around one."

"That leaves almost an hour, between midnight and one. What were Scott, Ella, and Lucy doing between midnight and one?"

I nod. "That's what we need to find out. Anyway, according to Scott and Lucy, Ella was still alive, albeit super drunk, at around one in the morning." I update my notes:

1:00

- *Scott carried Ella into the house, Ella still alive. Lucy left.*

QUESTION: *What were Scott and Lucy doing between 11:50 and 1???*

"Hmm. How do we know Naomi was really sleeping, even?" says Raquel. "She could have gone to their bedroom after Scott fell asleep and killed her."

I scratch my head. "Wouldn't it be difficult to get somebody to imbibe poison if they were already unconscious? We should read up on strychnine."

Rachel fires up her laptop and googles it. According to Wikipedia, strychnine, if consumed, is a fast-acting poison. Starting as early as ten minutes after exposure, the body's muscles begin to spasm. The convulsions progress, increasing in intensity until the person eventually dies by asphyxiation, two to three hours later.

"Look!" says Raquel, pointing at one spot on the screen. "*Poisoning can take place not only by mouth but also by inhalation.* So Ella could have been poisoned when she was unconscious by making her breathe it in. Or look, *injected directly into a vein.*"

"So it's still possible that Naomi did it." But I'm shaking my head even as I say it. Possible...but unlikely? There was still the matter of what the hell Naomi was doing with Ella's phone. It's probably not related, but it could be.

Or could that lurker we saw have stayed hidden until they all went in the house, and then snuck into the house afterward and made Ella breathe in (or injected her with) the poison while they were all sleeping?

Raquel is still scrolling down and reading. "*Although death usually occurs two to three hours after exposure to the poison, the symptoms—body spasms—start appearing much earlier. As early as ten to twenty minutes after exposure.* If she was never alone, then how could no one have noticed if she had body spasms?"

Could Scott have been so drunk that if she'd been having body spasms beside him in bed, it didn't even wake him up? Maybe. Or could he be lying about something?

Could both Lucy and he be lying?

"There are so many things we don't know." Raquel heaves a frustrated breath out.

"At least we know one thing for sure," I say, closing my notebook. "Naomi, Scott, and Lucy are all hiding something." Speaking of hiding things…why do I keep having the feeling that Isaac hasn't been completely honest with me either?

I find that I want to know more about his sister. Like who her bullies were. "Do you know anything about Isaac's sister?" I ask, changing the subject awkwardly.

Raquel shakes her head. "I don't really know how she is now. If you're asking about why she tried to kill herself, I don't know either. None of us really knew her. I wish I did. I wish I spoke to her more."

My phone buzzes, a text from my dad:

Maddy is asking if u need a ride home
from Raquel's

It's only a 15 min walk,
tell her no need but thx!

"I gotta go," I tell Raquel. "Thanks for helping with this."

"Of course!" She grins. "I mean, everything about this is horrible, but this part is"—her voice drops to a sheepish whisper—"*fun*. You know. The investigating."

On my walk home, my mind wanders back to Isaac's words that day by the lake. *She was being bullied in school. We only found out afterward, when we came across the comments on her social media.*

He said he didn't know who her bullies were.

So why can't I shake off the feeling that he's lying?

HANNAH

Hannah hits the floor hard, face-first. A sharp pain and the metallic taste in her mouth tells her that she's bitten her tongue. Luckily the floor is padded, otherwise she'd be hurting a lot more.

"Oof, are you okay?" says Ella, extending her a hand. Hannah hesitates, then takes it and lets Ella help her up. For a moment, she thought that Ella tripped her on purpose... She must have been mistaken.

Coach is frowning at her. "That was a basic cartwheel. How did you mess that up?"

"I...I don't—" stutters Hannah.

Coach cuts in impatiently. "I gave you a chance because you did well during the audition. It's not an excuse to slack now. Every girl here has to prove she deserves a place on the squad. I won't hesitate to kick off people who don't deserve to be here."

"I'll spot her until she gets it right, Coach," says Ella, smiling.

Coach nods and walks off as Hannah's heart sinks into her stomach. It's the second week of practice, and already she's screwing it up.

"Wanna try that one more time?" asks Ella sweetly.

———

Hannah is in the parking lot, waiting for her mom to come pick her up, when she realizes she's forgotten her cell phone in her locker in the changing room. She runs back in the building, back to the changing room. She pushes the door open, is about to go in when she hears her name.

"You tripped her today, didn't you?" Uneasiness twists inside Hannah's stomach as she recognizes Naomi's voice, and Ella's laugh.

"Wasn't it funny, the way she hit the floor face-first?" says Ella.

"What if she told Coach that you tripped her?" says Lucy.

"She wouldn't dare. And even if she did, it's her word against mine."

Hannah presses her hand to her mouth. Her head is swirling, and there's a roaring sound in her ears.

"What are you doing, Ella?" says Naomi.

"She shouldn't be here. I don't know what the hell Coach was thinking, letting someone like that on the squad."

"*Someone like that?*"

"You know what I mean," snaps Ella. "Look at her; she's not really cheerleader material, is she?"

Why did she come back? She should have left her phone here, come to get it tomorrow. What if Ella realizes that she's here, listening to them? She needs to get out of here. But she's frozen in place, like she's been transformed into a sweating statue.

"She's actually pretty good, when you're not tripping her," Naomi drawls. "Are you jealous of her?"

Ella gives a barking laugh. "Jealous of *her*? You gotta be fucking kidding."

"Oh my god, you are, aren't you?" says Naomi. "You're jealous of all the attention she's getting from Coach and the seniors. Coach thinks her tumbling is better than yours. You thought she was someone to be pitied, but she turned into a threat."

There's a silence, then Ella says, "Actually, I don't think she's going to last on the squad."

"What do you mean? It's not like you can get her kicked off or anything," says Lucy.

"We'll see, won't we?"

The sound of approaching footsteps. But Hannah can't move, standing in the doorway with the door half-open, unable to run. Then Ella's face: first shocked, then furious.

"What the f—were you eavesdropping on us?"

"No! I wasn't... You tripped me!"

Ella stares at her. "No, I didn't."

"You just said it! I heard you! I..." All she wanted was to be friends with these people. She'd even invited them to her house. Humiliation washes over her as she realizes that Ella, Naomi, and Lucy must have pretended they were coming, then purposely never showed. They were probably laughing at her the entire time. And Ella *tripped* her, caused her to fall and Coach to be angry with her. Worse, she *wants her kicked off the squad*. An unfamiliar feeling surges in her. "I'm going to tell Coach!"

Ella's face pales, and she grabs Hannah's arm in a painful grip. "Listen, bitch. It's your word against mine. Coach won't believe you. And if you try to spread lies about me, I'll destroy you. Now step aside, loser."

She gives Hannah a shove and stomps past, Lucy following quickly behind her. Hannah turns to look at Naomi, but she just shrugs and walks out too, and Hannah realizes that Lucy and Naomi don't give a shit about her, certainly aren't going to corroborate anything she might say to Coach or anyone else. Tears are streaming down her face, and she wipes them away with a shaking hand.

She stands there for another ten minutes or so, then makes up her mind. She starts walking to Coach's office.

DAWN

The next day at break, people are conspicuously missing from our table. There are only four of us here—the four of us who were questioned yesterday. It's like the other cheerleaders and footballers don't want to be seen hanging with us anymore.

"Scott," I say in a low voice. "Do you remember that person we saw that night? The one who ran away when you called out to them?"

"Yeah?" he grunts.

"I'd totally forgotten about them. Did you—"

"Did I tell the police about that person? Of course I did." Scott crushes his Coke can in his hand, frowning. "It was the first thing I told that detective yesterday. But he was so skeptical, like he thought I made that up or something. Wait, you didn't tell them about it?"

"I only just remembered yesterday evening. But I'm going to—"

"Goddamn it! No wonder they didn't believe me." Scott pushes back his tray and stands. "Yeah, tell them, please." Lucy reaches for his hand—but he snatches his away. "Leave me alone, Lucy," he snaps, before stalking away, leaving only Naomi, Lucy, and me.

Lucy sits back down, her bottom lip trembling. She shoots a glare at me, and I look away as she reaches for a slice of pizza and crams it in her mouth.

We stare at each other, mistrust evident on our faces.

While all this is happening, the rest of the cafeteria watches on. My skin is positively crawling with the number of eyes on me. I catch some people smiling, as if they're enjoying the show.

Lucy finishes off another slice of pizza. "Naomi," she says in a low voice. "The rat poison thing…"

"What about it?" snaps Naomi.

"Remember? What Ella said to…?" Lucy whispers, her face pale, eyes darting around.

Naomi's eyes widen as Lucy's voice trails off.

"What?" I ask, but they both ignore me.

"It's just a coincidence," Naomi says.

"What are you talking about?" I try again.

"Nothing," they both snap at me at the same time.

"Wow, fine," I mutter, raising my hands.

"Maybe she's haunting us," whispers Lucy, her voice wavering. Suddenly, she stares in horror at the third slice of pizza dripping oil down her hand, and she drops it back on her plate like it's burning her skin.

"She can't be haunting us, you idiot. First of all, there's no such thing as ghosts," Naomi hisses.

Haunting? Ghosts? I stare at the two of them. Am I in a gothic novel?

Naomi continues. "Secondly—" But the bell rings, and she breaks off. She stands up abruptly and hisses, "It's just a coincidence. She's gone." But her eyes dart around the cafeteria as she says it, as if to make sure this person/ghost/boogeyman isn't hiding somewhere nearby.

"Who?" I ask.

"God! Mind your own business, won't you?" snaps Lucy. But then the left side of her mouth curls up into a strange smile. "If you want to poke your nose into other people's business, why don't you start with your boyfriend?"

"My…" I can feel my face start to heat up. "I don't know what you mean."

"Aren't you dating him now? We all saw you sit with him and those weirdos yesterday."

I wish she'd stop calling people *weirdos*. "We're not dating. I was just—"

She cuts me off with a roll of her eyes. "Don't let his geeky exterior fool you. He's hiding something from you. I'm only warning you because we're friends." When I just stare at her, she continues. "I'll spell it out for you. You might want to ask him why he was banging Ella after how Ella treated his sister. I forget her name. Is she really a vegetable now?"

Lucy's words hit me like a bucket of ice water. She knew that Ella slept with Isaac? But more importantly, what did Ella do to his sister? Was Ella one of the people who bullied her?

As I sit frozen, they push their trays in my direction. "Help us return these, will you?" Naomi says sweetly as Lucy hurries out of the cafeteria like she usually does, running to the nearest restroom to purge her meal.

I'm the last one at the tray station when someone puts a hand on my arm, making me jump. It's Isaac. "Hey. Are you okay? I've been hearing lots of rumors." His green eyes are warm, full of concern.

"Can't talk. I have to get to class," I blurt out, and turn to go.

But he reaches out and grabs my arm again. "Dawn. Wait. Want to go to that spot by the lake after school? We can talk then."

I'm torn. I don't know how to feel after what Lucy just said. But for some reason, I also want to be there with him.

"I have practice after school," I say.

"After practice, then."

I stare at him. He waits patiently for my reply.

"Okay."

We're both silent as Isaac drives. Maybe he senses that I don't feel like talking, not until we get to the lake. I have the passenger window wound down completely, my eyes closed, letting the wind hit my face. It's freezing cold but it's good this way, numbing the skin on my face. If only it could numb my feelings too.

If only things weren't so complicated.

If only we weren't all keeping secrets.

For a moment, I allow myself to imagine what it would be like to be with Isaac. Throw what belongings we have in the trunk and drive somewhere far away. Somewhere where I wouldn't wake up every morning feeling the weight of my past mistakes.

We reach the usual spot, and Isaac parks and turns off the sputtering engine. Pine needles crunch under our feet as we walk the last dozen yards to the lake. It's a lot colder today than it was the other time we were here. Today's sun is completely obscured by the fog that surrounds us. The branches of the cottonwood trees, already half-naked, stretch forlornly against the gray sky. The lake itself is black today, malignant, its icy water full of secrets. I put my hands in my pockets to try to keep them warm, and we sit in silence until he says, "Is something wrong?"

"Was Ella one of the people who bullied your sister?" The question slithers out of me, rears its ugly head, ready to bite.

Isaac's face changes immediately. "I knew someone would tell you sooner or later." He looks away, back out at the black coldness of the lake. His expression is equally cold, and for a moment, I almost regret asking. But then he sighs and just looks sad. "She was," he says in a soft voice. "Ella, Lucy, and Naomi. But Ella was the worst one."

I don't know what to think. I don't know why, but I feel like crying. "But then why...why did you—"

"Why did I sleep with her?" Isaac laughs, a cold sound that chills me to the bone. "Because I wanted revenge for my sister. When I read the comments Ella wrote on her Instagram page, I…I lost it. I couldn't let her get away with what she'd done." Isaac whips a stone over the surface of the lake, and I suppress a shiver as it sinks into the cold black water. "She needed to be taught a lesson. I was going to teach her that lesson.

"For two years, I didn't know how I was going to do it. Then when I bumped into her at the end of summer this year at a friend's party, a ridiculous idea occurred to me. I flirted with her, and surprisingly, it worked. Maybe she was drunk. Maybe she fought with her boyfriend. Maybe it also helped that I'd grown four inches over the summer, and my skin cleared up. She was into me. So I slept with her. Then I dumped her." He sighs and rubs his face tiredly. "It didn't make me feel better, only worse. It didn't make my sister better."

So that's what happened.

"Do you want me to bring you back home now?" he asks.

"No." The word shoots out of me quickly, surprising me.

"You don't mind the company of someone who did something like that?"

I consider his question for a moment. "It was a shitty thing to do…but I guess I understand why you did it."

He throws a doubtful glance at me, and we sit in silence again. Then he says, "Do the police really think that Ella was murdered?"

I nod. "She died from, um, strychnine poisoning. Scott said that's *rat poison*."

"Jesus." Isaac shakes his head. "That's what I heard, but there are so many rumors floating around, I didn't believe it. What a horrible way to die."

"I know, right?"

"Didn't you leave early? Why did the police question you too?"

"Apparently, someone told them that I was the last person who talked to Ella and who gave her a drink before she died," I say, my voice trembling.

He throws me a startled look. "You were?"

"I don't know! I left as soon as I gave her that drink that she wanted. I don't know what happened after I left."

"You think that one of them may have lied to the police?"

"I don't know." I close my eyes. "All I know is she was fine when I left. And Scott, Lucy, and Naomi were still there. Oh! And maybe one more person."

Isaac's head whips up to look at me. "One more person? Who?"

"I don't know. We didn't get a good look at them. They were sort of lurking at the far end of the pool, in the shadows, but they disappeared when Scott called out to them."

We sit in silence for a few minutes.

"Maybe the police are making everyone think they're a suspect, some kind of interrogation tactic," says Isaac.

"Maybe."

"I just can't believe that someone killed her." Isaac shakes his head, as if he's trying to wrap his head around it.

"And that someone is one of us who was there at the party," I add, my voice hushed.

It's apt that he's brought us here, to this quiet, cold, foggy place, to talk about murder. The cold is creeping under my jacket, and I shiver.

"Weren't they all her friends? Why would one of them have wanted her dead?" he asks casually.

"Good question. That's what I'm trying to find out."

His eyes widen. "What do you mean?"

"I think some of them didn't like her very much." Quickly, I tell him what I saw and heard that night. Lucy's outburst. Scott's angry remark.

Isaac's face turns even paler than usual when I finish telling him what Scott said to Brett. *The bitch thinks I don't know.* All at once I get what he must be thinking and gasp. I don't know why I didn't think about it earlier. "You don't think…you don't think Scott might have found out that Ella cheated on him with you, do you?" I ask.

Isaac shrugs grimly. "Could be. Although, murder is a bit extreme even for that, isn't it?"

"I don't know. Maybe his ego couldn't take it. He sounded pretty furious when he said it." Did Scott find out and kill Ella in a rage?

The sun dips over the horizon, and the temperature immediately drops a few more notches. I start shivering for real. Isaac notices and frowns. "You'll need warmer clothes than what you've got."

"I know. I've forgotten how cold it gets here in Wisconsin," I say. He looks at me, confused, and I explain, "I've been here a couple of times before, with my parents to visit Maddy."

Isaac looks at me in alarm. "Your lips are blue."

"Why do you care about me?" I blurt out.

He shoots me a startled look. "Well, I don't want you catching pneumonia on my watch—"

"No, I mean…you came to ask if I was okay. In the cafeteria. Why do you care if I'm okay or not?"

He sighs. "Because this whole thing is so awful, and uh, we're kind of friends, aren't we?" I give a small nod, and the corner of Isaac's mouth twitches. "Well. I was hoping for a slightly more enthusiastic response than that, but okay."

"Sorry, it's been a long day."

"And you're freezing."

"And I'm freezing," I agree.

"Come on then, let's get you home before you turn into a Popsicle," he says, getting up and pulling me to my feet.

In the car, Isaac puts a CD into the stereo system, which I'm surprised works considering how old and beat-up the rest of the car is. An electric guitar riff starts, then rock music floods the car interior.

"What song is this?" I ask.

"'You Shook Me All Night Long,' AC/DC."

"Wow, I didn't know people still listened to rock music these days," I tease.

He grins. "Look, at some point you're just going to have to acknowledge that I'm deeply uncool, and I don't care who knows it."

I grin back at him. "That's okay. I'm uncool too."

———

When we reach Maddy's house, the words tumble out of me before I can stop them. "Hey, maybe we should exchange numbers or something. Since we're friends."

To my relief, he smiles and hands his phone to me. "Put in your number." I do so, little bubbles fizzing inside me like I drank an entire bottle of champagne. When I hand it back to him, he dials it, letting my phone ring twice before hanging up. He smiles at me, his dimples flashing. "There you go; now we're real friends who have each other's numbers and everything."

"Wow," I reply, grinning too. "Thanks, real friend."

"I think your aunt is going to burst out here if I don't go soon," he says, and I look up and catch Maddy's face in the window before she ducks away.

"Oh god, I'm so sorry about that," I say. "She's just worried for me."

"Of course she is, and there's no need to apologize. See you, Dawn."

I step out of his car, and then he's off.

What am I doing? Why do I keep getting closer to him? Why

am I so happy that we're now friends? And why do I want us to be more than that?

My phone rings again, jolting me out of my thoughts, but this time it's Raquel calling. I barely manage a *Hi* when she cuts me off, her voice breathless with excitement.

"I know what's going on with Lucy. You know, why she hates Ella."

"You do? Why? Tell me!"

"Scott and Lucy used to be a couple."

I'm speechless for a few seconds. Raquel doesn't say anything else, obviously enjoying the effect her news is having on me. Finally, I manage to muster an incredulous "*What?*"

"Yeah. They dated very briefly in sophomore year, like, just two months or so. I just remembered, they used to hold hands in the hall. Then he started dating Ella. Honestly, it was so brief I totally forgot about it, like everyone else, I guess."

Wow. Why didn't anyone on the squad ever mention this? Although that was possibly because everyone was afraid of incurring Ella's wrath by bringing it up. Or maybe because it was such a short-lived romance, they all forgot it ever happened, like Raquel.

Everyone except Lucy, who apparently never got over it.

HANNAH

Hannah stands outside Coach Davis's office, willing herself to knock on the door. Her courage, so new and unfamiliar, had gradually given out with every step she took until, by the time she reached the office, she was back to her usual timid, unsure self. Just as she's about to turn around and walk away, however, the door suddenly swings open.

"Hannah?" Coach asks, surprised. "Are you looking for me?"

"Ella tripped me," Hannah blurts out before she can regret it.

"What?"

"Just now during practice, when I fell while doing my cartwheel. It was because she tripped me."

Coach Davis just looks at her. Then she says, "I think you'd better come in. Close the door behind you."

Hannah follows her into the office. "Sit," Coach instructs,

gesturing at the chair in front of her desk as she sits down in her own chair. "Why didn't you say anything then, when you fell?"

Hannah perches uncomfortably on the edge of the chair. "Because I wasn't sure then, but I know now. I heard her in the locker room. She tripped me on purpose because she doesn't like me!"

Coach sighs. "Hannah. This is a serious accusation. I'll have to speak with Ella, ask her side on this."

Hannah feels herself turning cold. "No, don't speak with her, please—"

Coach shoots her a sharp look. "You want me to take just your word for it?"

"No, I…" Hannah squirms in her seat. She should never have told on Ella. If she finds out, she'll make her life even more miserable. Hannah feels like crying. "Can…can we forget I told you this?"

There is a long silence as Coach regards her coolly, until Hannah drops her gaze onto the floor. Then Coach speaks again, her voice chilly. "I don't think highly of people who make up stories, Hannah. Now, I have to go. I hope this doesn't happen again. And I hope for your sake that you try to get along with everyone else. We don't need this kind of drama in the squad."

———

The next day, it was clear Coach spoke to Ella anyway, asked her about the incident, because Ella corners her in the locker room before practice. "You little tattletale." Her face is a mask of fury as she grips Hannah's arm, nails digging into her skin.

"Let go of me." Hannah tries to pull away, but Ella is holding her arm too tightly. She looks around frantically, but the only other girls in the room are Lucy and Naomi, and they don't look concerned.

"Fat lot of good it did you though." Her lips pull upward in a triumphant grin. "I told you it would be your word against mine, and Coach believes me, not you. But you tried to get me in trouble, you bitch. You thought you could get me kicked off the team, huh?"

"No! I—"

"You're going to regret this," Ella hisses, and Hannah's insides shrivel up into a small hard ball.

———

It's two days later when Ella makes her move.

"How did your day go?" her mom asks as Hannah climbs into the Suburban's passenger seat after practice.

"Fine." She keeps her face turned to the window so her mom can't see her puffy red-rimmed eyes.

But her mom isn't so easily fooled, because after a few minutes, she tries again. "Everything okay with your new friends?"

"Yes, fine," she replies in a monotone, at which point her mom drops it.

Thinking about what happened just now makes her eyes well up again, and she digs her nails into her arms to stop from crying.

The morning started so incredibly when she found a note in her locker from Brett. She read the note quickly, her hands trembling. Then she read it again. And again.

Hey Hannah, want to go get ice cream or something after practice today? Meet me outside the guys' locker room at 5? Brett

Brett. Tall and handsome Brett, with his dazzling smile and that dimple in his chin, like a young Henry Cavill as Superman, but with sandy blond hair.

Her heart was doing little fluttering things in her chest, and her hands were sweating as she clutched the note tightly to her belly. When she felt like she could breathe again, she folded the note carefully and tucked it into her jeans pocket. Then she texted her mom to tell her that she was hanging out with her friends after practice and that she'd get a ride back home from one of them.

She reread the note over and over again throughout the day until she practically memorized it. She was going on a date with *Brett* after practice. A *date*. Going for ice cream together was a date, right? It would be her first ever. Nobody has ever been interested in her before.

But even Brett didn't change the fact that practice was awful. When their coach wasn't in the room, someone made snorting noises like a pig's whenever she attempted any move. She wasn't sure exactly who was doing it, but it came from the direction where Ella, Lucy, and Naomi were standing. When she whirled around to see who was making the noises, they just broke out in giggles.

Then when she tried to collect her uniforms, her pack wasn't there. It was the only one missing. Coach said she'd check again with the supplier. After Coach left the locker room, Ella smiled at her and said, "They probably didn't have your size."

"What's your size anyway? *XXL*?" Lucy added.

"I'm an *L*," she said, but Lucy just frowned.

"Do you just eat whatever you want?"

"I—"

"You know, some of us put in some effort."

You mean, rush to the restroom to vomit after every lunch break, like you? Hannah thought but didn't dare to say out loud, of course. It was obvious that Lucy and Naomi had turned on her too, sided with their friend.

"What are you going on about?" It was the head cheerleader, Katie. She was frowning, and had obviously overheard. "L is a perfectly normal size. And Hannah looks great. Don't pay any attention to them, Hannah."

Lucy and Ella mumbled something, slunk away.

After everyone else left, Hannah cried for a while. It was when she went to throw her used tissues in the trash that she found her stolen uniform pack, discarded in a heap inside the trash can.

When her eyes weren't red anymore, she headed to the boys' locker room to meet Brett. She pretended not to see the surprised sideways glances the other guys on the football team gave her as they came out one by one.

And then Brett was there, chatting with one of his friends as he walked in front of her, past her. He looked so cute with his still-wet hair curling slightly at the ends.

"Brett!"

"Uh…what?" he said.

Hannah smiled at him, but he seemed confused. That was when she felt her first twinge of doubt. "You…you asked me to meet you here. In your note?"

He frowned. "Note? What note?"

"You left a note in my locker. To go get ice cream together. Didn't you?" But even as she said the words, she realized that she'd been stupid. So, so stupid.

"Uh, no?" Brett said, the incredulity on his face broadcasting his thoughts. *Me, pass someone like* you *a note? To ask* you *out?*

She heard laughter as she turned and fled.

She ran back into the girls' locker room and hid until she was sure everyone else had gone. Then she texted her mom to let her know that she needed a ride home from school after all.

Even now, she can still hear their laughter ringing in her ears.

DAWN

My chance to find out more about Lucy and Scott comes the next day during lunch.

Scott doesn't come to join us at our table—electing instead to sit with Brett at a small table further away, by the window. Lucy is visibly upset; she's gorging herself on a second plate of fries, all while sneaking looks at Scott.

Finally, she gets up, goes over, and says something to him. She puts her hand on his shoulder. He shrugs it off, says something back to her. Brett, obviously uncomfortable, gets up to go. Scott gets up too and leaves with Brett. I'm watching it all with interest out of the corner of my eye while pretending not to notice—just like everyone else.

Lucy doesn't come back to join us. She walks quickly, stiffly, out of the cafeteria, abandoning her tray at our table.

I get up too and clear my tray. Outside the cafeteria, she's hurrying toward the nearest girls' restroom, and I follow.

The restroom is empty save one of the stalls, from which come retching sounds. Then, the sound of the toilet flushing. And finally, soft sniffling. I wait a few more minutes. When Lucy gives a particularly loud sob, I knock gently on the door of her stall.

"Lucy? It's Dawn. What's wrong?"

Silence for a few seconds. Then, "Go away, Dawn."

"You're obviously upset about something. Talk to me."

More silence.

I try again. "I'm not going away until I know you're okay."

Even more silence, punctuated by soft sniffles.

I'm just about to give up and leave when she unlocks the door and comes out, eyes puffy from crying. "It's Scott," she says, blowing her nose into a tissue. "He said that we shouldn't be together right now."

I give her what I hope is a comforting pat on her back. "What? Why?"

"I don't know. Some stupid thing about how it makes him look bad to be seen dating someone so soon, especially if that someone is Ella's friend."

"Oh my god, that's such bullshit," I say, hopefully looking outraged enough for her.

"I know, right?"

"Especially after how he treated you before."

She throws me a sideways look. "Oh, you heard, did you?"

"How he broke up with you for Ella? Yeah."

"Who told you?" Her lips are a thin line.

"I can't remember. Naomi, maybe. Or maybe someone else on the squad."

She sniffs. "Of course they did. Those gossipy bitches."

A girl comes in and stands in front of one of the mirrors, applying lip gloss. She doesn't seem to notice Lucy's irritation at her presence.

"Oh sweetie. That color makes you look ghastly," Lucy says. The girl throws her a startled look. Lucy just keeps smiling at her, and the girl hightails it out of here.

"What else did they tell you?" she asks as soon as the door closes behind the girl.

"Not much, just that."

"I don't know what you heard, but Scott was *mine first*."

She glares at me, her hands clenching into fists. I try not to think about or look at those sharp nails. Then she tears up again.

"He was my first boyfriend. We were both sophomores. I fell in love with him when I first saw him playing on the field." Lucy blows her nose again as I nod and make sympathetic noises. "We dated for almost two months. I gave him my virginity!" she cries, before bursting into fresh sobs. I pat her back again tentatively and she continues, the words rushing out of her like a flood bursting out of a dam. "Then Ella decided *she* wanted him." She turns, stares at herself in the mirror, clutching the sides of the sink with both hands so tightly that her knuckles turn white.

"I don't understand," I say, shaking my head. "Why would she do that?"

"I think she just liked the idea of having the quarterback as her boyfriend. She was so insecure. It's why she always craved attention, and why she was so obsessed with being the *best*. She didn't really love him; she just saw him as a trophy. Not like me. I've always only loved Scott," she says, blowing her nose.

I bite the inside of my cheek. *Sure, after two months.* "But why did he break up with you for her?"

"Because that bitch told him I cheated on him." She whips her head back to face me. "But I didn't! Chris was the one that kissed me. He was drunk. I pushed him away! But Ella spun this entire story to Scott about how I was the one who came on to Chris."

"Wow, that's awful," I say, shaking my head sympathetically. "How do you know that she didn't even love him?"

"If she did, she wouldn't have cheated on him, would she?" Lucy says, casting me a sly look. "You don't know about that, do you?"

I shake my head as if I have no idea what she's talking about. "She cheated on him? With whom?"

"With your new boyfriend," she says, barely managing to conceal her smile now. She's enjoying herself now. "She told me. Boasted about it. Said that loser was a good lay. But then he lost interest in her after that one time, and she started to get really obsessed with him. As if she was shocked someone like *him* had the audacity to lose interest in someone like *her*. That was fun to watch," she smirked. "Is it true? Is he a good lay?"

Heat surges into my face. My hand twitches with the urge to

slap her, and I fight to keep my expression blank. "I don't know. He's not my boyfriend."

"Oh? Could have fooled me."

"We just talk sometimes."

But Lucy is losing interest already, turning to the mirror to examine her face. "Ugh, this mascara is supposed to be water-proof! I don't have makeup remover on me. I can't step out of the bathroom like this," she says, wiping under her eyes with a tissue to remove the mascara that's smudged there.

"Here, use a bit of this lotion; it'll help get that off." I pass her the small bottle of lotion that I carry with me for dry skin emergencies.

"Thanks."

I watch her reapply her mascara and a bit of lip gloss, then ask as casually as I can, "Does Scott know that Ella cheated on him?"

Lucy turns back to me. "Why do you want to know?"

"Just wondering why you haven't told him, since you care for him so much."

Her eyes narrow. "That's none of your business."

"No, of course, it isn't—"

"You have a lot of questions, don't you?"

"I—"

"You won't tell anyone else what I've just told you, right?"

"Of course not."

"Good," she says, not taking her eyes off me.

The voice recording on my phone finishes playing, Lucy's voice still drifting in the air.

"Wow," breathes Raquel. "So Lucy definitely had a motive."

I nod. "Killing Ella would be killing two birds with one stone. Taking revenge on her, and getting Scott back at the same time."

We're huddled at the back of the computer lab. Miss Ward, our Computer Science teacher, is late, so I took the chance to play the voice recording I secretly did of my conversation with Lucy on my phone.

"If Lucy wanted Scott back so much, why hasn't she told him about Ella cheating on him with Isaac?" says Raquel.

Raquel has a point. It's obvious Scott doesn't know yet. Because if Lucy told him, he wouldn't have continued dating Ella, right? He was quick to dump Lucy immediately back when she supposedly cheated on him.

Unless, Lucy did tell him…but he didn't break up with Ella for some reason.

I have to find out for sure if Scott knows that Ella cheated on him.

———

Since Lucy has clammed up, and my instinct tells me that Scott would be the last person in the world who would tell me anything about that, the best way to find out would be to ask his best friend, Brett. It might be difficult to get it out of him, but it shouldn't be impossible. He's been flirting with me ever since I made the cheer squad.

Well, up till the night of the party when Ella died, anyway.

Guess a friend dying and your romantic interest becoming a murder suspect would kill anyone's mood.

Finding a way to talk to Brett alone turns out to be much harder than I thought it was going to be. We share a class—Algebra 2—but he sits on the other side of the room from me. Furthermore, I have to broach the subject without making him suspicious as to why I'm asking, which means I can't just stop him in the hall or wait for him after football practice and start interrogating him or something. I'll need to get his guard down, lead him into it.

Besides, with the days turning colder—late October in Wisconsin means temperatures hovering in the midfifties in the afternoons—cheer practices are now always held indoors in the dance room, not on the field.

The only time I ever get close enough to Brett to talk is during lunch, but then of course everybody else is also there, which makes it impossible.

———

It's only when Naomi brings up Halloween that the seed of a plan forms.

"Halloween is going to be sooo different this year, isn't it?" Naomi says, poking her congealing lasagna glumly with her fork.

Lucy has been sneaking forlorn looks at Scott—sitting at the other end of the table, where he'd relocated to with Brett after his sort-of breakup with Lucy—as usual, but the mention of Halloween catches her attention. "I know, right?" she says with a sigh. "The thing about Ella is, she knew how to throw a party. What are we going to do this year? Stay home?" But then she perks up. "Hey! Why is Ella the only one who can throw a party? Maybe one of us can throw one for Halloween this year."

"And who's going to come?" asks Naomi, rolling her eyes. "Nobody wants to be seen with us now. Or haven't you noticed?"

She's right. Ever since we became murder suspects, other than Brett, nobody else in school would be caught dead with us. Sierton High's social elite have become social pariahs. Not for the first time, I feel a warm glow of affection for Raquel, who has never stopped being my friend.

"Who cares about them anyway?" continues Naomi. "They'll all come crawling back trying to suck up to us once this stupid thing is over."

But she does care. It's in the way she flushes when she walks into a room, hunching her shoulders slightly—when she used to sashay in like she owns the place, second to no one... except Ella, of course. It must be so irritating for her that she only got to enjoy being the new queen bee for a few weeks after Ella died, until the police spoiled it all that day by showing up at Sierton High.

"Hey, you know what..." I say. "Maybe a Halloween party is exactly what we need."

Naomi frowns. "What do you mean?"

"So we're all murder suspects, right? What better hook than that for Halloween?" I say.

The two girls stare at me for a while without speaking. Even the guys are intrigued, stopping whatever they've been talking about to turn and look at me.

"The four murder suspects…having a Halloween party," says Lucy slowly, her eyes starting to light up.

"Everybody will be *dying* to come," I say with a grin.

"I bet they all will. I love it," says Naomi, her smile even bigger than mine. "I could do with a distraction, after all this murder suspect shit and the shit at home…"

"What shit at home?" asks Lucy.

"Never mind, it's nothing." Naomi shrugs, swatting away Lucy's question. "I'll throw the party at my house. You two can help organize it."

"Of course," I agree, deferring to her like I once did to Ella.

But then she frowns again. "Can we pull it off though? Halloween is next week Tuesday."

"Of course we can," chirps Lucy.

"A party! Cool," says Brett. "Will be nice to just have some fun again."

Lucy is sneaking another look at Scott, and when he shrugs and says, "Why not?" she bursts into a radiant smile.

I smile too because it's the perfect opportunity for me to finally get Brett alone.

HANNAH

In her room, fresh out of a shower, Hannah stares at herself in the full-length mirror on her closet door.

She was warming up with jumping jacks like the other girls during practice today, when a voice floated over. *Is there an earthquake? Oh, it's just her doing jumping jacks.* A few girls giggled and Hannah froze up, eyes on the padded floor, her heart suddenly thudding even faster than when she was doing the exercise. She didn't dare to look around and see who said it, but there was no mistaking the voice. It was Ella.

Hannah thought about telling Coach, but in the end she didn't. Coach would simply choose not to believe her, just like the last time.

She's been keeping her head low, trying to stay out of Ella's way. Maybe if she doesn't do anything to further anger the girl, she might forget about her declaration of war.

She stares at her tummy, which, unlike the other girls on the squad, isn't completely flat and toned. At her thighs that jiggle when she moves, unlike their long, lean, muscly limbs. Maybe this is why they don't like her. She hadn't thought there was anything wrong with her body, but the comments from Ella—hell, her own mother—are starting to worm their way in.

It's becoming clearer every day that she'll never have any friends. She'll never be like them—these perfect, beautiful girls— even if she kills herself trying.

She can't talk to her parents because they won't understand. Her parents always made friends, it seems, easily, effortlessly. They have fond memories of high school. She can see their thoughts as they stare at her, their faces puzzled. *Why isn't their daughter like them?*

She was stupid to dream that she could reinvent herself in high school.

———

The first mean comment appears on her Instagram page a week later. How did normal people produce such ugly offspring, someone writes under a photo of her with her parents, taken last winter. She looks like an alien, somebody else writes. Hannah's heart is thudding in her head, bursting out of her chest as she blocks them. She realizes Ella has begun her attack for real. The profiles are obviously fake—accounts created moments before they posted the comments. She takes down the photo, but someone else leaves a comment on another photo of her at summer camp: Bet you had no friends there too. And then that person actually slides into her DMs: The whole school laughs at u when u stand beside the other cheerleaders. U look nothing like them. Ur just a wannabe. Hannah blocks that account too, makes her profile private.

Still, she cries for hours that night.

DAWN

"So who should we invite? Or can anyone who wants to come just come?" asks Lucy, swinging her long bronze legs at the edge of Naomi's bed excitedly like a kid.

The three of us are gathered in Naomi's bedroom, Lucy and I summoned there after practice on Friday to help plan the party.

Sitting on the quilted bench at the foot of Naomi's bed (I didn't even know that these things existed outside of fancy hotel rooms), I look around curiously. Her room looks like something straight out of an interior design magazine: hardwood flooring, an expensive-looking queen-sized bed with a dusty rose velvet headboard, and a designer armchair in the same dusty rose velvet fabric.

Naomi, perched cross-legged in that armchair facing us, frowns as she considers. "I want everyone to *want* to come, but not necessarily *everyone* to get in."

"Uh…you mean, like a party at the hottest club?" asks Lucy.

"Exactly."

"Maybe we can get someone to act like a bouncer at the door? Let in the coolest, the best-looking, the best-dressed?" I say.

Naomi perks up. "That. Is. Brilliant. We'll get the word out in school, and people will get all dressed up and try to get in!" She beams at me, obviously already seeing how that will catapult her right back to the number one spot on the popularity ladder at Sierton High.

"You're sure your parents don't mind you throwing a party on a school night?" asks Lucy.

"Yeah," I say. "Especially after…" *Especially after Ella died at hers.*

But I don't have to complete my sentence. They immediately get what I'm trying to say.

"I still can't believe it," says Lucy, her voice dropping to a whisper. "You know, I googled strychnine poisoning, and it's a *horrible* death."

"I googled it too," admits Naomi.

"So did I," I say.

"At least the police have left me alone ever since my parents retained a lawyer for me," says Naomi.

"Yeah, same. Maybe that means they have nothing to go on and are going to leave us alone from now on," says Lucy hopefully.

I doubt that's going to happen. They're probably building cases against all of us right now, including me. But I keep quiet.

Naomi turns to examine her flawless face in the mirror on her table. "Anyway, I asked my parents just now. They're fine with the party as long as Andy is here to keep an eye on things, and everyone clears out by one in the morning latest. And nobody trashes the place."

"Andy?" I ask.

"My brother. He's twenty-one."

"What about your parents?" asks Lucy.

"They won't be here that night. My mom's going out with some of her friends, and my dad's going to be in LA. Some work thing." Naomi starts running a brush through her already-glossy brown hair. "They support me in whatever as long as I keep up a perfect GPA." Her eyes flicker to a crimson and black scarf draped over her table.

"What's that?" I ask.

"Just my dad's old Harvard scarf," Naomi says with a casual shrug. Her right hand reaches out to touch it, her fingers caressing the old fabric tenderly.

"You're sure to get in," says Lucy.

"I'd better. Harvard is the best, and I deserve the best," says Naomi modestly.

"I don't know how you maintain a four-point-oh GPA," says Lucy, pouting. "I can barely get mine to stay above three."

Naomi shrugs. "It's not that hard, Lucy. You just have to spend a bit more time studying and a bit less time pining over Scott. I'm serious. You have to watch it, or you're going to end up in some community college."

CINDY R. X. HE

"Bitch," says Lucy. "What's your GPA, Dawn?"

"Uh, three-point-four, I think?" I say.

"See?" says Naomi pointedly at Lucy. "You need to buck up."

"Okay, Mom," says Lucy, rolling her eyes. "Seriously though, didn't you get several Cs in Physical Science last year? How the hell are you getting four-point-oh for your GPA?"

"Only for two tests, and Whitlock let me retake them at the end of the year," Naomi snaps. "Now can we go back to the party planning? It's in four days. Okay, I'll procure the drinks. As for food, Lucy, can you find a caterer that'll do Halloween-themed stuff?"

"On it," says Lucy, pulling out her phone.

Naomi turns to me. "Dawn, you'll help with the decorations. I'm thinking...*haunted asylum*."

"Oooh," Lucy and I both breathe.

A door slams down the hall, making all of us jump. Then, raised voices:

Jesus, do you always have to be such a bitch? This is why I can't stand to be around you.

Right, blame me. Work meeting in LA, my ass. You think I don't know you're going to see that woman?

Startled, I glance at Naomi. Her face is red, and she won't meet my eyes. She stands up abruptly. "That's all for the party planning right now. I think you two should leave."

"Thanks for coming to get me," I say as I climb into the passenger seat of Maddy's car.

Maddy's lips are pressed together so tightly they're thin lines. "I don't know about this Halloween party," she says, shooting me a sideways look while driving. "Someone died at the last one, remember? And the four of you will be at this one too?"

No. If she persuades my parents not to let me go, I won't be able to get Brett alone to speak with him. I try to quell the panic surging in my chest. "I know you're worried. But we need this. You don't understand what it's been like these past few weeks at school. Everyone is avoiding us like we've got the plague or something."

Maddy is quiet for a minute, then she sighs. "Okay, I'm trying to understand. I really am. But I still think it's a bad idea. Will Naomi's parents be there at least to chaperone?"

"Maddy, you know how uncool that would make the party. Naomi said they won't be there, but her older brother will be there to keep an eye on things. He's twenty-one."

"I wish there'd been someone at Ella's party to keep an eye on things," she mutters. She casts me a worried look. "Look kid, I know you want to fit in, but you're spending so much time with those girls. Especially after what happened. Don't you have other friends in school?"

"Of course I do."

Maddy looks like she wants to say more, but thankfully, she doesn't.

Ugh. If she's so freaked out about this party, how am I going to convince my parents to let me go?

But when I speak to them in the evening, my parents are surprisingly cool with it.

"That sounds fun. Whose idea was it?" asks my dad.

"Mine," I admit. "So, um…you're okay with me going to this party?"

"Of course," says my mom. "You're young; you should go and be with your friends. Don't be stuck at home with us. We know you're not going to do anything to get yourself in trouble."

———

The next morning, I wake up to a text from Naomi.

> Meet Lucy and me in an hour at Deco World

I look for Maddy to ask if she can give me a ride, but she must have gone out already, because she's not in the house and her car's not in the driveway. My parents aren't around as well. Maybe they have a doctor's appointment and Maddy took them. Then I see the note:

Be back this evening, there are leftovers in the fridge

I suppose I could try calling for an Uber or something, but I don't really want to. I text Naomi back.

> My aunt's not here & I don't have a car. Swing by & pick me up?

Ugh forget it, ur place is on the other side of town. Lucy n I can get the stuff by ourselves.

> Sorry

I text back in relief.

Don't think ur getting out of the setup next week!!!

> R u kidding? Of course I'll be there! This party is going 2 b so epic!

Ikr?!!

I have cereal with milk for breakfast, then impress even myself by getting all my assignments for the week done by noon. As I heat up leftover casserole in the oven for lunch, I pull out my notebook again and stare at what I've got so far.

What I need to figure out is what motives they each might have for wanting Ella dead.

The timer on the oven beeps, and I sit down with the dish and my notebook, and set to work on both.

Motivations

Scott: Ella cheated on him (does he know?)

Lucy: 1) Hates Ella for stealing Scott from her. 2) To get Scott back.

Naomi: To be cheer captain/queen bee?

If all goes according to plan, I'll find out at the party on Tuesday whether Scott knew.

As for Naomi...the motivations I have for her so far look ridiculous, but who knows? People have killed other people for even more inane things, according to those murder shows that Maddy likes to watch on Netflix.

Suddenly, I feel ridiculous. What the hell am I doing? Even if I manage to find out that these people have their own motivations for wanting Ella dead, would it even do any good? Somehow, I doubt that Mulchaney or Doyle would take my notes and thank me effusively for helping them to solve their case.

I flip my notebook shut and get up to wash the casserole dish and fork, feeling irritated and antsy. I go up to my room and change quickly into a sports bra, another T-shirt, leggings, and pull on a hoodie. Run back downstairs and put on my sneakers, and get out of the house.

It's cold outside—the air nips at my nose and ears—but I

warm up quickly as I start jogging. Something that my mom can't ever do again. Without realizing it I jog faster and faster until I'm flat-out sprinting. But no matter how fast I run, I can't outrun my past mistakes.

I'm gasping when I reach home half an hour later, a stitch in my side making me bend over, but my head is still a mess. I need something to distract me. I pull out my phone and tap out a text to Isaac.

> Hey.

My heart starts racing again. We've texted each other a couple of times ever since exchanging numbers, but so far it's just been random chat, nothing like what I'm about to say.

I stare at my phone. The minutes seem to crawl by. He must be busy because he doesn't reply. Back in my room, I throw my phone on my bed, ignoring the sinking feeling in my stomach, and jump in the shower so that I don't keep staring at my phone screen.

When I'm done with my shower, the first thing I do—still dripping wet with only a towel wrapped around me—is to check my phone again. The notification message on the screen sends my heart lurching, and I open it immediately.

> Hey back at u. What's up?

> Nothing much. Went for a run. U?

> Just listening to some music

> I have the house to myself till evening

I type, sending the text before I can delete what I've written. Immediately, anxiety grips my chest and stomach—so strong it actually physically hurts. A minute goes by. Two minutes. I'm regretting ever texting him when he finally replies:

> R u inviting me over?

> I don't know. Do u want to come over?

I text, my heart beating triple time in my chest.
His reply comes back almost immediately:

> Yes

Followed by:

> When?

> Half an hour?

I text back, my fingers trembling.

Ok

I throw my phone on my bed and fling myself onto it as well, burying my face in my pillow.

I didn't expect to meet someone I'd like, coming here. This is all so unexpected, and I don't know what the hell I'm doing, but I just can't help it.

HANNAH

She's feeling weak and light-headed all day because she only had a glass of orange juice for breakfast, and then half an apple during lunch break. But she reminds herself that it's all going to be worth it when she's thinner. So she ignores the hunger pangs and the rumbling from her stomach.

A bit harder to ignore are the remarks the others make during practice after school.

"Is that your stomach growling?" says Naomi, shooting her an incredulous look when Hannah's stomach gives a particularly loud rumble.

"God, you're just hungry all the time, aren't you?" That's Ella, of course.

"Why are you looking at us that way? Are you thinking of eating us?" squeals Lucy, pretending to be afraid.

"What the hell is wrong with all of you?" says Katie. "Hannah, I have an energy bar, do you want it?" Hannah shook her head.

"Quiet down, girls," says Coach as she walks into the room. "We're going to continue practicing stunting today. Katie, can you take the others over there to practice twisting? Thanks. Okay, bases, back spot, in position."

Lucy and Hannah step forward, and Naomi stands a little further back. With Katie gone, they resume their attack. "She should be the base all by herself, she's so *big*," Lucy murmurs sullenly as Coach is speaking to someone else, and the other girls around her break out in giggles.

Coach returns and claps her hands. "Remember all: safety first. Alright, bases, stand with your feet hip-width apart, a tight core, shoulders up, and backs tall! Let's go!"

Hannah struggles over the next thirty minutes. She normally has the strength to stunt, but today she just feels too weak. Her arms shake so much that even the other girls start to notice.

Ella, the flyer, is struggling to maintain her balance. "Hey, watch it! You almost dropped me!"

"Maybe you're just too heavy," says Naomi. "I should be on top; I'm lighter than you."

"Shut up and keep your eyes on my hips," says Ella.

"Stop talking!" says Coach. "You all need to concentrate. No, you're wobbling too much. Okay, stop. Let's get you down—"

Hannah's arms give out just then.

Ella falls to the floor with a shriek. Luckily, the floor is padded—but Ella must have landed badly, because she lies on the floor, crying and clutching her leg.

"It's broken! It's broken!" she screams.

"I'm so sorry!" says Hannah, wringing her hands. "I'm so—"

"Let me see!" Coach pushes her aside, crouches beside Ella. Prods her swelling ankle. "Okay, I don't think anything's broken; it just looks like you've sprained it."

"It was her!" says Ella, pointing her finger at Hannah. "She dropped me on purpose! She was trying to kill me!"

Hannah takes a step back. "What? No!"

"Calm down, Ella," says Coach. "I doubt that anyone was trying to kill you. Although"—she frowns at Hannah—"that was terrible stunting. You seem very distracted lately. Come to my office after today's practice." She turns back to Ella. "I'll get the school nurse. Just wait here."

Hannah staggers. The room spins around her. Why does Coach want her in her office?

"You bitch!" shouts Ella as soon as Coach leaves. "I won't be able to cheer for weeks! You did this on purpose!"

Hannah starts to cry. "No..."

"You did; we all saw you," says Naomi.

"You dumb ass," says Lucy.

"I'm sorry—"

"You're so stupid and useless," says Ella, her every single word hitting Hannah like a punch in the face. "You're going to pay for this. You'll wish you were dead."

"Woah, woah, woah, what the hell?" says Katie, coming over from the other side of the room. "Everyone calm down—"

Hannah stumbles out of the room. She feels sick. She runs out of school, only stopping to dry retch on the grass outside.

Everyone hates me, she thinks. *I hate myself. It's never going to change.*

She stumbles home on foot. She doesn't go to Coach's office after practice. She knows Coach has been regretting her decision to let her on the squad. Coach must have decided to throw her off the squad. It must be why she's called her in her office. It doesn't matter that she's usually the best in terms of motions, cheers, and tumbles. She made one terrible mistake, and now she has to pay.

Worst of all, she knows Ella will find a way to punish her for dropping her and injuring her. Ella is convinced that she did it on purpose. Probably because if Ella was the one at the bottom, she would have done it on purpose to someone else.

What is Ella going to do to her now?

DAWN

I spend the next fifteen minutes anxiously changing from one casual-enough-for-hanging-out-at-home-but-still-hot outfit to another. This pale pink tank top is cute enough, but should I wear these heather-gray cotton shorts or these pink-checked cotton pajama pants? The shorts are cuter and show off my tanned legs… but also the scars. Screw it. The shorts it is. It's okay if Isaac sees the scars on my legs.

I pop in my contacts, then spend the remaining fifteen minutes blowing out my hair and putting on a tiny bit of mascara. Two minutes left… Oh no, I can still smell the casserole I had for lunch on my breath. I rush to brush my teeth. And swipe some deodorant under my arms.

I'm just spraying the tiniest bit of perfume behind my ears when the doorbell rings, and I'm so nervous I almost trip on my way down the stairs.

Isaac is waiting on the porch when I open the door.

"Hi," I squeak.

He smiles shyly back at me, his dimples flashing in and out. "You look cute."

"Oh. Thanks. You look cute too." And he does—even if his clothes are just as ill fitting as always, in a baggy black sweater that's too big and blue jeans that are just two inches too short—and he must have also just taken a shower because his dark brown curls are still slightly wet at the ends. He smells good too, that familiar mix of soap and citrusy shampoo that now drives me quite mad.

"So you're all alone at home, huh?" he says, looking around.

"Yeah, my parents and my aunt left me a note saying they'll be back in the evening." I shiver slightly as a breeze blows through the open door into the house, my skimpy outfit not giving me much protection from the cold. Isaac notices immediately because he steps in—brushing up against me—and closes the door behind him.

"So. What are we going to do?" he asks casually.

"Wanna watch a movie?" I ask equally casually, even though my legs feel as strong as jelly and just about as likely to keep me standing.

"Sure. You choose the movie."

"Really? If I choose a romantic comedy, you'll watch it?"

Isaac eyes me dubiously. "I guess we'll find out."

We grab some drinks and snacks from the kitchen and settle on the couch, a careful distance between us. Not too near, but near enough. I end up choosing an old horror flick, *Carrie*.

At first, it's hard to concentrate on the movie. I'm too conscious of his presence beside me. I sneak a look at him on my left, study his side profile. The shape of his lips. The way a dimple pops in his cheek when he smiles at something. He must sense he's being watched, because he suddenly glances at me and we lock eyes before I tear my gaze away and back to the movie, my face hot.

I get sucked into the movie. I'm enjoying it, especially the ending, but when I sneak another look at Isaac, he's frowning. "What's wrong?" I ask.

"I get that her crazy religious upbringing instills in her the belief that vengeance is right, or should I say, *righteous*," says Isaac. "But that's just not true."

"You don't believe in the righteousness of revenge? Oh man, better not watch *John Wick* with you, then. You'd *ruin* the movie for me."

Isaac laughs. "Hey, I love *John Wick*. I love all of Keanu's movies, just so you know."

"Even *Bill and Ted*?"

"Even *Bill and Ted*. But yeah, real life isn't like in the books or movies." He looks away. "Revenge just isn't worth it."

I know he's thinking about what he did with Ella. I fidget awkwardly. "Do you regret doing it?" I ask.

"Yes. Like I said, it didn't change anything. Didn't bring my sister back. Just made me feel shitty about myself. I wish I'd made peace with the past sooner." He lifts his head, looks at me. "But better late than never, right?"

I stare at him. Can I do it? Make peace with the past?

Since the accident, I've contemplated some very dark thoughts. But maybe things don't have to be this way.

Maybe I *can* move on.

As the thought sinks in, something swells in me, gentle and light. It dispels the darkness that's been weighing on me ever since the accident.

I think I can. Move on.

My stomach interrupts rudely with a loud rumble.

"Sorry," I say.

Isaac laughs. "I'm hungry too."

"Want to get pizza?"

"Sounds great."

I ring our local pizza place and order two pizzas—pepperoni and mushrooms, and sausage and mozzarella. I have one big slice of each, and Isaac has *five* slices.

"Another movie?" he asks.

I smile. "Sure, you choose."

Isaac chooses a comedy. We settle back on the couch, and he throws his right arm casually over my shoulder. This time, we're sitting very close to each other, sides practically pressed against each other. He's removed his sweater and is wearing a plain white T-shirt. It's a bit too small, like most of his clothes, but this time this works to his advantage, showing off his arms, which I've just noticed are quite muscly. I can even see the shape of his chest and abdominal muscles under his T-shirt. Like I said, it's a great T-shirt.

He turns and catches me looking at him again. Heat surges into my face, but before I can turn away, he says, "Thanks for asking me over."

"That's what friends do," I mumble.

"This is nice. Hanging out with you," he murmurs.

"Yes, it is." My heart is thumping so hard, I think I might pass out.

His lips curve into a smile, and his gaze drops to my mouth.

I've only ever kissed one boy before. It was the same boy who taught me how to surf, back in Santa Cruz. That's about as far as we got.

What would it be like to kiss Isaac?

He looks into my eyes again. And then our faces are moving toward each other almost exactly at the same time, and we're kissing. His mouth is warm, his kiss gentle. His right hand slides around the base of my head. He tastes like peppermint. My heart is skipping and stuttering behind my ribs. I'm not aware of having consciously raised my hand, but I tug gently at his hair.

Isaac's left hand strokes my right leg lightly, the feathery touch sending electrical currents shooting up my thigh, up my spine, making me shiver. His fingertips trail lightly over the raised ridges on my leg.

He pulls slightly away, breaking our kiss. "How did you get these scars?"

"Car accident." *Please don't ask me about it.*

Luckily, he doesn't pry. He takes my face in his hands, kisses my lips gently. "I'm glad you're here."

"Me too," I murmur. So glad, for the first time.

I don't know how this second movie ends, because Isaac and I spend the rest of the time making out, which is more than okay with me.

Okay fine, it's the best day of my life.

When we finally break off our kiss, my lips are swollen and tingly, and I'm breathless. My hands are still clinging on to the front of his shirt. I make myself let go. He runs a hand through his hair. "When did you say your parents are coming back?"

I glance at the clock on the mantelpiece. "Ugh. Anytime now."

"I guess I should go." He sounds as reluctant as I feel. "See you at school tomorrow?"

"Yes," I breathe.

We share one last lingering kiss at the door, then he grins sheepishly and gets in his car. My entire body is light, bubbly, ecstatic.

I'm just watching him drive off when something raises the hair on my arms. Something pulls my eyes to the car parked across the road just opposite, a brown sedan that I've never seen in the neighborhood before. Someone is sitting in the car, not moving.

I make out the woman's features. It's Detective Mulchaney, her brown hair tied in that distinctive knot at her nape. And she's watching me.

My skin crawls, and I slam the door shut. *What the hell?*

Why is Mulchaney parked outside my house? Are the police seriously keeping tabs on me? How long have they been watching me, and why?

What are they hoping to catch me doing?

But then anger replaces the initial alarm, and I open the door again. Storm out to Mulchaney's car. Tap on her window and gesture for her to wind it down.

"It's perfect that you're here," I say. "I need to tell you something about that night at the party that I forgot earlier."

"Oh?" she says impassively, her face carefully not giving anything away.

"Yeah. It was just before I left. Scott and I saw someone there that night. And I don't think they were invited."

"Who?"

"I don't know," I admit. "I couldn't see their face; it was dark and they were standing in the shadows. On the opposite side of the pool. And they were wearing a hoodie that covered their head."

To Mulchaney's credit, she takes out a pen and notebook, and jots in it. "Why don't you think this person was invited?"

"Because they were wearing a hoodie, and none of the guests were that night. And because they ran away as soon as Scott called out to them."

She writes that down too. "Okay. Is there anything else you want to tell me?"

Yes, that it's creepy that you're staking out my house. "No, that's it."

"Okay." She flips her notebook shut.

I turn around stiffly and march back into my house, feeling her eyes on my back the entire time. When I turn to close the door, her car is already gone.

HANNAH

Hannah doesn't have to wait long for Ella's revenge. The next morning, she wakes to discover that someone has created a "Hannah the Loser" account on Instagram. Somehow, overnight, it already has 508 followers. The account is posting photos of her on Stories. The photos are photoshopped to make her look terrible. The texts on the photos say things like Everyone hates you and Waste of space and You don't deserve to be on the squad, tagging her in all of them. The posts are all like these, without text captions, the cruel words only superimposed on the photos themselves.

People start leaving comments like Is this who I think it is? And What's going on? and Come on, these are obviously photoshopped.

Hannah tries reporting them, but Instagram doesn't take them down.

She blocks the account, then she unblocks it again, for fear that it might post something really horrible without her knowing about it.

And she needs to know.

———

The next day at lunch, Hannah heads to a table in the corner of the cafeteria instead of the long table, carrying her tray of a salad instead of the spaghetti Bolognese that she really wanted. Unfortunately, her path takes her past the long table, so she looks down, fixes her eyes on the floor so she doesn't have to see anyone at the table staring at her.

But a foot shoots out, tripping her. She falls clumsily, dropping everything with a loud clatter.

The foot turns out to be Ella's. Ella is sitting at the long table with Naomi and Lucy; none of the other cheerleaders or football players are there yet.

"Oh, wow, are you okay?" says Ella.

"Why are you doing this?"

"Doing what? What are you accusing me of doing, Hannah?"

"Tripping me! The Insta account!" Hannah's voice cracks. She's dangerously close to crying.

Ella smiles, and Hannah knows immediately that her suspicions were right, even as she says, "What Insta account?" Beside her, Lucy shrugs, puts a fry in her mouth. Naomi's eyes won't meet hers.

"Why are you doing this?" says Hannah again.

Ella lowers her voice so that it's barely above a whisper. "You should have stayed in your lane. But you squeezed yourself somewhere you don't belong. You kept squeezing yourself in front of me, sucking up to Coach and Katie, and then you told lies to Coach to try and get me in trouble. Then you *dropped* me so I'd break my ankle—"

"I didn't do it on pur—"

"You crossed the wrong person. I don't forgive, and I don't forget. I'm going to make sure the rest of your life in Sierton is hell."

A treacherous tear breaks free and rolls down Hannah's cheek, followed swiftly by another, as she stares at Ella. But Ella is done talking to her and has already turned back to her two friends, who are still carefully pretending they don't see her, didn't hear anything.

Hannah dumps her tray, almost makes it out of the cafeteria when she bumps into Coach Davis, who frowns at her.

"Why didn't you come see me in my office yesterday like I told you to?"

Hannah can feel her face burning as she stares at the floor, her eyes still hot and filled with tears. She stares at Coach's foot tapping impatiently, once, twice, and then the woman sighs.

"I can't have this kind of attitude, Hannah. You're off the squad." She walks off.

Hannah finally looks up, stares in growing confusion at her

retreating back. Why does it sound like Coach has only just decided to kick her off the squad? Wasn't that the reason she told her to see her in her office yesterday?

Unless…

All around her, other students are starting to whisper and stare. She runs out of the cafeteria, not bursting into tears until she's locked herself safely in a girls' restroom stall.

———

That night, there is only one post on the Instagram account—of her face being crossed out with a big red *X*. The caption reads She got herself kicked off the squad! Frankly, we're all just surprised it took this long. Spoiler: Nobody's going to miss her.

Hannah taps out a DM with shaking hands.

> I'm already off the squad.
>
> Stop posting about me!

The reply comes back less than a minute later.

> Lol no way, this is too much fun

> What do u want me to do so that u stop???

Hannah types, crying.

The reply comes casually:

> Maybe if u swallow some rat poison and kill urself 😃

DAWN

"Everything. Is. Perfect!" squeals Naomi, twirling around in the center of her living room, which we've transformed to look like an old abandoned asylum.

"It *is* perfect," I agree, looking around me. We worked on the props yesterday after school till late in the night. Coach agreed to reschedule today's practice to tomorrow, and Lucy, the other cheerleaders, and I rushed over to Naomi's house again today to finish all the decorations. The guys came over after football practice to help with the setup for the party.

We've cleared out most of the usual furniture, stored it safely in the attic for the time being. Only the big sectional couch is left, and we've placed a fake wheelchair beside it. We've also placed a fake hospital bed complete with spooky straps to strap someone in against their will. A large drinks table lines the wall where a bookshelf stood, decorated with syringes and skulls. The room is lit up by flickering florescent lights lining the walls, and there's even a giant disco ball on the ceiling.

"You've all brought your costumes, right?" asks Naomi. "Come on, Lucy, Dawn. You can change in my room."

In her room, Naomi changes into her sexy doctor's costume. She pairs it with fishnet stockings and three-inch pumps as red as the bloodred lipstick she's wearing.

"Remind me again why you get to be the sexy asylum doctor, but Dawn and I have to be nurses?" says Lucy, staring at the costumes Naomi chose for us.

"Because we don't need two doctors," says Naomi curtly.

Lucy's mouth snaps shut. She knows better than to pick a fight with Naomi. Naomi's been in a particularly bad temper the entire day, often staring at her phone moodily, as if she's waiting for some bad news to hit.

Naomi finishes applying her lipstick and heads back downstairs with Lucy. I finish changing into my costume and am just about to go down to join everyone when I get a text on my phone. It's Raquel, and my heart sinks when I see her message.

> Is it true Naomi's throwing THE party of the year at her place, and everyone's invited? Why didn't u tell me???

I didn't tell her because I know Naomi has no intention of letting her in if she comes.

> It's just some dumb party. I didn't
> think you'd be interested.

I reply.

> I'm on my way!

She replies immediately.

Shit. Okay, I'm just going to have to find a way to sneak her past whoever's the bouncer when she comes.

When I head back downstairs, everyone else is also dressed. Another girl on the squad and her boyfriend are Harley Quinn and the Joker—which I thought was particularly inspired, but Naomi's mouth presses into a thin line when she sees them. She's probably pissed off that Harley Quinn looks incredibly hot.

Scott hasn't even bothered with the theme—he's wearing a sweater vest and a pearl necklace.

"Who are you supposed to be?" asks Naomi.

"Harry Styles," says Scott.

"So cute," squeals Lucy, and Scott rewards her with a smile.

Naomi rolls her eyes, then turns to Brett, who is wearing a transparent rain jacket over a suit and holding an axe, his hair all slicked back. "And you?"

"I'm Patrick Bateman from *American Psycho*, duh," Brett says, grinning.

"Why do I even bother coming up with such a cool theme if you're all just going to ignore it? Ugh, whatever," says Naomi, as the doorbell rings. "Well, Patrick Bateman, you can be the bouncer to start."

Brett scratches his chin. "What am I supposed to do?"

"Just let people in, and keep the losers and weirdos out. Now go. Please."

As Brett sidles out—mumbling under his breath something about *bossy girls*—Andy, Naomi's brother, comes hurtling down the stairs two steps at a time.

"You have to get dressed up too if you want to join the party," says Naomi, eyeing his polo shirt and jeans.

Andy rolls his eyes. "I'm not joining some stupid high school party. I'm just getting something to eat. I'll be in my room the whole night. Don't trash the place."

"We won't," says Naomi, and he disappears into the kitchen.

Naomi hooks up her laptop to the sound system, and "Heads Will Roll" by the Yeah Yeah Yeahs blasts out of the loudspeakers.

Sierton High's other students start streaming in, clearly impressed with the setup—Naomi, Lucy, and I in our sexy asylum costumes here to greet them—and the party starts.

———

It's a huge success, of course. Who could resist coming to a fabulous Halloween party thrown by the four beautiful people suspected of murder?

Naomi and Lucy bask in the attention, soaking it up like cats preening in the sun, as the other students fight for their attention. Somebody asks them for details about that night, and Naomi describes the pool party and how Scott screamed the next morning when he woke up next to Ella's body. Lucy's eyes dart around, but Scott isn't aware he's being gossiped about; he's hanging out in a corner of the room with some of the other guys talking about football, a blond Harry Styles looking infinitely cool.

I grab two beers and head outside to find Brett. He's venting his frustration at being assigned gatekeeping duty by telling two guys—a zombie and a goth—that they're too lame to go in.

He perks up as soon as he sees me and the beers in my hands. "Thanks, Dawn, you're the best." He chugs down his beer as I sip at mine.

"I'm so sorry you're missing the party. I can take over if you want to head inside."

My words have the intended effect, as Brett's smile grows even warmer. "I'm good now that you're here," he says. "I'd rather be out here with you than inside with the rest of them anyway. By the way, I love that nurse's outfit on you; you look really good."

His eyes travel slowly down my body, and I suppress a shudder, smile at him. "I love your costume. You look so *dangerous*."

"Oh yeah? The psychopathic serial killer vibe does it for you, huh?"

I giggle. "Maybe." Brett flushes slightly, and I offer him my beer as well. "Here, take mine too. I've already had several inside."

"I can't believe you don't have a boyfriend," he says, taking the bottle from me. "You're really cool, Dawn."

"That's so sweet. Thanks," I say, lowering my eyelashes and smiling at him as if his thinking that I'm cool is the highlight of my day. I guess I'm a hell of an actress, because his grin widens even more. "The past few weeks have been so crazy though," I sigh, pouting slightly.

"Tell me about it," he says.

"Do you think it's really one of us who did it?" I whisper, my eyes wide.

"I don't know… It seems impossible, but then again, not really." He frowns. "I don't want to talk bad about somebody who's dead, but…"

"But?"

He shrugs. "But then Ella was a bitch. So who knows?"

"Was she? I'd only known her for three weeks before…before it happened."

"Oh yeah."

But then he stops talking, and there's a few seconds of awkward silence.

Shit. He's so close to saying something, I can feel it. I have to go for it. "I heard Scott saying…something at the party that evening. Was he talking about Ella?"

Brett casts me a sideways glance as he takes a swig of his beer. "Overheard that, did you?"

"I didn't mean to, I'm sorry."

"Hey, it wasn't your fault you heard Scott talking." But he stops again, looks away.

Crap. How can I get him to talk to me? I bite my lip, then shoot him a hurt look. "I understand if you don't trust me to keep it a secret."

"That's not what I…"

"It's fine," I say coldly. "Sorry for bothering you. I'll just go back in now." I turn around, take a step. Shoot a quick prayer into the universe.

"Dawn, wait." Brett grabs my hand, pulls me back to him. "Look, if you have to know…yeah, he was talking about Ella. She cheated on him with some other guy in school, and Scott found out when Lucy told him."

I knew it.

I look up at him with wide eyes. "Wow, that's horrible. But… why didn't he break up with her? He must have been so mad."

"I know what you're thinking, but I don't think Scott did it." Brett exhales. "Killed her, I mean. He was angry with her, and he wanted revenge, but…"

"But?"

"But not like that."

He stops talking as someone comes up to us.

"Dawn! Hi, um, Brett, right?" says Raquel. She's wearing a tank top and shorts, and carrying a watermelon, of all things.

"Who are you," says Brett, "and why are you carrying a *watermelon*?"

"I'm Baby! From *Dirty Dancing*, obviously…" says Raquel, her voice trailing off.

CINDY R. X. HE

"What the hell is *Dirty Dancing*?" asks Brett.

Raquel's shoulders droop. "Never mind."

"Look, you can't come in. Naomi will be so pissed if I let you," says Brett.

"Why? I'm Dawn's friend," says Raquel.

"You are?" Brett glances at me in surprise.

I turn to him. "Please, can we let her in? There are so many people inside; Naomi won't even notice her."

Brett looks at me. Looks at her again. Sighs. "Fine, I guess you can go in."

Raquel grins and slips past him before he can change his mind, giving me a hug as she passes.

"I'm so sick of this bouncer shit," says Brett.

"I'll go and find someone else to replace you," I say quickly and head back in, mulling over what I've learned.

So my suspicions were right; Scott did know that Ella cheated on him, and the *bitch* he was talking about *was* her. And he didn't break up with her because he wanted to get back at her. Why did Brett say he wanted revenge but *not like that*? What kind of revenge did he have in mind? I decide that it's definitely possible the revenge he had in mind was murder.

I locate Naomi dancing with Lucy and Scott, and go up to her. "Brett's getting tired of door duty," I say.

"I guess he's done his part," says Naomi. "Scott, can you take over for Brett, please?"

Scott tosses back the remainder of his beer and heads outside, and Naomi starts grinding against some guy who is grinning with a *I can't believe this is happening* look on his face. Lucy lets out a loud exhale and heads to the drinks table, and I follow her.

"I'm so sick of her ordering us all around," says Lucy, glaring at Naomi. "She's like Ella version two-point-oh. I didn't want to be a nurse. Why couldn't I be a doctor too?" From the way she sloshes her cup around as she talks, and the slight but perceptible slurring of her words, it's obvious that she's had a few drinks already. For a moment I'm reminded of Ella's party, when she got drunk there too.

"Well, you do look super cute, if it's any consolation," I say.

"Thanks. I guess you do too. Selfie?" Lucy takes out her phone, and we both pose for the camera, me imitating her pout as best as I can.

"We are *so* cute. Posting this right now so everyone who isn't here can eat their little envious hearts out," she says, tapping away on her crystal-encrusted phone.

"Tag me so I can repost. Wow, I love your phone case so much," I say.

"Thanks! They're real Swarovski crystals."

"It's cuter than Naomi's pink one."

"What?" Lucy blinks at me, confused. "Naomi's isn't pink. It's blue."

"Oh, I could have sworn I saw her holding a phone with a pink case."

"Really? When?"

"At Ella's party."

Lucy blinks at me again, then laughs. "That's Ella's phone. And Ella would never have let anyone else touch her phone. Especially Naomi."

But I've rattled her. She frowns now, glancing at me again. There's something she's not saying.

So I push on. "Why wouldn't Ella have let anyone else touch her phone?"

She makes a little scoffing sound. "You'd let other people go through your phone?"

"Well, fine. But you said, 'Especially Naomi.' Why did you say that?"

Lucy smirks to herself. She's dying to spill. Her eyes dart around us to make sure nobody else is near enough to overhear us. "Ella had stuff in there."

"Stuff?"

"Stuff that she could use against people."

I blink at her. "Do you mean, like…blackmail stuff?" Wow. *Wow wow wow.*

She laughs, her upper lip curling. She knocks back the rest of her rum and Coke. "How do you think she got to have everyone to do what she wanted? Most of us didn't even like her that much. We were all afraid of her," she slurs.

"Did she have something on you too?"

"No, of course not," Lucy says a little too quickly. Then she smiles again. "But she might have had something on Naomi."

"Ooh, what makes you think that?"

"Because Ella wasn't the most popular girl freshman year or sophomore year. Naomi was. Not just because she's prettier than Ella. I'm sure you must have noticed by now that Naomi's also better at acting nice. Anyway, one day, Naomi just started, uh… What's that word when someone lets someone else win?"

"*Surrender? Concede? Capitulate?*"

Lucy side-eyes me. "What are you, a walking dictionary? Yeah, that. She started, uh, capitulating to Ella, in everything. Like, when someone asked her what she thought about their outfit, she'd just look at Ella and then agree with what Ella said. And when it was time for Coach to choose a new captain, Naomi openly supported Ella, over herself."

That is *super* interesting. "When did Naomi start acting like that?" I ask casually.

"Hmm, I think sometime in the middle of last year? I think Ella probably had something on her and took over being queen bee." Lucy eyes me. "You sure you saw her with Ella's phone?"

"Yeah, I think so. I could be wrong."

"Hmm," says Lucy.

My head is swirling. If Ella had something on Naomi, that gave her a much-stronger motive to get rid of Ella. I'm pleased with everything that I've found out here tonight. Scott, Lucy, and Naomi are all looking super suspicious with strong motives to have wanted to kill Ella. I revise my list mentally:

Motivations

Scott: Ella cheated on him and he knew, but didn't break up with her. He planned to get back at her. Could he have decided to kill her?

Lucy: 1) Hates Ella for stealing Scott from her. 2) To take Scott back.

Naomi: 1) To be cheer captain/queen bee? 2) Was Ella blackmailing her?

"There you are." Brett's voice breaks in, scattering my thoughts. "Thanks for getting Scott to replace me."

Lucy shoots me an annoyed look. "You suggested that to Naomi? Ugh. This whole bouncer thing is so stupid. It was your idea in the first place, wasn't it?"

"It was a stupid idea, I'm sorry," I say, but she stalks away before I can say anything else.

Brett grabs another beer, then sidles up to me and places one hand proprietorially around my waist. "Wanna dance?"

I sigh inwardly but muster a smile. "Sure."

Brett grins, flashing those perfect white teeth, and grabs my hand. I let him pull me to the makeshift dance floor, and we dance to Billie Eilish's "Bury a Friend."

He pulls me close to him, his hands sliding over my back to my hips. "Dawn," he says, his breath hot against my cheek. "God, I can't get over how hot you look in that nurse's outfit. Hey, want to see if we can find a room upstairs to be alone?"

No thanks, I want to scream, but I force myself to smile back at him. It isn't his fault. I've been flirting with him, leading him on to get information out of him. And he *is* cute. He's just not my type anymore. In fact, I realize I now have a very specific type. The pale-skinned, messy-brown-curls, green-eyed, geeky-but-tattooed type. That I can never be with.

Brett starts nuzzling my neck. He's pressing himself against me now, his excitement hard and insistent on my left hip. "Actually, I'm not feeling very well. I might have had too much to drink," I murmur. But he presses his lips on mine, his tongue darting into my surprised mouth. I shudder, almost gag. I push him away.

And catch Isaac's eyes, staring at me from across the room.

The look of utter shock on Isaac's face makes me want to cry. I freeze in place, unable to do anything other than stare back at him.

He's standing near the front door with his two friends. Scott must have been shirking bouncer duty. Isaac is wearing a black leather outfit with silver studs and buckles, his dark hair teased into wild, messy spikes, and he has long scissor blades attached to his fingers. He's a completely gorgeous, heart-throbbing Edward Scissorhands. I don't even know what his friends are dressed as because all I see is Isaac. Whose look of shock has now changed to hurt, his mouth twisting into a grimace, his eyes dark pools of accusation.

He spins around and heads out the door, ignoring his friends' surprised questions. That jolts me out of my frozen state as well. I pull myself away from Brett's grasp ("Hey, where are you going?") and run outside after Isaac.

He's already some distance further down the road beside his car, pulling off the scissor blades attached to his hands.

"Isaac! Wait!" I call, my voice breaking as I run to him, reaching him just as he's opening his door. "That wasn't what it looked like!"

"It's alright. You can kiss anyone you want."

Isaac's voice is so polite, so cold, that hot tears flood my eyes. "I didn't kiss him. He kissed me." But my protest sounds weak even to me.

He doesn't look at me as he throws the fake blades into the back seat of his car. "You don't have to explain yourself to me."

"Please, don't go," I say. "You just arrived."

"I shouldn't have let my friends talk me into coming. I just… I guess I wanted to see you." He sighs, as my heart twists at his words. "This was a mistake. Have fun. Don't let me ruin your night." He slams his door shut and drives off, leaving me staring after him, shivering in the freezing night air in my ridiculous costume.

I blink away my tears. Everything is just wrecked. And once again, it's all my fault.

I don't want to be here anymore. I've found out everything I came to find out, and there's nothing left for me here. I'll say goodbye to Naomi, Lucy, and the rest, and text Maddy to come get me early.

As I walk back to the party, I finally notice the brown sedan parked just across the road from Naomi's house. Sitting inside are Mulchaney and Doyle, watching everyone who's going in and out of the house. Doyle sees me and we lock eyes, and the realization that they're actually staking out Naomi's house, staking out our party, washes over me.

Looks like I'm not the only one investigating tonight.

I take a shaky breath and force my legs to take me back into the house. I locate Naomi standing in one corner of the living room and make my way over to her to tell her I'm leaving.

"Naomi, I'm sorry…"

But Naomi doesn't seem to hear me, doesn't even look up. She's staring at her phone, her hand gripping it so tightly her knuckles are white.

"Naomi? What's wrong?"

"What's wrong?" She finally looks up at me. Her eyes are shiny, and I realize with a shock that she's crying. "My stupid parents are getting a divorce, that's what's wrong. My mom just texted me. She couldn't even tell me in person." She wipes at her tears angrily with her other hand. "I guess I saw it coming, especially after their fight this morning before my dad left for the airport."

"I…I'm so sorry," I stammer, but she's already looking past me, glaring at something just behind me, and I turn around.

"This party is so great!" says Raquel, beaming. "I love your costumes!" *Oh no.*

"Who," hisses Naomi. "The fuck. Let you in?"

Around us, people stop dancing, turn and look.

Brett walks up to her, followed by Lucy. "Dawn asked me to let them in." He glowers at me. I guess he isn't too happy at the way I ditched him and ran after Isaac.

"She did, did she?" Naomi turns to me. Her face is pale with anger. "We'll talk about this tomorrow."

Raquel is starting to realize something is wrong, her eyes wide like startled deer caught in a car's headlights. "Sorry, I heard that anyone could come… I'm just g-going to go—"

Everybody has stopped dancing now. They're gathering round, a few people in the crowd snickering as Naomi smiles slowly. "You're right. You're welcome to stay."

"I am?" says Raquel, her voice high with both relief and confusion.

"Yeah. I'm really happy you're here. Because you can help us with the game I've planned."

I glance at Naomi in confusion. Game? What game?

"It's called Seek and Kill. You'll have two minutes to find somewhere to hide, and then the rest of us will look for you. It'll be so much *fun*. It's like hide-and-seek, except…" says Naomi, her red lips curling up at the side. At that moment, in the dark room, lit by the flickering lights, she looks truly frightening, like a beautiful but insane character from a horror movie come to life.

"What will happen if I'm found?" whispers Raquel in a hoarse voice.

"We get to kill you," says Naomi to shocked silence. Then she bursts out laughing, and everyone else joins in as well. "Kidding! We won't *really* kill you; we'll just *pretend* to. Anyway, if we find you, you lose and you have to leave. But if we don't manage to find you after half an hour, you win and you get to stay for the rest of the party. Unless you're too chicken for the challenge?"

"Naomi—" I say, but Raquel cuts me off, her chin jutting out.

"Sure, why not? Sounds fun."

Naomi claps her hands. "Cool! Lucy," she says, and as Lucy leans in, she whispers something into her ears. Lucy nods and heads toward the stairs. "Okay, listen up! Here are the rules. Number one: we can go anywhere in the house; no room is out of bounds. Number two: all the lights must stay off. And number three: don't touch any of my stuff, or my parents' stuff, in our rooms. Seriously, don't."

I look around. Everyone is murmuring, fidgeting, excited. Just then, Lucy comes back down the stairs with Andy, who adds in a resigned voice, "Hands off my stuff too."

Naomi smiles that red-lipped smile again. "Everyone close your eyes. I'll start the countdown, and then the hunt will begin."

Everyone closes their eyes obediently, and Naomi whispers to Raquel, "Better start hiding." Raquel nods determinedly and darts off. Naomi turns to me. "You should close your eyes too."

Reluctantly, I close my eyes as she starts the countdown on her phone.

As the seconds tick down, the excitement in the room is palpable: thick, red, and pulsating. Fanged. Hungry.

I beat down the feeling of dread. What she's proposed sounds like completely innocent fun.

And yet.

Why does it feel like something horrible is going to happen?

Her phone sounds, making me jump. I open my eyes. Ghouls and zombies stare back at me, smiling, bloodthirsty. Someone laughs, an excited, almost hysterical sound.

"Go," whispers Naomi, and there's an almost-imperceptible

collective shudder, then everyone breaks off into different directions, as David Bowie's "Scary Monsters (and Super Creeps)" trails off, and the thumping beat of Michael Jackson's "Thriller" starts playing.

I realize that almost everybody has their phones out; some are using them for light, but most are recording videos of their search. My own phone vibrates with an incoming text message—a text from Maddy.

> Ready to go?

I'm torn. All I want to do is go home and curl into a small ball in bed, especially with those detectives watching us...but I can't leave until I know that Raquel is going to be alright.

> Not yet. In the middle of a game.
> Should be done by midnight. Ok?

> Ok

I look around me. Only a few people have remained in the living room—Andy is lounging on the couch with his phone, obviously not caring about the game—the rest have all broken up into small groups of twos or threes and gone to explore the rest of the house. And there's a lot of it to explore; in addition to the three levels of rooms and bathrooms, there's a basement and an attic.

Naomi and Lucy are heading to the kitchen, followed by Scott, a giggling witch, a cat, and a zombie. I follow as well, to see Naomi handing out knives to Lucy and Scott.

"Can I have one too?" asks the witch, her eyes wide.

"No, only the cool murder kids get knives," says Naomi.

"What the hell?" I say.

"Relax, it's just to scare her when we find her. Here, take one."

"I don't think it's a good idea to have people walk around with knives. Those are sharp. What if someone gets hurt?"

Naomi rolls her eyes. "Oh my god, will you chill out? I just want to blow off some steam, okay? I had no idea you were such a party pooper. No one's going to get hurt. Are you going to stab someone with that?" she asks, to a chorus of *No*s. "See, they're not going to stab anyone. Okay?"

"Yeah, chill out, Dawn, jeez," says Lucy as she pushes past me, leading the zombie and the witch toward the door that goes to the basement.

"I'm going to go check my room first, just to make sure that freak isn't in there," says Naomi, also pushing past me, followed closely by Scott and the cat.

I hesitate, then follow them up the stairs. In the dark, I pass pale ghoulish faces and leering, bloodied faces, all creeping around, their footsteps masked by the thumping music. Somebody trips drunkenly, prompting a round of fiendish cackles and giggles from others. My heart starts racing as unease trickles down my back.

Scott breaks off into another room, as Naomi heads into

her bedroom and begins to look everywhere with the cat: in her closets, under her bed, in the adjoining bathroom. To her obvious disappointment and my relief, they find nothing.

But it's only been less than five minutes, and this is Naomi's house. Where can Raquel hide that Naomi, with the help of several dozen other people, can't find her?

Too late, I realize what Naomi is doing. What we're all doing. We're terrifying Raquel and recording it so she can be publicly humiliated by everyone later as well.

"Stop! Stop taking videos!" I say, but nobody pays me any attention.

Someone roars, "Come out, come out, wherever you are!" Another says, "We're going to get you!"

On the speakers, Alice Cooper shrieks a welcome to his nightmare.

I feel like I'm stuck in a nightmare as well, but not my own.

And then from the attic comes a bloodcurdling scream, and everyone rushes to the scene.

Raquel is crouched on the dusty floor. She was hiding under a tarp, which Naomi flung aside, gleefully brandishing her knife like she was about to stab her. Raquel is crying, cowering, and gasping between sobs. She wasn't expecting the knife.

Everyone is surrounding her, pointing and laughing, filming her with their phones. "I got it!" shrieks another girl, who was also in the room. "I got it all on my phone! Oh my god, it was awesome!" she laughs. "I'm uploading it to TikTok right now!"

Already, I know that tonight there'll be at least a dozen videos of this "game" uploaded to all the social networks.

"Did you have fun?" asks Naomi, and everyone laughs.

"Please. I just want to leave now," says Raquel, her breath hitching between sobs. As they continue laughing at her, she gets up shakily and stumbles to the stairs, almost tripping in her need to get away.

I look around me, at Naomi and Lucy, their red-lipped mouths twisted in jeering laughter, white teeth flashing. At these beautiful girls, these monsters.

I go down the stairs too, all the way downstairs, not stopping until I step through the front door into the freezing night. I walk to the curb and close my eyes. As soon as I do, I see Isaac's shocked face again, those accusing dark eyes.

It'll be at least another fifteen minutes before Maddy arrives to get me, but that's okay. I'd rather freeze out here, under the staring eyes of Doyle and Mulchaney, than spend another minute in that house.

HANNAH

She can't let her parents think anything is wrong if she wants her plan to work.

So she chats with them after school as if everything is normal. She helps make dessert (a walnut pumpkin pie). She laughs at her father's lame jokes—which admittedly isn't such a great idea, because he gets suspicious and asks why she's in such a good mood, so then she has to dial it down a little.

After they go to bed, she stays up, replaying the comments under today's latest post in her head, over and over again.

> She's so stupid

> Lol i still can't get over how someone like that was on the cheer squad 😆

> There's something wrong with her, has anyone else noticed? I'm serious!

> I agree, she gives me the creeps.

She doesn't know why her eyes are leaking tears nonstop, because inside, she feels nothing. Like there's a hollow, empty hole in the middle of her chest where her heart used to be.

She checks the time on her phone: 2:18 a.m. Her parents should be sleeping by now. All the same, she opens their bedroom door slowly, as quietly as she can. Peers in at them before entering.

Her mother is on her back, her eye mask on as usual; her father on his side, facing the wall, snoring lightly.

She creeps into their room, bare feet cold on the floor, tears streaming down her face. Her nose is blocked with snot, so she breaths through her mouth. The door to their bathroom is open. Hannah goes in and closes the bathroom door behind her—so slowly and gently that there isn't even a *click*—shuts herself in complete darkness.

She unlocks her phone, uses its flashlight to illuminate the medicine cabinet. There it is, her mother's Valium. A small prescription bottle, almost half-full.

She takes it in one trembling hand, switches off the flashlight. Opens the door just as quietly as she closed it. Tiptoes back out of the bedroom, her sleeping parents none the wiser.

Back in her own room, she shakes the contents of the bottle onto her bed and counts the pills. There are twenty-three of them. Is that enough to kill herself with?

Suddenly, she has the most horrible doubt. What if twenty-three aren't enough? She really doesn't want to have to resort to other, more painful means.

She grabs her phone again, googles how much Valium OD, and finds the answer on addictionresource.org ...if Valium is taken in combination with alcohol or opioids, a dangerous overdose may occur...

That's it.

She goes downstairs to the kitchen and grabs the bottle of brandy that her father keeps in the cupboard, the one he occasionally brings out after dinner when they have guests over. Back in her room, she struggles for a few minutes to unscrew the cap, grimly laughing at the thought that her plan might be thwarted by a too-tight cap.

Luckily, she manages to get it off. The smell of brandy drifts out, warm and spicy. She throws the cap on the floor, lifts the bottle lip to her mouth. Takes an experimental sip, swallows. It burns a little going down, and she coughs.

She reaches for a pill. Her hand is shaking, but only a little. Holds it up to her mouth.

Then before she can chicken out, she swallows it, washing it down with a gulp of brandy. Then another two at a go. Then three, four at a time, each time washing them down with brandy, until they're all gone.

She takes one last swig of the brandy, puts the bottle down quietly on the floor. Her chest and stomach are burning warmly with the alcohol, and her head is already starting to spin.

She lies back on her bed and closes her eyes.

Soon, there'll be no more problems.

No more beautiful, perfect girls who laugh at her, hate her.

No more of anything.

DAWN

I try to catch Raquel's eye the next day in American Lit, but she studiously avoids looking at me. She avoids looking at anybody, staring down at her book the entire time, trying to pretend she doesn't see or hear everyone else whispering and laughing at her.

And I don't blame her. This morning, the latest video that popped up on my TikTok was titled "Party Crasher Gets Scared Shitless." I can't even imagine how she must be feeling right now.

Actually, I can. Which is why when the bell goes, and Raquel shoves her book into her bag and slinks out of the room, I run after her.

"Raquel, wait," I call, but she only walks faster. "Raquel, please!" I chase after her in the hall until I catch up with her and put my hand on her shoulder.

She spins around, shrugging it off. "*What?* What do you want? Are you going to laugh at me too?"

"No!"

"Why not?" Her eyes flood with tears. "Your friends are."

My own eyes are wet too. "I…I'm really sorry. For what they did to you."

"And yet, it's not like you did anything to stop it last night."

"That's not fair. I didn't know what they were going to do until they did it. And I told them to stop taking the videos. Nobody listened," I say, but my protest sounds weak even to me.

"Oh, well. I suppose I should thank you then, for *trying* to stop them." She starts walking away.

"Raquel, please, will you please listen to me?" I say, my voice going a bit louder than I intend, and several people turn to look at us. I grab her wrist and pull her to the side of the hallway.

She shakes my hand off and hisses, "Let go of me! Why don't you go back to your cheerleader friends and leave me alone?"

"They're not my friends."

"Oh yeah? Could have fooled me."

I know I deserve her anger. I know I didn't manage to protect her like a real friend should have. I despise myself too. I may have lost her friendship after what happened last night; this whole thing is so messed up…but I still need her help. "I was only at the party last night to try and find out more stuff. And I did. About Scott. About Naomi," I say in a low voice, the words rushing out of me before she can walk off again. "And I need your help."

195

"Why should I help you?"

"Because I need your help to find out what Naomi Chen is hiding. Ella was blackmailing her about something. I can drop by your place after cheer practice today to explain everything."

Raquel's eyes widen. I can see she's struggling between telling me there's no way in hell she'll help, and wanting to find out what Ella was blackmailing Naomi about. Then, reluctantly, she nods. "Okay."

Gratitude surges in me. "Thanks."

"Oh my god, isn't that the girl who's on that video?" a girl standing a few feet away whispers, pointing at Raquel, and her two friends nod and giggle.

"Oh, go away," I say, and the girls glare at me.

Raquel's lips disappear into a thin line, and she spins and walks off stiffly, disappearing around the corner.

———

After practice, I'm in the changing room shouldering my bag, just about to leave, when Lucy and Naomi corner me, boxing me in on both sides.

"What are you playing at?" asks Naomi, tilting her head, her eyes sharp like knives.

My heartbeat picks up immediately, hammering a staccato beat in my chest. "I'm sorry, what?"

"Don't play dumb," says Lucy, her upper lip curling.

"I—I'm not," I stammer, even as my mind starts racing. *They know what I've been doing.*

"Why did you invite that loser last night, and then ask Brett to let her in?" asks Naomi. "Yeah, he told us everything. Were you trying to sabotage my party?"

"What? No!" I say, as relief surges through me. So *that's* what they're confronting me about.

"You knew I didn't want losers there, and yet you did that."

"I wasn't trying to sabotage your party."

Naomi narrows her eyes. "I don't know whether to believe you, the way you've been acting recently."

I gape at her, and then at Lucy, who's smirking. "What do you mean?"

"Why didn't you sit with us at Ella's funeral?" asks Lucy.

"I hate funerals. I just couldn't. Couldn't sit all the way up there," I say.

"Then last night you led Brett on, then ditched him for Isaac," says Naomi.

"Yeah, we saw you running after him; everyone did," says Lucy. "You think you're too good for Brett. And you think you're better than us too."

"No! I don't—"

"Especially when you acted like you were so shocked with the knives. Or when you were shouting at people to stop recording videos," says Naomi.

They stare at me, daring me to contradict them.

"I'm not better than you," I say quietly.

They glare at me.

"I don't know what you're up to, but we're keeping an eye on you. So you'd better watch your step. Come on, Lucy," she says, and they both stalk out.

———

Maddy drives me to Raquel's house. She seems a bit preoccupied with her own thoughts, and I wonder if she's had another fight with her boyfriend again.

After she drives off, I walk up the short driveway to the front door of the gray and white duplex and ring the doorbell. When Raquel opens the door, distrust is still shining clearly in her eyes. She hesitates for a moment, as if debating whether or not to slam the door in my face. Then she sighs and steps aside. "We can talk in the living room. My parents aren't home with my sisters yet. It's just us."

"So how do you know that Ella was blackmailing Naomi about something?" she asks as soon as we're seated.

I tell her what I found out from Lucy last night.

Raquel's eyes widen. "You think Naomi might have killed Ella because Ella was blackmailing her about something?"

"I don't know. It may not have anything to do with Ella's murder...but it might. That's what I'm trying to find out," I explain. "How bad the secret is. And what she was doing with Ella's phone, the night Ella was murdered."

"Okay, so…" Raquel says slowly, "Lucy thinks Ella had stuff on her phone, stuff that incriminated people, including Naomi. How on earth are we going to find out if Naomi stole Ella's phone that night to delete something on it?"

"We all have stuff on our phones backed up somewhere, right? Ella had an iPhone," I say.

Understanding dawns on Raquel's face. "That's what you want my help with. Are you serious? That's illegal."

"Please, Raquel," I say.

"I can't hack into Ella's iCloud," Raquel says grimly.

DAWN

I doubled-checked last night on Apple's support page. All files on an iPhone should normally be backed up to the user's iCloud account. When someone deletes photos and videos, they go to the Recently Deleted album for thirty days. It's only after thirty days that they're deleted permanently.

"If Naomi deleted something from Ella's phone, it should be stored in her Recently Deleted album on her iCloud," I say. "Ella died on the seventh of October. That's twenty-five days ago. Please. I know you can do it."

She shakes her head. "It doesn't matter if I technically can or not—"

"So you think that it can be done?" I say.

"You're not listening. I *can't* do this. Hacking into someone's account is illegal. If I get caught, I could go to *jail*."

Shit. I just know that Ella had something on Naomi, something *bad*, and whatever it is is right there, almost within reach.

"Look," says Raquel. "There's an ongoing police investigation. Maybe the police already checked Ella's iCloud."

"I doubt they have because what reason would they have to go looking in the Recently Deleted album of her iCloud account? I only know there's something there, and the significance of what it could mean, because of what Lucy told me," I say. "Even if they have, and seen whatever it is, they wouldn't know the context of it. That Ella was blackmailing Naomi."

"So why don't you just tell the police what Lucy told you?"

"Then they'd ask Lucy if it's true, and she might deny it," I say, frustration bubbling over.

Raquel gets up and starts pacing the room. "Okay. Let's say that I hack into her account and find something. Something big. How would that help?"

"If we find something like Lucy has hinted, then maybe I can confront Naomi, get her to talk somehow."

She takes a deep breath. Lets it out. "It *would* be nice to dig up dirt on Naomi, after what she did to me last night," she mumbles.

Hope surges inside me like a champagne cork popping open. "Look, you don't have to be the one actually doing the hacking. Just teach me how to do it and I'll do it myself, on my own computer. If I get caught, I won't mention you at all."

Raquel sighs. "Can I think about it?"

I try to suppress my anxiety. "Okay, but we have only five days left before it disappears forever."

―――――――

Maddy and I are finishing up doing the dishes when the doorbell rings.

Maddy looks astonished. "Who could it be?"

"I'll go see."

I open the door to find Raquel on the doorstep.

"Fine, I'll help," she says. "But if you get caught and you mention my name—"

"I won't, I swear."

"Let's see what Little Miss Perfect is hiding," she says, grinning.

Maddy enters the hallway as I step aside to let Raquel in. "Oh hey, Raquel, right?"

"We're doing a group project together, and we need to finish up on it after doing some research," I say quickly.

"Oh, okay."

Maddy wanders back to the kitchen, and I start leading the way up the stairs. "Let's work in my room," I say in a low voice. "But keep your voice down because my parents have already gone to bed."

I bring my laptop on my bed and power it on.

Raquel joins me on the bed. "Okay. First, you have to install this app…"

Forty minutes later, we're staring at the files on Ella's iCloud account on my laptop screen.

"Damn, Raquel," I mutter. "I knew you were some sort of computer genius, but I didn't know you could do all this hacker shit."

She shrugs. "It's easy with the right hacking application. With luck, no one will even notice. Specifically, the police. At least…I, er, hope not."

I double-click on the Recently Deleted album and scroll slowly through all the stuff that was deleted.

Selfies. Hundreds and hundreds of selfies. Wow, that girl really loved taking selfies. I double-click one that looks like a video, and Ella pops up on my screen, on her bed in a black lacy bra and panties, pouting. "Hey, baby, I miss you. Here's a special little something for you…" She sucks her finger, pouting again, then pulls down her bra.

"Eww," says Raquel.

I close the video, keep scrolling. Stop. "Oh my god. Is that…?" I double-click on the file, and then we're staring at a photo of two people kissing. They're in some living room, and the photo is slightly blurry, as if it was taken through a window. I don't recognize the man, but the female in the photo is clearly identifiable.

It's Naomi.

The man's right hand is on her ass, and her right hand is on his crotch.

"Holy shit," whispers Raquel. "It's Whitlock."

The name is vaguely familiar, but for a moment I don't remember where I've heard it before. "Who's Whitlock?" I ask.

"He teaches Physical Science. Wow. *Gross.*"

I open the next photo. Whitlock is sitting on a couch, his pants down at his ankles, and Naomi is straddling him. She has her top off, and his hands are on her breasts.

So that was how she managed to get her perfect GPA despite the "several Cs" she got in Physical Science last year.

"This was last year, which means Naomi was a minor when they did this." Oh my god. This is *huge.*

"We need to report this!" says Raquel, bouncing up and down on the bed in agitation. "A teacher can't be allowed to take advantage of a student and get away with it! He needs to be fired! And go to jail!"

"No!" I say. "I mean, yes, we'll have to report this eventually. But not right now."

"What? Why not?" She sputters the words out like I just asked her to betray her moral code. In all fairness, I probably just did.

"Because I need a bit more time to see if I can find out anything else that might be related to Ella's death. Please! I'm so close. I just need a bit more time."

Raquel shoots me a dubious glance, but she sighs and mutters, "Okay. But we *are* going to report this eventually."

"We definitely are," I say, which seems to appease her for now.

I check the next photo, but it's another selfie of Ella making a duck face in her car. It's only those two photos, but they're enough. I download them, then exit the account and close the app.

"Maybe you should also wipe the app completely from your laptop. Here, I'll do it," says Raquel, taking over.

"Ella must have followed Naomi to Whitlock's house and taken those photos," I say, thinking aloud.

"And Naomi killed Ella because she was tired of Ella holding that over her!" Raquel shuts my laptop. "All wiped."

"We don't know that," I say. "All we know is she got hold of Ella's phone to delete them. That gives her a motive, sure. But it doesn't mean she killed Ella."

"What? It seems like a pretty damn strong motive to me!"

"She's not the only one with a motive," I say.

She gapes at me. "What do you mean? Oh, wait, you said something about finding out something about Scott too, right?"

I nod. "According to his best friend, Scott knew that Ella cheated on him. And he didn't break up with her because he wanted to take a bigger revenge on her than just dumping her."

Raquel gapes. "Did Lucy, Naomi, and Scott *all* hate her?"

"It looks like it. But who killed her? I've managed to find out stuff, but it's not enough. Not yet. I need to dig further." I look at her. "I'm really sorry about what happened yesterday."

Raquel sighs. "I shouldn't have gone there in the first place." Then she perks up. "Hey, the next time Naomi is a bitch, can

I at least hint that I know that she's been doing the dirty with Whitlock?"

"Not unless you want to risk her killing you for it?" I say. Her eyes widen, and she shudders.

I follow her downstairs, lost in my thoughts. I've learned a lot in the past month about Scott, Lucy, and Naomi. Not only did each of them have the opportunity to kill Ella, each one of them has their own motivation for wanting her dead.

But this is where I'm stuck. Unlike the police, I can't take each of them into custody and interrogate them until they confess.

Or can I?

Maybe I should just turn over everything I've learned to Doyle and Mulchaney right now, let them do whatever they want with the information. After all, that's the reason I started digging into their secrets in the first place—to take the heat off myself. So they stop trying to pin it on me.

Will they even believe what I tell them? How do I even explain how I'm in possession of those photos?

I open the front door, but Raquel doesn't move. She's staring at her phone, her mouth hanging open.

"What is it?" I ask.

"Oh my god," she breathes. "My sister just texted me. She just heard it from her friend Jamal."

"Heard what?"

"Jamal only knows because he lives across the street from him, and he was putting the trash outside when they came—"

"Knows what? Raquel, I have no idea what you're talking a—"

"The police! They came to his house! They just arrested him a few minutes ago!"

"What? Arrested who?"

"Isaac Caldwell! It must be for killing Ella!"

The room seems to tilt slightly, and I feel sick.

They arrested Isaac? How can the police have gotten it so wrong? *He wasn't even there that night.*

"Dawn? Are you okay? You're breathing funny—" says Raquel.

"Are you sure?"

"Well, I don't see why Jamal would make up something like this, so yeah."

I can't breathe. It's like something is clutching my throat, cutting off my air supply. "It's not him. It's not possible. He was the one who told me we shouldn't dwell on the past. They've got it wrong."

The memory of Mulchaney parked outside my house resurfaces. What if the person she was watching wasn't me, but *Isaac*?

I don't know what Doyle and Mulchaney think they know, but they're wrong. They've messed up, arrested the wrong person. Isaac wasn't even there that night...

Was he?

DAWN

Isaac isn't answering my texts.

I toss and turn for hours that night, managing to fall asleep only in the small hours of the morning.

When my alarm sounds, I jolt awake—my heart in my throat, exhausted. A headache pounds in my skull as if I haven't slept at all. My eyes are so dry that putting my contacts in sends stabbing pains shooting to the back of my eyeballs, and the lenses sit on my eyes like gritty flecks of sand.

I only manage to summon up the energy to drag myself to school through the sheer hope that Raquel's sister and her friend might have been wrong, and that I might see Isaac in school today.

Morning classes are an absolute torture. Who cares about Algebra 2 or Economics with everything that's going on right now? Staring at my textbook, I bite my lower lip. I want to scream.

But that's not going to help anything, so I try to push the frustration and anxiety down. Half a dozen thoughts are twisting and chasing each other around in my head.

Do they think he did it because Ella bullied his sister? It's true that it doesn't look good for him, the way he got close to her afterward. And slept with her then dumped her. But the fact remains that he wasn't even at the party. Ella never invited him. Could she have invited him without telling the rest of us?

No, he wasn't there that night. I was and I didn't see him.

Did they handcuff him? Did his mom go with him to the station?

Thankfully, the bell for lunch sounds. I snatch my book and bag and run out of class.

I rush to the cafeteria, but Isaac isn't here, of course. I'm one of the first students to arrive. I take a tray and queue up to get some food, even though I have no appetite at all.

I realize I don't know where to sit. It's like my first day here again, this uncomfortable feeling of being out of place. I don't know if I should sit at the table with Lucy and Naomi anymore, after our confrontation yesterday. As I hesitate, the two of them enter the cafeteria and give me baleful looks that strengthen my anxiety.

I just can't handle them. Not right now. But if I go to sit with Raquel, I'll be openly declaring myself on the side of the school's outcasts. Which—while I don't give a shit about my reputation or what other people in school think of me anymore—would probably make it impossible for me to get back in with the rest of the cheerleaders or with the guys on the football team, which would in turn make it difficult to continue with my investigation.

As I stand there, biting my lower lip, a messy-haired, lanky, green-eyed boy walks in. *Isaac came to school after all! They released him!* There's a hint of stubble on his face, and he looks pale and tired. He moves slowly, like he got even less sleep than me, which could very possibly be the case.

Without thinking about it, I go up to him immediately. Balancing my tray awkwardly in my left hand, I reach out to touch his arm with my right. "I heard about what happened last night."

Isaac looks at me. Stiffens. "Oh? Is the entire school talking about it?"

I drop my hand back to my side. "N-no! Raquel told me last night, someone she knows lives across the street from you; he saw it—"

"Great," he says, dropping down to sit at his usual table, not looking at me.

Heat floods my face. His friends—I hadn't noticed them standing behind him before, so focused was I on him—are staring at our exchange, but I don't even care. I need Isaac to talk to me. I put my tray down and sit opposite him, then turn to the two of them. "Please, will you let me speak to him alone?"

They exchange glances. Then to my relief, the girl shrugs, and they walk away.

"I know you didn't do it," I say. "The police have got it all wrong. I don't know why they're trying to pin it on you, but I've found out many things. Things important to the case. I'm going to talk to Doyle and Mulchaney, tell them they have the wrong person." Isaac laughs softly, but I carry on speaking. "You weren't even there that night!"

"But I was," he says.

Cold washes over me. He's staring at the table now, not meeting my eyes.

"W-what?"

He looks up, looks at me. "I was there that night."

"I don't understand." But even as I say that, realization begins to dawn on me, and I start to tremble. The figure who'd been lurking by the pool that night. Cold tendrils of alarm snake down my spine.

It couldn't be. He couldn't have been that shadowy figure lurking at the party that night. Watching us from the dark.

Isaac closes his eyes and is silent for a few seconds. Then he opens his eyes, stands up. Starts walking out.

I hesitate for a moment. But I need to know. I chase after him, catching up with him as he's cutting across the grass to the parking lot, and grab his arm. "Isaac, wait! Where are you going?"

"Look…just leave me alone, okay?" He shakes my hand off. "I don't even know why I'm here. I shouldn't have come to school. I only came because my mom wanted me to." He laughs again, that same soft humorless laugh that he did in the cafeteria. "But what's the point, when I'm being investigated for murder?"

"I know you didn't do it," I say again.

Isaac blinks, shakes his head. "Why are you so sure, when I lied to you?"

"Because I know you. You're the one who keeps telling me that we shouldn't dwell on the past. That revenge is useless." I reach out and take his hand in my own shaky one. "Now, please tell me what really happened that night."

He runs a hand through his hair and lets out a gust of air. "I'd been ignoring all Ella's texts, like I told you," he says slowly, reluctantly. "But that night, she texted me again. She begged me to go over. She said that if I didn't, she'd...she'd kill herself."

So that's what happened. Annoyance at Ella's blatant emotional manipulation surges inside me. "What time did she text you?"

He rubs his eyes with the palm of his free hand. "Around a quarter past eleven. When I saw her text I just...panicked."

I think I understand. "Because of your sister."

He nods tiredly. "I didn't want her to do what my sister did, even if she was part of the reason my sister tried to kill herself. So I finally replied to her. I told her that I'd come, and not to do anything foolish. I drove down there so fast.

"But when I arrived, she seemed perfectly fine. She was sipping a drink, lounging in a pool float. Laughing. That's when I realized she was just messing with my head. Saying shit to manipulate me into coming down."

"So you *were* the one we saw standing in the shadows," I whisper.

He nods sheepishly. "When Scott called out, I knew it was

going to be so bad if he realized I was there. Already, I regretted going down. And anyway, I told myself that Ella would be fine with her boyfriend. So I left. The music was so loud no one ever heard my car arriving or leaving."

"You went back home?"

Isaac nods. "I just went back home and went to bed." He rubs the side of his face ruefully. "I didn't tell you because...well, first of all, it was so stupid. But especially because..." He sighs. "I was afraid to let anyone know I'd been there. I knew the police wouldn't like how it looked. And I was right, wasn't I? The first time they called me down to the station, it was because they'd found her texts to me, and my reply saying I was coming. I told them that I didn't go in the end. That I'd changed my mind." He scowls, then his shoulders slump, and he just looks defeated and scared. "But then, somebody told them that I did leave my house that night."

"Who?"

"My neighbor. She's this old widow who lives in the house just on the left of ours. The police must have gone round questioning everyone on our block. And Mrs. Nowak told them that she'd woken up that night to use the bathroom, that she'd gone to the kitchen to get a glass of water and happened to look out of her kitchen window, the one over the sink, and saw me leaving in my car. And that she remembers wondering where I was going so late at night."

"But...but what motive could they possibly think you have for killing her?"

"Someone told them about what happened to my sister," he says, his voice flat. "They think I schemed to get close to Ella, close enough to kill her. To get revenge on my sister's bully."

"But...you didn't. Did you tell them that, um...that...?"

"That the only revenge I took was sleeping with her and dumping her? I did, but that didn't seem to go down very well. I think it just helped them make up their minds that I'm a major asshole with ulterior motives who can't be trusted, who's probably lying about that now."

I feel flustered. "But you're not the only one with a motive. Scott, Naomi, and Lucy all hated her, and they had just as much opportunity to kill her. Did you know it wasn't even Ella who sent you those texts?"

Isaac throws me a startled look. "What?"

"When you got those texts, someone else had her phone. It was Naomi. She must have sent those texts, pretending to be Ella."

Quickly, I tell him how I went looking for Naomi and how I found her in one of the bathrooms in the main house with Ella's phone.

Isaac stares at me, uncomprehending. "But why would she—"

"She took Ella's phone in order to delete something on it. Something that Ella had been using to blackmail her with. She must have gone through Ella's texts and seen her texts to you and decided to mess with the two of you. Get you to come down, and then enjoy the messy scene between you, Ella, and Scott." I pause, remembering the way she set up the Seek and Kill game at her

Halloween party. "She hated Ella for blackmailing her. And she knew that your sister had attempted suicide…"

"And she knew that was the way to get to me." Isaac's mouth twists in disgust.

"I don't know; I'm just guessing at her motive. But one thing's for sure, it was her who sent those texts to you, not Ella. Because I came back with Naomi to the pool, and I saw her put Ella's phone on the table. And Ella was in that float in the pool all that time, until I left at a quarter to midnight."

Isaac is quiet for a while as he digests everything that I've just told him. Then he sighs. "It doesn't make any difference anyway, who sent the texts. It got me to go down to Ella's house that night. And because I lied about it to the police at first, and they know I got with Ella even though, no, *because* I hated her because she bullied my sister…I'm their biggest suspect now."

"But, if they arrested you last night, how did you manage to get them to release you?"

He shakes his head. "They didn't arrest me. They wanted me to go down with them to the station last night for more questioning. So I went down with them."

"Oh…" Relief surges through me, relief and irritation with this Jamal. Talk about spreading rumors. "So…they haven't charged you?"

"No. I think it's only because there isn't any actual proof that I was there. The police must still be trying to get things to match up."

The two of us fall silent. Then Isaac says, "When you said

you found out many things, things that might be important to the case…you're talking about Naomi being blackmailed by Ella?"

I nod. "And Lucy hated Ella because Ella stole Scott from her. And Scott knew for sure that Ella cheated on him. Brett confirmed it." I bite my lower lip. "It's what I was trying to find out from Brett that night, on Halloween. I…I flirted with him to get him to spill."

Isaac stares at me, dumbfounded for a moment. Then, his mouth widens slowly into a grin. "So that's what you were doing." Suddenly, he laughs, as heat floods my face. "Poor Brett. He never had a chance."

"Stop," I mumble. "It wasn't my finest moment."

Isaac just continues grinning at me. "Look, I know I have bigger problems right now, but…" He takes my hand. "You have no idea how happy that makes me. Knowing you're not really into that guy."

I smile up at him. "I confirm that he's not the one I'm into."

Isaac tugs me nearer to him and we're kissing again, little champagne bubbles popping in my belly. Everything is okay again between us, and it makes me dizzy with happiness.

But only for a moment because reality sinks in quickly. Because everything is not okay for *him*.

Then an idea comes to me. "You haven't admitted that you were there? You didn't tell them everything that you just told me, did you?"

"No, I refused to answer any of their questions. Doyle looked like he personally wanted to murder me."

"Okay, listen to me. You came to the party that night, but you never went to the pool, okay?" Isaac's eyes widen as I continue. "This is what happened. When you drove up to the house, I was just arriving in the driveway to wait for my aunt to come pick me up, and when I told you that Ella had fallen asleep, you got back in your car and left. Okay? Remember, because our stories have to match."

I know this version of events is fudging the truth slightly, but it was only *slightly*. Isaac didn't do it, and I can't stand by and let him take the fall for it.

———

I'm an anxious mess the rest of the day as I head to the rest of my classes. Which is understandable because after practice I'm going to go down to the station and change my testimony to the police.

When Maddy comes to pick me up, I get straight to it as soon as I get in her car.

"Maddy, could you drive me to the police station, please? I have to speak with the police again about Ella's case."

She shoots me a look of alarm. "Why? What's happened?"

"It's just I've found out some new stuff, and also I have to clarify some other stuff."

Maddy stares at me, obviously wondering why I'm being so vague. "Oookay. You're not in more trouble, are you?"

"Not me, but my friend is."

"Would this friend happen to be Isaac Caldwell?"

My face grows hot, but I meet her eyes. "Yes, and he's innocent. And I need to speak with those detectives."

"Kid, I don't know—"

"If you won't drive me there, it's okay. I can call for an Uber."

Maddy shakes her head, then sighs. "Fine. Let's go."

As Maddy drives, I go over what I intend to say in my head. But when we arrive, she insists on coming in with me, throwing me off guard.

"There's really no need—"

"You're still a minor."

"Okay, but it's really not necessary."

She gives me one of those looks. "I think it is."

I know better than to try to argue, so I don't. I head to the front desk, Maddy a few steps behind me. There are two officers, a woman seating behind the front desk, and a man standing beside her. Their heads swivel to me as I walk up to them.

"Excuse me, but…I need to speak with Detective Doyle or Detective Mulchaney, please."

The female officer raises an eyebrow. "What is this concerning?"

"I'm Dawn Foster… It's about the Ella Moore case."

She eyes me dubiously. "They're busy right now, talking to some other witnesses. It might take a while."

Other witnesses? Unease creeps over me. "It's okay. I can wait."

"Take a seat," she says, nodding at the row of chairs in the waiting area. Maddy and I sit down to wait.

Who could Mulchaney and Doyle be talking to?

After a while I realize my right leg is jittering and make myself sit still.

Fifteen minutes later there's the sound of approaching footsteps, and then Mulchaney comes around the corner, *followed by Lucy and Scott.* I stare at them as they walk past me on their way out. Scott avoids my eyes, but Lucy turns to me and throws me a sly smile, and my stomach twists into knots.

Did Doyle and Mulchaney ask them to come down to question them again about what happened that night? Scott and Lucy don't even know that Isaac was there that night. So they wouldn't have changed their stories now...right?

But my thoughts are interrupted when Mulchaney comes to stand in front of me. I look up to see her frowning at me. "Can I help you, Ms. Foster?"

I take a deep breath. "I have new information that might be important to the case."

She raises her eyebrows. "In that case, follow me."

Mulchaney leads Maddy and me to the same small room we were in the first time I was here. It's as cold and claustrophobic as I remember, and I shiver.

Doyle joins us. The two detectives sit across me from the table, and Maddy stands beside and a little behind me, just like before. We're in the same positions as the first time, like we're reenacting it, and I have such a strong sense of déjà vu the hair on the back of my neck stands.

Doyle nods at me. "You said you have new information?"

I clear my throat. "Yes. I've found out some things. About Scott and Lucy." The two detectives don't say anything, their expressions stay unnervingly unchanged. I take a deep breath and plunge on. "They hated Ella. They have motives for wanting her dead."

Mulchaney lets out a little exhalation. "Yes, you already hinted that the second time we spoke. But you refused to elaborate then."

"Because I didn't know for sure then! But I do now."

And then I tell them everything that I've learned about Lucy and Scott.

How Lucy hated Ella because Scott had first been her boyfriend, and how Ella stole him from her by telling Scott Lucy had cheated on him. How she still hated Ella all this time, her drunken confession to me that night by the pool.

I play them the recording on my phone:

Then Ella decided she *wanted him,* we hear Lucy's voice say, loudly and clearly.

I don't understand… Why did he break up with you for her?

Because that bitch told him I cheated on him.

Next, I told them how Scott hated Ella too, because he found out that she cheated on him with Isaac. How he called her a bitch that night by the pool. How he wanted revenge.

"Brett Young can confirm all of that," I say.

I don't tell them about Naomi being blackmailed by Ella, because she went into the house and was less likely to have had the opportunity to kill Ella. Also, I need to keep her secret under wraps for a while longer in case this doesn't work out. Because I don't like the way Lucy and Scott were here, talking to Mulchaney and Doyle, and something tells me I should have a plan B.

But what I've told them about Lucy and Scott should be good enough. What were they doing alone with Ella between midnight and one, *an entire hour*, before going to bed? If they're investigating Isaac, then they should investigate Lucy and Scott too.

"That's all very interesting, Dawn," says Doyle, "Thanks for coming in."

"What?" I bristle. "That's it? What I've found out changes everything! Lucy and Scott had motives for wanting Ella dead! They were alone with her for—"

"New evidence has emerged. We have cause for suspicion, enough for an arrest," says Doyle.

He must be talking about Isaac's neighbor's testimony. The old widow with the Polish name. But...*cause for suspicion, enough for an arrest*? I don't have to fake my confusion as I say, "What evidence? Arrest who?"

Mulchaney smiles grimly. "Someone else who was also there that night."

"Oh."

My flat response draws the two detectives' attention, and they look at me sharply, like hounds scenting game.

"You know who I'm talking about?" asks Doyle.

I nod. "You mean Isaac? I didn't think—"

"Didn't think what? That it was important to tell us?" says Mulchaney, her black eyebrows knitting together into a frown.

"You saw him? Why didn't you mention it before when I asked you to tell us everything?"

"Because I didn't think it was important," I shake my head, as if confused, as I slide into the story I'd prepared with Isaac. "He drove up just as I arrived in the driveway to wait for Maddy."

"And then?" asks Doyle impatiently.

"I asked him what he was doing there, and he told me that Ella asked him to come. But I told him that Ella had a lot to drink and had fallen asleep in the pool float. And that Scott was with her. So he changed his mind and got back in his car and left before Maddy arrived."

My voice trails off, and the two detectives stare at me for what seems to be an eternity as I sit there, sweating despite the cold. There, I've done what I came to do. My hands are clammy and trembling slightly, and I clasp them together as I wait for the detectives to speak.

"Are you sure that's what happened?" asks Mulchaney carefully.

"Y-yes. I didn't think it was important. Isaac didn't even go to the pool area. He was there for literally only a minute."

The two of them are frowning now. Finally, Doyle says, "That's not what happened, according to other witnesses."

A plummeting sensation, like the drop in a roller coaster ride after the climb. "What? Other witnesses? What did they say?"

Mulchaney smiles thinly. "A few other people had a change of heart. They now testify they saw Isaac Caldwell loitering by the pool area."

"*What?*" I gape at him as I fight a rising panic. It must be Lucy and Scott. *The little shits are making this up.* "They're...they're lying!" I say.

"It's your word against theirs. What reason have they got to lie now?" She eyes me shrewdly. "Whereas you have a reason, don't you?"

"What...what do you mean?"

"Isaac Caldwell is your boyfriend, isn't he?"

"No!"

"Obstructing an officer is a misdemeanor punishable by a fine up to ten thousand dollars, or up to nine months in jail, or both Miss Foster," says Doyle.

"I'm not—"

"You should be glad we may have found the real person who killed Ella Moore. Because before we had these statements from these witnesses and physical evidence tying Isaac Caldwell to the scene of the crime—"

"Evidence? What evidence?"

Doyle continues as if he hadn't heard me. "—this might have gone unsolved."

Maddy's hand grips my shoulder so tightly, I wince. "Kid, I think we should go now."

"But—"

"*Now,*" Maddy hisses, and she pulls me up and out of the room.

———

Maddy is furious. She doesn't say anything on the drive home, but her lips are pressed together so tightly they're just a thin line, and her knuckles are white on the steering wheel.

That's fine. I can't speak either.

Unfortunately, ten minutes before we reach her house, she finds her voice. "I don't think you should talk to this Isaac Caldwell anymore."

"They're making a huge mistake! It wasn't him; those two are *lying*—"

"*Stop it!*" she shouts. "Just...stop. You just tried to *lie to the police*!" She expels a gust of air. "I'm trying my best to be understanding, okay? But you really need to stop trying to interfere with a goddamn homicide case. Okay?"

I'm really upset, she doesn't understand at all. But if I try to argue with her, she might tell my parents what I just tried to do. I bite the inside of my cheek and nod stiffly. Maddy shakes her head, obviously not believing me, but she doesn't say anything more.

As soon as we reach home, I run past my parents who are watching TV in the living room, ignoring their *Hey, how was school today?* and *Is something wrong?* up the stairs to my room. I don't dare to text Isaac, because I don't want Doyle and Mulchaney going over our texts, so I call him.

Isaac answers on the third ring. "Hey. How...how did it go?"

His voice is hesitant, worried—and I want to cry. But I hold myself together.

"I told them what I said I would, but…"

"But?" he says flatly.

"Lucy and Scott were there too. They told Doyle and Mulchaney that they saw you."

"What?" he says, surprise making his voice go up. "But Lucy didn't see me. And you said Scott didn't recognize me either."

"They're lying. To pin Ella's murder on you."

But why now? How did they know Isaac was there that night?

"Fuck," Isaac says in a low voice.

"What?" I ask.

"Someone just rang the doorbell. Hang on—I'm coming," he calls. Then he says, his voice thick with panic, "My mom is calling for me. I think...I think the cops are here. I'll...I'll try to call you later. If I can."

Isaac hangs up, and I'm left holding my phone to my ear. But I know he won't be calling me back.

Because they've come to arrest him, and this time, it's for real.

DAWN

I'm in a cold, dark room. It's the interrogation room at the police station, except Isaac is also there, in a cage. I tell him I'm going to get him out, and he nods at me sadly. But I can't figure out how to unlock the lock, a baffling contraption full of hundreds of spinning numbered dials.

Something is coming. It's creeping up behind me...but I have to focus, open this lock. Isaac is pointing behind me, his green eyes wide with fear. He's telling me to go, to run, but I have to open this lock. It's my fault he's in here, I can't leave him, and the thing behind me is here, and I want to turn around, finally *see* what it is. But I can't look back, if I look back, it'll eat me—

My alarm rings, jolting me awake.

I must have fallen asleep. My phone is still in my hand. I check it again. Nothing. Dread bubbles in my guts as, unable to stop myself, I call Isaac again. It rings and rings, but he never picks up.

I call Raquel, and she confirms what I already know. "Yeah, Jamal saw them."

It was the police, and this time, they really did arrest Isaac. They took him away in handcuffs. His mother cried and screamed as they pushed him into the police car.

"It wasn't him. He didn't do it," I whisper.

"I don't know," says Raquel. "He does look very suspicious. I heard that he snuck into the pool party uninvited that night."

My heart feels like it's sinking to the bottom of my feet. "Heard from where?" Lucy and Scott couldn't have already moved so quickly...could they?

"Some people from school. This kind of news spreads fast. It tracks, Dawn. Ella bullied his sister, whose life is ruined. He has the biggest motive of all."

"It wasn't him," I repeat again, but despair has a choke hold on my throat, and I can barely get the words out.

"We've been looking at the wrong people," Raquel says quietly. "I think you're not seeing it because you like him. It was him all along, Dawn."

———

The morning is blisteringly cold and grim, the sky gray with low menacing clouds. It's so cold that on the way to school, it begins to snow. Tremulous flakes drift in the air, melting as soon as they reach the ground or the windshield of Maddy's car. By the time I reach school, though, they've turned into angry stinging raindrops, so cold on my face it turns my skin numb as I run the few yards from the parking lot into the building.

The news that the police arrested Isaac for Ella's murder sweeps through Sierton High that day like a virus spreading through an overly crowded city. Everywhere I go, there are students whispering—their shock, often mixed with glee, barely contained in their hushed voices.

He snuck down to her party and killed her when no one else was around!

He'd been planning his revenge for years, you know what Ella did to his sister...

Oh my god, I can't believe I thought he was cute...

They're enjoying the drama, as if it's a show on television. No matter how I try to tune them out, their sibilant whispers chase me everywhere.

Lucy is at her locker. Before I can help it, I'm there beside her. She jumps slightly when she notices me.

Talk about a guilty conscience.

"What do you want?" She glares at me, but as I meet her eyes, hers slide away.

"Why did you and Scott tell the police that you saw Isaac at Ella's party?"

She smirks. "Because we did."

"No, you didn't."

She tilts her head at me, that infuriating smile on her face. "Are you calling us liars?"

My heart is racing, but I stand my ground. "Yes."

She rolls her eyes. "God, Dawn. Just let it go, okay? I mean, I'm sorry for your boyfriend, but if he was unlucky enough to be there right at that time…"

I stare at her, speechless, but she continues.

"You should be thankful we changed our statements. The cops will leave us alone from now on." She shrugs. "Just find another guy. There are other cute guys in school. Guys who don't come along with baggage like vegetative sisters." And then, she smiles slyly again. "Actually, I should be thankful to you for getting Isaac to admit how he was there that night."

Understanding rocks me, hits me like a blow to the chest. "You overheard us."

"It was so dramatic, the way you chased after him out of the cafeteria yesterday. I had a feeling your conversation would be interesting. And wow, it really was." She grins again, even as I fight the urge to slap her, strangle her. "It was too perfect. All Scott and I had to do was tell the cops we saw him." She shrugs again. "So we didn't really see him. But that's just a minor detail, isn't it? After all, he was there. As far as we know, he really was the one who killed her."

"You…you…"

"I, I, what? Don't act so scandalized. You're the one who was going to tell a bigger lie to get him off. You chose him over us, you traitor." Lucy takes a step forward, her face coming right up to mine. "Fuck that. And fuck you."

I gasp as she gives me a hard shove.

"Don't get in my face again, or you'll see what I can do to you, bitch." She walks off, bumping me hard with her shoulder.

I have to speak with Scott. Maybe I can persuade him to admit to the police that he didn't see Isaac that night—that Lucy put him up to lying about it.

I have no idea how I'm going to do that, but I have to try because I don't know what else I can do right now.

By the time English—the last class of the day, and also the only class I have with Scott—rolls around, I've convinced myself that I can talk him around. Thankfully, neither Naomi nor Lucy is in our class.

After the bell rings, I make my way over to Scott and intercept him before he can leave. "Scott, wait," I put my hand on his arm. "Can we talk?"

He frowns, stares at my hand. Shakes it off. But like the other day at the police station, he doesn't meet my eyes. Instead, he focuses his gaze over my head, somewhere past me. "What do you want? I have to get to practice."

"It's about Isaac," I start to say, and he glances around quickly at the other students near us, who are still gathering their books and bags, or lingering behind in the classroom chatting. I get the hint and stop talking until everyone else is gone.

When we're finally alone in the room, Scott exhales irritably. "What about him?"

"Please, you can't tell the police that you saw him that night when you didn't."

Scott scowls, finally looking at me. "I did see him. I saw him by the pool, remember? You were there too."

"But we didn't see who it was! We couldn't make out his face. Please, you can't—"

"*Who cares?*" He's shouting now, his face red. "He admitted to you it was him yesterday. Lucy told me. You were going to tell the police that he never even went to the pool area, weren't you? Just to get that asshole off. Well, I think he did it."

"He *didn't*! He left when you called out to him. When I went back out front to wait for my aunt, his car wasn't there anymore!"

"He probably parked his car somewhere further down the street, hung around until we were all asleep, and then snuck in and killed her."

My mouth snaps shut. I hadn't considered that possibility, and his words hit me like being doused with a bucket of ice water.

"Wake up, Dawn! He blamed Ella for what his sister did to herself. That's a hell of a stronger motive than what you think I have." Scott is breathing hard now, his face pale except for two angry red spots in his cheeks. "I know you think I did it. Brett told

CINDY R. X. HE

me you were digging around, poking your nose into my business. Yeah, I knew that she cheated on me with that asshole. And yeah, I was planning to get back at her. If you have to know, I was going to break up with her at prom, humiliate her in front of the entire school. I was looking forward to it, actually. But then she died, so..." Scott shrugs. "So I'm not that sad that she died. She kind of deserved it. But I wasn't the one who killed her. And I'm sure as hell not taking the fall for it." His lips compress into a grim line. "To be honest, I don't care if it was that asshole who did it, or Lucy, or Naomi. Or you. As long as the police leave me alone from now on. You too. Leave me alone, Dawn."

Scott pushes past me and stalks out of the room. I can only stare after him, then sit down and bury my face in my hands.

DAWN

It's still raining on Saturday morning: a cold, relentless drizzle that washes the entire world gray and shows no sign of stopping as I huddle under the shelter of the bus stop outside Sierton's public library, waiting for the bus that will take me to Isaac's house.

I don't know if anyone will be home, or what exactly I'm going to say to them if they are. But I have to do this because I have to know what's happening, and how he is. Also, doing something—anything—makes me feel less helpless.

Isaac's house is a small single, painted off-white, with a detached garage and a little patchy lawn covered with soggy dead leaves. His old rusty car sits in the driveway; seeing it sends my heart lurching. The memory of being in it with him comes to me so strongly I can almost hear the coughing sputtering of the engine, smell the citrus of his shampoo, see the angel's wings on the back of his neck.

Steeling myself, I walk up the porch and ring the doorbell. I wait for a minute, but nobody comes. I ring the doorbell again, then put my hands in my pockets for warmth. If no one is at home, should I give up and go home, or should I wait out here until someone returns? If I wait, would whoever comes back think I'm crazy? Also, how long can I stand out here before I become hypothermic?

I'm about to try ringing a third time when I hear soft footsteps approaching from behind the door. It opens, and a woman looks out at me.

"Can I help you?"

Her voice is thick, like she has a cold. She has curly shoulder-length dark brown hair. My eyes meet her striking green ones. She must be Isaac's mother. For a moment I just stare. She's probably starting to wonder if she should close the door in my face when I find my voice. "Hi. I'm Dawn. I'm Isaac's friend. I just…I just wanted to know if…" *If he's going to be okay* is what I'm about to say, but of course he isn't, and I'm stupid for asking. "Is he here?"

It's then that I notice her eyes are red rimmed, her face is all blotchy, and her clothes are rumpled, as if they were what she'd worn to sleep the night before. If she'd slept at all.

"Isaac isn't here." She looks at me silently for a moment before speaking again. "Did you walk here in the rain?"

"No. I mean, yeah, but just from the bus stop."

"Would you like to come in?"

I nod, and she opens the door wider and steps aside. She leads me down a narrow hallway into a small living room, where a girl is sitting in a wheelchair. She's pale and has the same brown hair, cut in a pixie style, and startling green eyes like Isaac.

Her gaze slides over to me as I enter, but her expression doesn't change, nor does she reply when I say hi.

"My daughter doesn't speak anymore. Not since..." Mrs. Caldwell's voice trails off, and her lips press together into a firm line. Then she shakes her head and indicates with her hand for me to sit, so I sink awkwardly onto a faded couch. "What can I get you to drink? I think there's some Diet Coke. And Dr Pepper. Or do you prefer coffee?"

"I'm alright, thanks. Maybe just a glass of water."

She nods and heads back into the hall. I look around me. Even though the house is small, and the furniture in this room is spartan and mismatched, everything is clean and neat. Except for the few wads of used tissues on the side table. Isaac's mother must have been crying just before I came. Isaac's sister seems to have lost interest in me, because she's gone back to staring out of the window.

Mrs. Caldwell comes back with a glass of water for me and a cup of coffee for herself, which she places on the small wooden coffee table between us.

"Thank you, Mrs. Caldwell."

"Call me Corinne. Oh, I'm sorry about that mess," she says, leaning over to scoop up the used tissues. She dumps them in a wastepaper bin in the corner of the room before returning and sinking down heavily in her armchair.

My eyes drift to a framed picture on a sideboard against the wall. It's a photo of Isaac, his mom, and his sister, who looks shockingly much more alive in the photo. Isaac looks a bit younger than he is now, and the skin on his neck is clear; there's no tattoo there yet. They're outdoors; I can see trees and what looks like a tent in the background. Isaac is stretching his arm out in front; he's the one holding the camera for a selfie, and his mom and sister are brandishing marshmallows on sticks. They all have huge smiles.

Corinne follows my gaze to the framed photo. "We were camping by Lake Michigan. That was three years ago. The summer before…" Her voice breaks off, but she doesn't have to complete her sentence. It was the summer before her daughter's attempted suicide.

"Are you Isaac's girlfriend?" she says suddenly.

"No! I mean… I don't… We…" I feel my face grow hot. What exactly are we, anyway? We aren't dating. We've never gone out on a date. But we kissed. Did him coming over to my house that day count as a date? Has Isaac said anything about me to his mom?

"You care about him," she says, looking carefully at me.

"I do. Was he really arrested yesterday evening? Is he still—"

"Yes." Corinne's voice is thick with emotion, and to my alarm, her eyes fill with tears. "I can't believe they handcuffed him." She reaches for another tissue and covers her eyes with it, and then starts crying softly into it. "I'm sorry. I'm just… It's just so shocking. The worst thing is, he turned eighteen in September, so they're going to try him as an adult. They charged him with first-degree murder last night."

My heartbeat is pounding in my head, and the room swirls around me. *They charged him with first-degree murder.* It can't be happening. It's just not possible. My vision blurs as my eyes fill with tears.

Corinne is sobbing quietly now. "They won't let me bail him out. They're going to keep him locked up in the county jail until he faces trial. But he didn't do it! He would never do anything like that!"

"I know," I whisper.

"I've called and spoken to a few attorneys today. I'm going to meet up with one tomorrow morning." She's rambling now, twisting her fingers around each other. "I don't want them to assign him a public defender; I've heard they're usually overworked. I'm going to sell my car to help pay for it."

My entire body feels numb, except for a constant squeezing in my chest. Isaac has been charged with first-degree murder. I guess that up until a few moments ago, I've been unconsciously holding on to the belief that the police will realize that they've made a mistake and let him go.

I can't bear to be in her company anymore. *It's my fault.* I jump up. "I'm so sorry. I have to go." Everything is spinning. I lurch out of the room, down the hallway, back toward the door. Grab the knob and twist it, throw open the door. Icy raindrops hit my face as I half stumble, half run out, running down my sweating, clammy skin.

I don't stop running until I reach the end of the block and turn the corner. I can't see through all the rain in my eyes. Or maybe they're tears.

I think about everything: one action leading to another, dominoes falling over, cause and effect.

And now Isaac is locked up, waiting to face trial for first-degree murder.

I take out my phone, and my trembling hands drop it immediately. I snatch it up off the soggy grass, wipe at the wet screen. Google the penalty for first-degree murder in Wisconsin. It's the most serious crime, and if found guilty, Isaac faces life imprisonment. *Life imprisonment*, for something that he didn't even do.

I have to see him.

I pull out my phone again and google *Sierton county jail*, check their visiting hours and rules. Standing in the rain, I make an appointment to visit him.

HANNAH

Something jolts her into consciousness. She doesn't want to wake. She's so tired. She wants to slip back into the darkness, where it's peaceful, quiet…

But again it comes—the hard tap to her face—almost a slap. And a voice, shouting her name.

"Wake up!"

Obediently, Hannah opens her eyes a little—funny how that requires such a tremendous amount of effort—and winces as the too-bright lights hit her eyeballs. She closes them again, but that someone slaps her face and shouts at her again. "You have to wake up!"

Irritation and resentment surge through her. Who the hell is this, and why do they keep slapping her? She opens her eyes again, squinting, sheer annoyance giving her the energy to look and locate the person—a stout, middle-aged woman with shoulder-length, dyed-red hair who is glaring at her.

Hannah opens her mouth to tell this bossy woman to leave her alone, but all that comes out is a croak. The woman, however, grabs her by the jaw and says, "Good! Keep your mouth open!" and then *shoves* something into her mouth, something hard and scratchy. She pushes it further until it hits the back of Hannah's throat, and then keeps pushing. Hannah coughs and raises her hands automatically to clutch at her attacker's hands, but someone else grabs her hands and pins them to her sides.

"Stop fighting!" the red-haired woman shouts at her, pushing the thing even harder against the back of her throat, and Hannah retches, her eyes filling with tears. Somehow, she manages to get her hands free, and she shoves the woman away, and mercifully, the thing in her mouth comes out too.

"What—" she rasps, stopping to cough. "What…?"

"We have to pump your stomach!" the woman shouts, still glaring at her.

"I don't know what you want me to do!" The tears run down Hannah's face as she glares back at this stupid, horrible woman.

"Oh." The woman blinks at her. "We have to get this down your throat." She holds up a long tube thing.

"You should have just said so," Hannah says tiredly. How had she come to be here? Is it still the middle of the night? How had her parents known?

"Okay, let's try again. Swallow when I try to put it in."

She opens her mouth, and the woman puts the thing in again. It hits the back of her throat—she tries to swallow, and it hurts her throat terribly—but this time it goes down. The woman feeds it further and further in—she can feel it sliding down—she keeps feeling the need to gag, or retch, but she suppresses it. And then there's a cool sensation in her stomach as they start to pump something in, and she closes her eyes again.

She is so, so, tired, she just wants to sleep.

———

The next time she wakes, she's in a different room. It isn't as bright as the previous place, with its blinding white florescent lights. This time, she's lying in a bed with a thin blanket drawn over her body up to her chest.

A soft sobbing sound alerts her that she isn't alone. She turns her head to the right; her parents are sitting on chairs beside her bed. Both of them are crying.

Her mother starts crying harder, then grabs her hand. "*Why? Why did you—*"

Hannah doesn't know where to start. Or what to say. She's so tired. She just wants to sleep. Her mother is gripping her hand so tightly that it hurts, so she pulls it away. "I'm sorry," she says, her voice raspy from a sore and bruised throat. Is that the right thing to say? Her eyes drift shut again.

This time it's her dad who speaks. "We just want to know why—"

"I'm really tired. Can we talk later?"

But her mother grabs her hand again. "No! We need to talk about this now."

Her mother is so agitated, Hannah knows she isn't going to leave her alone. She looks around desperately, locates the call button, and mashes it.

"If your mother hadn't woken up in the middle of the night, and decided to check on you in your room…" Her father's voice breaks off, and he actually *sobs*.

Hannah starts crying too. There's a part of her that feels terribly, horribly, bad for hurting them. But she's been disappointing them all her life, nothing new there. A bigger part of her is more upset that her attempt failed.

There's a knock on the door and a nurse enters.

"I'm very tired. Please tell them to leave," says Hannah.

"We're not leaving!" says her mother.

"I'm afraid you need to leave if the patient wants to rest," says the nurse firmly.

Scraping sounds as her parents stand up, pushing their chairs back. And then, mercifully, they leave.

Hannah closes her eyes again, and slides slowly back into the quiet dark.

The next time she opens her eyes, her mother is back again, this time with a young woman in a white coat, her flaxen hair pulled back in a ponytail. How long have they been standing at the foot of the bed, looking at her?

"Your father is stuck at work, but he'll be back this evening." Her mother's smile is too wide, too determined.

The woman smiles at Hannah, showing even teeth. "Good morning. I'm Doctor Lundgren. The good news is, despite the massive amount of diazepam that you ingested, your parents got you here in time for us to flush most of it out by gastric suction. We also administered flumazenil to counteract the respiratory depression..." Her voice drones on, and Hannah tunes it out until the doctor finishes, looking at her over the top of her glasses. "I don't know if you understand how lucky you are not to have died."

"Lucky me."

Dr. Lundgren frowns, her blond eyebrows knitting together. "Overdosing on a drug like diazepam is no joke. You're lucky because we acted in time, and also because you're young and a young body is more resilient, able to bounce back from an overdose that could kill an adult, or at least have caused massive organ failure, or brain damage."

"Is she going to be okay?" asks her mother.

"She appears to be stable for now, but—"

"Oh good, so she can come home with us now?"

Dr. Lundgren frowns again. "I'm afraid not. For cases like

this, we'll need to keep her here under psychiatric hold for at least another twenty-four hours."

"So she can be discharged tomorrow?"

"Yes, but on the condition that she speaks with a professional about her suicide attempt. The nurse will provide you with a few recommendations for therapists."

"I understand," says her mother quickly. "We'll arrange that. As long as she can be discharged tomorrow."

The hospital discharges Hannah the next day.

The car ride home is full of silence until twenty minutes from home when, stopped at a red light, her mother asks, "What do you want for lunch?"

"I don't know. Up to you," Hannah mumbles.

"We can get anything you want. You must be sick of all that hospital food."

"Whatever, Mom. A burger and fries."

They pull into a Culver's and her mom gets them two ButterBurgers, cheese curds, and frozen custards.

They drive the rest of the way back home in renewed silence.

"Why aren't you eating?" asks her mom.

Hannah tries taking a bite of her burger, but her stomach is clenching too badly for her to enjoy eating. Tomorrow is a school day. "Do I have to go back to school tomorrow?"

"I don't know," says her mom. "Maybe it's better if you don't go back to that school."

———

Hannah doesn't go back to Sierton High.

She waits for her parents to tell her she has to start going to therapy, but her parents never follow up on arranging counseling sessions with a therapist for her. Maybe they don't believe in the healing powers of therapy. Or maybe they just want to pretend that there's nothing wrong with her.

"The best thing for you is to start afresh somewhere else. A completely different school in a different city," says her father.

Her father applies for and gets a transfer to another office in another city, and they up and relocate.

A new city, a brand-new life, right?

They enroll Hannah in a new school, this one much bigger than Sierton High. It's somewhere she can get lost in, just another face among the thousands of faces there. Nobody there will know she tried to kill herself.

Her parents start acting as if it never happened.

"Hey, kid. You should join an extracurricular. It's a good way to make new friends!" says her father. "Just maybe not cheerleading."

"Maybe next year," says Hannah.

"Are you making any friends?" asks her mother.

"I'm trying."

She tries not to notice their disappointment, again.

———

The days pass as she goes through the motions of going to school, doing her assignments, eating, sleeping. But she can't seem to get out of whatever this is that she's sunk into.

First of all, she can't stop crying. Only in private, of course, in her room at night when her parents are sleeping.

She has no appetite. She only eats when she's at home, and even then, she barely touches her food.

But her parents don't seem to notice. Maybe they want so desperately for things to be back to normal, that they don't see whatever they don't want to see.

———

It gets harder and harder to get up in the mornings. Hannah feels exhausted all the time. If her mother doesn't make sure she wakes up, she just keeps right on sleeping. When she gets back home after school, she goes right back to bed and sleeps until her mother calls her down for dinner.

But when night falls, strangely enough, she isn't able to sleep. Many nights, she lies awake almost the entire night, listening to the sounds of the city below.

She can hear her parents talking about her at night when she's in bed, when they think she can't hear them (she can, because the walls here are thinner than the ones back in their old house in Sierton). They sound worried, but also irritated. What's wrong with her? Why can't she be more...normal, like other teens her age? Why does she have to be so difficult?

Hannah wants to be normal too, instead of this...this loser with no friends. This sad person. But she'd tried, and failed, and now she can't see the way out.

———

She doesn't know she's going to do it until the split second before she does it.

She's waiting to cross the road after school as she normally does, to the bus stop on the other side. The street is busy with traffic as usual at this time, with all the people rushing to get home from work. Hannah still finds the sheer amount of noise and activity surprising. It's so different from a small town like Sierton.

She isn't sure what makes her look up at that moment, at the truck as it rumbles toward her. It's white with some company logo on the side, just some unsuspecting delivery truck.

Just as it's about to pass where she stands, she steps off the curb in front of it.

Time seems to slow down at that moment.

The dull gleam of the chrome bumper.

The stink of exhaust fumes from the traffic.

The pale face of the man high up in the driver's seat, his mouth a comical O as he locks eyes with her.

The scream of the woman on the pavement opposite.

A loud metallic screech.

The bone-breaking pain as the front of the truck hits her. An explosion of lights behind her eyes. She's faintly aware of more people screaming. The world is turning red. Before she passes out, she's dimly conscious that it's because her eyes are full of blood.

Then finally, thankfully, no more of anything.

DAWN

I sneak glances at Maddy as I eat my cereal. Her eyes are red and slightly puffy, like she'd spent a good part of last night crying. She must have been fighting with Liam again.

I don't look much better than her anyway, with the dark circles under my eyes, because I'd spent most of the night coming up with my plan.

"Maddy, may I borrow your car this morning, please?"

Maddy is so surprised she drops her spoon back into her bowl of cereal, splashing milk onto the table. "Why do you need it for? I thought you hated driving?"

"I do, but I think it's time I got over that. I feel bad that you have to be my designated driver all the time."

"Oh...it's not that big a deal, really—" Maddy starts to protest, but the relief in her voice is clear: she's tired of it too.

"No, really, it's just… I want to get over my fear of driving. I was thinking that I could maybe practice driving a little this morning. And then maybe I could look into getting a little secondhand car for myself. I mean, if you trust me with your car."

"A little practice driving, huh?" Maddy considers it for a while, frowning. "Well, I'm not going anywhere this morning, so I guess you can practice with my car. When do you want it?"

"Umm, right now?"

"Okay."

I try not to let my surprise and elation show. That was easier than I thought it would be. I'm just starting to congratulate myself when she adds, "Just give me half an hour to finish my coffee and use the bathroom."

Shit. I think frantically. "Oh, you don't have to sit with me in the car. I can just practice driving by myself. I mean, I have my license. I just want to ease myself back into it. Besides, I want to take my time, and I don't want to bother you."

She frowns again, and I hold my breath. To my relief, she finally shrugs. "Okay, kid. Just…don't crash into anything, okay?"

"I won't. Thanks! I'll be back before lunch. And I'll make sure to top up the gas." I get up and hug her, then run upstairs and back to my room before she can change her mind or suspect that I'll be using her car for anything else.

Our family owns a log cabin by Lake Michigan, super charming with two levels and three bedrooms, a bathroom, and a fully equipped kitchen. I used to love going there with them every summer when I was younger.

I dig out the keys to the cabin from the envelope in my important documents file folder. I also make sure to bring my ATM card because I'll need money for supplies. Then I head back downstairs, grab Maddy's car keys from the mantelpiece, and head out.

I break into a cold sweat as soon as I get into the driver's seat. My mouth is dry, my hands slippery with sweat. I can hear my heart pounding in my ears. A wave of nausea hits me. I close my eyes and lean my head against the steering wheel. I need to pull myself together; I don't have time for panic attacks.

After a few minutes, the nausea subsides, and I turn on the ignition. My hand is shaking only slightly as I input the address into the GPS.

I take my time to reverse out of the driveway, then start down the road so slowly, if someone was watching me, they might think that I'm a geriatric driver with extremely bad eyesight. Luckily, Maddy's car is an automatic, so I don't have to bother with changing gears. By the time I get to the end of the street, I'm more or less okay.

Until I hit the first intersection where there are multiple moving cars. The edges of my vision go black, and it's like my heart seizes up. I breathe in ragged gasps. The car behind me honks. I wasn't aware that I'd hit the brakes. The light is green for me, so I take my foot off the brake and step on the accelerator.

Once I'm past the intersection, it's a little better. I follow the directions on the GPS until I arrive at Sierton County Jail, a dismal concrete lump of a building. If I don't look at the exterior too closely, it might be a particularly austere-looking school… except for the barbed wire running along the top of the high gray walls.

I park in the visitors' parking lot, flip down the sun visor, and check my reflection in the mirror. Run my fingers through my hair (funny how I'm still concerned with my appearance at this point). Check the time. It's 8:45. I'm right on time for my visitation at nine o'clock that I scheduled by appointment yesterday.

Inside, signing in, the ruddy-faced guard stares at my driver's license. At my face, then back down at my photo.

Heat floods my face. "It's an old photo. I know I look a bit different now."

Luckily, he doesn't ask me for a different piece of identification because I haven't thought to bring another one. He checks the form, stamps it. A russet-skinned guard with her hair cut in a severe bob gestures for me to follow her.

She leads me to the visiting area. "Number three," she says, pointing at a booth.

Two minutes later, Isaac walks in.

He looks the same, and yet somehow different already. His eyes are duller, as if some light in them has gone out, been extinguished in the last few days. There are dark bruises under his eyes, and his shoulders are slumped as he ambles over. But he smiles at me as he sits down on the other side of the glass. His smile cracks open something in my chest. I only have fifteen minutes with him. We lift the receivers almost at the same time.

"Well, this is a nice surprise," Isaac says. "Thank you for coming."

"Are you okay?" I say stupidly.

There's a little pause as he formulates his reply. "I've been better." He grins at me as if it's funny, but the smile doesn't reach his eyes. His brows furrow slightly as he tilts his head. "I didn't know you wore glasses."

"Yeah, I usually wear contacts." I shrug. "Can't cheer with glasses on."

He keeps staring at me. "It's funny, I could have sworn that your eyes were—"

I cut him off. "I just wanted to… I went to your house yesterday. I was worried when you didn't call me back. Or show up in school. I saw your mom. And your sister." The words tumble out of me in a rush, stumbling over each other.

"You met my mom and Gracie?"

Gracie. That's his sister's name. I can't believe I never asked before. "I'm sorry. I wasn't… I had to find out if you…"

"No, I understand."

We stare at each other. There are so many things I want to say to him. I want to touch him so badly. The seconds tick by; according to the clock on the wall behind him, we have twelve minutes left.

"So um…" Isaac scratches the side of his face. "What did you and my mom talk about?"

"Well, she, uh…asked me if I was your girlfriend," I mumble as my face grows hot.

His mouth twitches a little at the corner. "What did you say?"

"I don't remember," I say. Then, "No. I said no."

He gives me a little smile. "Probably best you don't have a murderer for a boyfriend."

"We both know you didn't do it."

Isaac sighs and rubs his eyes. "Other than my mom, you're probably the only other person who believes that right now."

"Your mom told me they've charged you with first-degree murder." The words feel poisonous; they leave a bitter taste even after they leave my mouth. "Do you think they've really got a strong enough case to convict you?"

"I don't know. The fact they caught me lying at the beginning…maybe?" He doesn't look at me as he talks. He looks more tired than ever, and for a moment, I glimpse the scared boy underneath the brave act he's putting on.

"You're not going to be convicted," I say.

"I wish I could be as confident as you."

"You didn't do it, and you're not going to take the fall for it. Don't worry. Everything will be fine."

I tried to keep my voice steady, but Isaac must have caught the odd tone that crept in because he throws me a startled look. "How are you so sure?"

I look down. I don't reply.

"Are you thinking of doing something?"

"I know who did it," I say. "I'll fix things."

"What? Who? What do you—"

"You won't take the fall for it," I say again and stand up, even though we have ten minutes left. Blink back the sting of tears.

"Dawn, what are you planning to do? Wait!"

"I'm sorry," I choke out. "I'm sorry. It will be fine." I turn and start walking to the door. The guard there opens it for me.

"Dawn!"

The door swings shut behind me, cutting off Isaac's voice.

I drive to my next destination, a small mini-mart not too far away.

It takes quite a few hours to get everything ready, and I'm thankful I headed out early. I even have time to stop at the parking lot at the grocery store a few streets away to clean off the mud and leaves from the wheels and bottom of the car before pulling back into Maddy's driveway just before one. Just in time for lunch, like I promised.

After lunch, I retreat back into my room and gather my thoughts, then I call Naomi.

"What do you want?" Naomi's voice is irritated but also surprised. I know she only answered because she's curious as to why I'm calling.

"Hi, Naomi. Can we meet up today? We need to talk."

"About what?"

"About how Ella died."

She laughs. "What's there to talk about? The police have who did it. Isaac Caldwell."

"They have the wrong person. It wasn't him."

"Whatever. Look, I know he was, like, your boyfriend or something, but this doesn't concern me—"

"But I'm almost certain I know who did it. Who killed Ella. And it isn't him."

She's quiet for a while. When she speaks again, her voice is high with curiosity. "Really? Who?"

"I need your help in filling in the last blank. We all know parts of it, bits and pieces. You, me, and Lucy. But none of us have been telling the entire truth. That's why we need to meet. All three of us. So I can piece together the final pieces."

"Why the hell should I—"

"Because I'm so close to figuring it out. Ella was your friend. Don't you want to know too?" Anxiety squeezes my chest as I struggle to keep my voice calm. She *has* to agree to meet me, otherwise everything falls apart.

"Actually, not particularly. Even if it's not Isaac Caldwell, like you say. I don't really care."

I can't believe her. *I don't really care?* I guess I have no choice but to pull out my last card.

"You know what else I know?"

"Hanging up now, Dawn."

"How you got Mr. Whitlock to change your grades for Physical Science."

The silence is so full of electricity, I can almost hear it crackle. When Naomi speaks again, her voice is tight, nervous, angry. "I have no idea what you're talking about."

"I have the photos. You thought you got rid of them, but Ella sent them to me before the pool party," I lie.

I can hear Naomi's sudden sharp intake of breath. "You're lying."

"I could send them to Raquel. After the way you humiliated her at your party, she'd love to broadcast them to the rest of the school. And the school board. And your parents."

"You *bitch*. Are you *threatening* me?"

"Look, I don't want to show them to anyone. Especially not the police, since you were a minor when you did it. I just want us to meet up and talk. I want to solve this case. Isaac didn't do it, and he doesn't deserve to be framed for it."

Naomi breathes in little pants. The silence stretches out for a full minute. Two. Finally, she growls, "Where the hell do you want to meet?"

"Somewhere quiet where we can talk without anyone overhearing us. I know the perfect place. I'll show you when you come to pick me up."

"You have got to be kidding me!"

"Sorry, I don't drive, remember? I'll text you my address and the time after I call Lucy, okay?"

"Fine," she snaps before hanging up on me.

I dial Lucy's number next. It rings and rings, but she doesn't pick up. I wait a few minutes, then try again, but she still doesn't answer. So I text her:

> Call me back unless you want the entire school to know how you were getting it on with Scott on the night your supposed best friend/his girlfriend was murdered.

Lucy calls me back less than ten seconds after I hit send. "Oh my god! What the hell is *wrong* with you?"

"We need to talk."

"Oh yeah? Well, I have no idea what you're talking about." Her voice is defiant.

"You and Scott hooked up after I left while Ella was passed out on that pool float, didn't you? It's why Scott didn't bring her into the house and why you didn't go home until one o'clock."

"Says you—"

"You've always wanted him back, and he was pissed off with Ella for cheating on him. It explains what you two were doing from midnight to one. Whose idea was it? Yours or his? Imagine what everyone in school will think when they hear about that."

I know I've hit the nail on the head when Lucy is silent for a long time. Then she actually shouts, "What is your problem?"

"I told you, we just need to talk," I say. I give her the same speech that I gave Naomi, then finish with, "Naomi is coming."

"She is?"

"Yeah." No need to tell Lucy I had to blackmail Naomi too for her to agree.

She's quiet again. Then, "You're not actually going to tell people at school about...about Scott and me."

"I don't want to. But I will if you don't help me figure this out and help Isaac."

"Fine! God, you're such a fucking pain in the ass!"

"Naomi's going to come pick me up, then we'll come get you, okay?"

"Whatever." Lucy hangs up on me.

My hands are so sweaty as I text Naomi my address that I almost drop my phone twice. She doesn't reply, but the status changes to read. Then I sit down at my desk to write a letter, and then another one.

It's not too late. I can still save him. And I know what I must do. I put my contacts in and head downstairs.

DAWN

"You're so lame, honestly," says Naomi as I climb in the passenger seat of her BMW. "Why don't you have your own car?" She's wearing expensive-looking leather booties with little heels. Those booties are going to be ruined.

"I have a fear of driving."

"A *fear of driving*? Why are you so dorky?"

"GPS says turn right up ahead to go to Lucy's house."

Naomi clicks her tongue. "I know." She stops at the red light and turns to look at me, smiling pleasantly. "You know, I'm going to get you for this."

"Sure. Whatever."

"You really like Isaac, don't you?"

I don't answer.

"I hope he likes you back, since you're burning your entire

social life at Sierton for him. Oh yeah, you're going to pay for this." Naomi tosses her hair and smiles as if she's already planning how to make me pay, and enjoying the thought of how I'm going to suffer when we go back to school tomorrow. We ride in silence for a while before she speaks again. "You have the photos on your phone? Since I'm here like you want, I want to see you delete them. Right now."

"Later."

"I don't think so—"

"After we talk and I have the information I need. And don't bother trying to take my phone to delete them. I have them backed up both in my email and in iCloud. Don't worry; I'll delete them in front of you afterward."

She glares at me, then accelerates with a jerk that has my head hitting the headrest.

Lucy is waiting on the curb outside her house, her face black like thunder. She climbs sullenly in the back. "I was supposed to go to the movies with Scott, you asshole. Where are we going anyway?"

"My aunt's cabin, it's just by Lake Michigan."

"*Lake Michigan?*" says Naomi.

"It's not that far, and we can talk there without anyone overhearing our conversation." I wave my phone at them. "I have it on Google Maps. We can drive right up to it."

I give directions to Naomi. Soon we're out of town and surrounded by pine trees on both sides of the road as we head into the forest.

The two of them complain almost the entire drive to the cabin.

"Forty minutes' drive, for fuck's sake," Naomi grumbles.

"Why do we have to come all the way here? Why can't we just talk, like, in your room?" asks Lucy.

"Because my aunt might overhear us. Besides, I don't want us to be interrupted until I find out exactly what happened that night."

Lucy sighs. "Are there at least drinks and snacks there?"

"Yes! I think there's milk and cocoa powder. Maybe some cookies." Lucy rolls her eyes, so I add, "And maybe some Bacardi Breezers. And bourbon." I knew that would appease her, and she goes back to texting on her phone, presumably to complain to Scott.

As we get gradually nearer to the cabin and the lake, fog rises up seemingly from the ground, growing thicker and thicker until it eventually swallows us up. Naomi flicks on her fog lights and slows down reluctantly to a less terrifying speed.

Lucy taps on her phone frustratedly. "Ugh, do you guys have any reception?"

"I don't *know*, Lucy. I'm *driving*," snaps Naomi.

"Reception can get really glitchy around here. It's even worse when there's a fog like this. Don't worry; there's a landline at the cabin if you need to make any calls," I say.

"Fine. Just great," says Lucy, dropping her phone back into her Louis Vuitton handbag and sighing theatrically again.

Eventually I lose the signal on my phone too, so I can't check the GPS anymore, but that's okay because I know the way. After all, we used to come up here all the time. "There's a fork in the road coming up soon… Slow down or you'll miss it… There! Turn right here."

The road starts climbing gently after the turn, curving up the hill in sometimes large bends, sometimes sharp ones.

"We can't see anything out there in this shitty fog," says Lucy. "Not even the road. Slow down, Naomi."

"I'm already super slow. Do you want to get there or not?"

"Yes, but in one piece."

"How much further?" asks Naomi, her patience obviously stretched paper thin.

"Just continue along this road for another ten minutes or so, and we'll be there," I say.

When we finally arrive at the top of the hill at four, Naomi and Lucy blink at the cabin. "Oh. It's not too bad," says Naomi.

"Were you imagining a horrible little cabin in the woods, like in some horror movie?" I ask.

Naomi glances sideways at me and rolls her eyes. "I still think we could have just stayed in town somewhere, but whatever. We're here now; let's get this over with so I can get back to civilization."

We step out of the car into the fog. It envelops us, clinging on to our exposed skin. It brushes my face, reaches down my neck with cold, wet fingers, and I shiver. Naomi shudders too and pulls her cashmere cardigan more tightly closed. As we trudge toward the front of the cabin, the naked white limbs of the paper birch trees and the dark straggly black walnut trees loom over us, shrouded in the mist, deformed and grotesque. Other than the little snap and crackle of twigs and pebbles crunching under our shoes, the place is completely silent. Almost as if it's holding its breath, waiting for something to happen.

By the time I fish the keys out of my pocket and unlock the door to let us in, we're all damp and shivering. But it's just as cold inside as it is outside, our breaths condensing in the still, slightly musty air in little white puffs.

"Is there a heater in this place?" asks Lucy, stamping her feet for warmth.

"No, but there's a fireplace. Look, get on that couch and wrap up with the blankets. I'll get us something to drink to warm us up, and then get a fire going."

They head to the large gray sectional couch, over which several wool blankets are draped, and I go into the kitchen. By the time I come back with a tray of three mugs of hot cocoa and a bottle of bourbon, the two of them are snug on the couch with blankets wrapped around them.

"No Bacardi Breezers, but I did find a bottle of bourbon."

Lucy's eyes light up as I pour a shot of bourbon into one of the mugs of cocoa. She takes it and takes a long sip, licks her lips, then grins. "Okay, maybe hot cocoa isn't such a bad idea."

Naomi smirks. "You only like it because of the bourbon."

"I'm just trying to warm up."

"Right," I agree. "Do you want a shot of bourbon in yours?" I ask Naomi.

She shrugs. "Why not?"

I pour a shot in each of the remaining mugs. As she takes one, I go over to the fireplace and crouch down in front of it.

"You know how to get a fire going?" asks Naomi, taking a sip of her cocoa. Then she grimaces. "This is a little bitter."

"Sorry. I couldn't find the sugar, so there's just cocoa powder and milk. And yeah, my dad showed me how when I was young. Let's see if I remember how to do it."

There's everything I need to make a fire, either neatly stacked beside the fireplace or placed on the mantel above it. I take a few logs from the basket on the left and put them into the fireplace, and then arrange a few thinner logs on top of those. Then I tear up a few pages of old newspapers for kindling and heap that on top of the logs. Finally, I grab the box of matches from the mantel and strike one, then light the kindling. I blow gently until more of the kindling catches fire. It takes some time, but eventually I manage to get a nice fire going.

"Impressive," says Naomi.

"It's not that hard."

"And cozy. If only I were here with Scott instead of you," says Lucy. She tosses back the last of her cocoa and puts the mug down on the coffee table impatiently. "Look, this impromptu little getaway is nice. But mostly weird. What the hell do you want to talk about?"

I take a deep breath. "Isaac didn't do it. The police have got the wrong—"

"You've said that already," Lucy cuts me off. Her eyes are gleaming, and her upper lip curls into a little sneer. "But I don't agree. I think he *did* do it. He crashed our party. He must have hidden himself somewhere and killed her after I left. Why did he go there, if not to kill her? He wasn't even invited."

"But he was. Naomi begged him to come," I say.

Lucy blinks, confused. "What? When? Why?"

"Do you want to tell her? Or should I?" I ask Naomi.

"I have no idea what you're talking about," she says coolly as she puts her empty mug down. "I didn't even know that he came down."

I cross my arms. "Come off it. I know you were the one who texted him. That's why you took Ella's phone. I saw you with it in her bathroom. You texted him, pretending to be her, and demanded that he come."

We glare at each other. Then she shrugs. "It was just a joke."

"Yes, a very funny joke. And the reason why Isaac is in jail right now," I say. "Makes me wonder if you planned the whole thing, then found a scapegoat for it."

"What?" she sputters. "That's ridiculous! Of course I didn't."

"Then why did you text him pretending to be Ella and beg him to come?"

"I told you, it was a fucking *joke*."

I cross my arms. "But you *really* wanted him to come. To the point where you pretended that Ella would kill herself if he didn't. You knew that would make him come, after the way his sister attempted suicide."

Naomi throws off her blanket and laughs angrily. "Are you seriously accusing me not only of killing Ella, but plotting to frame Isaac for it?"

"Did you?" asks Lucy, her brown eyes large in her face.

"No! God!" Naomi turns to Lucy. "I just wanted to put that bitch in a tight spot, watch her squirm and explain to Scott when Isaac showed up! It would have been funny!"

"Funny, like the way you engineered that little game on Halloween with Raquel?" I say softly.

Naomi sneers at me. "Yeah, exactly. That was *hilarious*."

Lucy giggles. "It was awesome. Do you know one of the videos has over a million views on TikTok right now?"

Naomi ignores her and continues as she stares at me. "Anyway how could I have killed Ella? I was the first to leave the pool, remember? When I left to go inside the house, she was still fine." She turns back to Lucy. "After Dawn left, it was just you and Scott with Ella. What the hell were you all doing?"

"Lucy and Scott hooked up," I say.

Lucy's face is now flushed pink. "That's...that's none of your business. And anyway, you have no proof."

"You slut," says Naomi with a little laugh. Then she gasps. "It was the two of you, wasn't it? The two of you poisoned her, then went off to fuck."

"What?" sputters Lucy, her eyes bulging almost out of her head.

"Oh, just admit it," says Naomi with a big yawn. "The two of you killed her, then you gave each other alibis. It's why you were so happy to pin it on Isaac Caldwell."

"That's ridiculous!" squeals Lucy.

As the two of them argue, I stand up quietly. I walk over to the front door and lock it. It's one of those old-fashioned locks that you lock with an actual key, even from the inside.

"What are you doing?" asks Lucy. She yawns, then looks surprised.

"Just realized I forgot to lock the door just now," I say as I pad back to the living room and stand in front of the fireplace. The fire roars gently in the fireplace, throwing light and shadow dancing around the room. It's warm in the cabin now, almost too hot. I hold my hands out to the fire. I wonder what the flames would feel like, licking my skin.

Naomi yawns again. "God, I'm so tired. Can we go now? Honestly, I don't care who killed Ella. She was such a bitch."

I turn back to face them as Lucy blinks stupidly and rubs her eyes. "Yeah, she deserved it, didn't she? Hey, you didn't drink your cocoa."

"It's okay; I'm not cold anymore," I say.

They stare at me, and I stare at them. "You sound different," says Naomi.

"Do I?"

"Your accent…it's changed."

"Ah. Yeah." I shrug again. "It's tiring to pretend all the time."

There's no avoiding it. No escape. I planned it from the

beginning, and it's only because I was so silly and naive that I started having second doubts, changed my mind.

It was because I met Isaac. *Revenge just isn't worth it*, he said, and I allowed myself to believe him. Started daydreaming that there could be another ending for me.

But now I know better. There can be no happy ending. People like me are too broken for happy endings. I should have stuck to the plan. I realize now that there was never any other choice. It's the only way to save Isaac. And I kind of owe it to him. It was my fault this all happened.

"That's not true," says my dad. "We told you, it wasn't your fault."

"You know whose fault it is," says my mom.

"Yes." I tell them. But… "Wait. How are you two here?"

"What? Who are you talking to?" says Lucy.

I stare at Lucy, then at my parents, who are right there beside us. "My parents. Don't you see them?"

Lucy's eyes are huge. "Uh. No."

Oh. I guess they're dead after all.

"It doesn't matter. Don't get distracted now," says my mom.

"You know what you have to do. Like we discussed. No more changing your mind now," says my dad.

"It's the only way to put things right," says my mom.

I guess I've always known I was going to do it. Perhaps I've already made up my mind, long ago, and have just been pretending to myself that I haven't.

But I know now for sure that I have no other option.

"Do it. Do it now," says my dad.

I turn around again and throw the key into the fire.

"Hey! What are you doing?" asks Lucy. Her voice is squeaky with shock and alarm, which makes me laugh a little.

Naomi gapes at me. "What are you laughing at? Did you just *throw the key in the fireplace?*"

"We don't need it anymore," I tell her, still giggling. "And you should care about who killed Ella. Because it was me."

HANNAH

Everything hurts.

Hannah opens her eyes to a plain white ceiling. Her eyes are gritty, and her tongue lies thick in her desert-dry mouth. She tries to swallow, and even that hurts. It feels like she's been sleeping for a long time.

The first thing she feels is surprise. Surprise that she's not dead, again. *Jesus.* It's getting ridiculous.

Surprise is swiftly followed by disappointment. Then anger, which leaks out of her in the form of hot tears. They're the first emotions she really feels in a while, piercing through the all-encompassing fog of nothing that has been her constant companion for the past few months.

She looks down. She's wrapped in bandages, her right leg raised in some kind of pulley thing. Her parents are standing near the foot of her bed, and a tired-looking gray-haired man with dark circles under his eyes and wearing a white coat is standing nearer beside her.

"I'm Doctor Singh. You just came out of a seven-hour operation on your leg and hip. How are you feeling, Hannah?"

Hannah swallows again. "Like I just got hit by a truck." Her voice comes out in a raspy croak.

Dr. Singh smiles, but her mother bursts into tears.

"Your condition is stable now, but you have some serious injuries. You have a concussion and skull fracture from when your head hit the windshield, and multiple bone fractures, including your collarbone, four ribs, your pelvis, and your right femur," says Dr. Singh, listing her injuries off the chart that he's carrying.

"Luckily, the driver reacted immediately and managed to brake enough so the impact wasn't as bad as it could have been. It's why you haven't suffered more horrific injuries, like a brain hemorrhage or other organ ruptures." Dr. Singh looks from his clipboard back up at her. "What happened to make you fall off the curb? Did you feel faint? Did somebody push against you?"

Hannah stares at him. "I…I tripped."

"When can she be discharged?" asks her mother.

"Oh, she'll need at least a week to recover from the operations, maybe two. Then she'll need daily physical therapy. She'll walk again, but it'll take some time. Luckily she's young, so she'll recover more quickly than other patients with these kinds of extensive injuries."

Hannah stares at the middle-aged woman in a white uniform—the tag on her chest reads TRACEY BROWN, PHYSICAL THERAPIST—who stands beside her bed, and the walker that she's brought with her.

"You want me to *walk*? But it's just been a *week*—"

Tracey Brown nods briskly. Everything about her is so brisk, so no nonsense, it's scary. "You have to do it. It'll help speed up recovery."

"But…but I can't!"

"You can and you will. Come on now, I'll help you up."

The PT practically drags Hannah out of bed, ignoring her feeble protests and cries of pain.

"Okay. Use the walker—put your hands here—and walk out of the room. We'll just need you to walk along the corridor for fifteen minutes. Come on, let's go."

Somehow, Hannah manages to limp and hobble her way out of the room, a monumental effort that leaves her soaked in sweat. The pain in her hip and legs is unbearable, her legs are shaking with every small faltering step, but Tracey Brown will not let her stop, no matter how she begs, how she tells the PT, tears rolling down her face, that she can't take one more step.

"It's necessary," insists her stolid-faced torturer.

When Hannah has hobbled enough to satisfy the woman, the PT helps her back into her room and into bed, announcing cheerfully before she leaves, "I'll leave the walker here. From now on, you should be able to use it when you have to go use the bathroom by yourself. See you again tomorrow."

"Tomorrow?" Hannah shakes her head. "I have to do that again tomorrow?"

"Yes, every day until you're discharged. And then you can continue your physical therapy at an outpatient center."

Hannah crumples under the weight of all those promised hours of future torment as Tracey Brown leaves the room, whistling cheerfully.

At least she has painkillers. Speaking of which, the nurse who is supposed to come give her her next dose is late. Gritting her teeth against the pain that flares up as she twists and reaches for the call button, she smashes it hard. Five minutes later, the nurse—a young curly-haired intern named Charlie—comes in and gives her the painkillers. They only give them to her one dose at a time, when it's time to take them. Charlie makes sure she swallows them, instead of squirreling them away somewhere, before leaving.

They also check on her constantly, as if she can somehow kill herself by strangling herself with her bedsheets or something.

Which is fair enough.

———

Another week later, Hannah is discharged in a wheelchair. But just as Dr. Singh and Tracey Brown warned, she has to go for physical therapy every day. She knows better than to complain, especially when her mother has to drive her to and from the therapist's office every day.

The first two times she goes, she's the only person there, but on her third visit, there's another girl sitting in the waiting room.

Hannah peeks at the other girl, who has her face in a book. She's petite with straight black hair and a small elfin face. It's easy to sneak looks at her, because she doesn't look up from her book— in fact she acts as if Hannah isn't even there. It doesn't matter. Hannah doesn't feel like making small talk with anyone anyway.

Still, she wonders what the other girl is there for.

Ten minutes later, a little hunched elderly woman shuffles out of the therapist's office with a walker, and the black-haired girl leaps up to help her. That must be her grandmother. The old woman must be the patient, and the girl just there to accompany and help her.

———

The next few times Hannah bumps into the black-haired girl in the waiting room, she still doesn't try to make any small talk with Hannah, or even eye contact. Unlike all the other people Hannah encounters in the waiting room who do, which makes Hannah so uncomfortable, she's started resorting to wearing headphones to pretend that she's listening to music, and keeping her eyes locked fixedly on either her phone screen or in the pages of a book. She doesn't want to make any small talk, doesn't want to talk about herself or tell people the cause of her injuries.

Is it possible that the black-haired girl is even more socially awkward than her? Hannah finds herself starting to become more and more curious about her.

It's only after another week or so that the black-haired girl lifts her eyes and gives Hannah a small nod when she enters, which Hannah returns shyly.

Another week later, the black-haired girl says in a soft voice, "Hi."

"Hi," Hannah replies, strangely pleased.

A few days later, the black-haired girl puts down her book when Hannah sits down. "I'm Chiyo," she says softly, almost apologetically.

"I'm Hannah."

"My grandmother had a stroke."

"Oh, I'm sorry. I was hit by a truck," Hannah volunteers.

Chiyo's eyes widen slightly, but to Hannah's relief, she doesn't ask for more details like many other people do. And thank god for that, because it would be too embarrassing and horrible to disclose that she'd stepped in front of said truck intentionally, and it was so uncomfortable the few times she's lied about it.

Chiyo says, "I'm a junior at Pacific Charter."

"Oh! That's just a few blocks down from my school."

Chiyo is a native, born and raised in California. She doesn't surf, but her brother does. She herself prefers to read and write;

she likes poetry in particular. And she too likes catching Pokémon in *Pokémon GO*.

Slowly, falteringly, the two girls become friends.

———

Something happens that Hannah isn't expecting. She isn't just recovering well physically; somewhere along the line, the dark cloud that has been hovering over her—choking her—has somehow vanished.

She starts coming out of herself. She has an appetite for food again, attacking her mother's cooking with relish, much to her parents' delight. Her parents approve of Chiyo and her brother, Taigen, who promises to teach Hannah to surf as soon as she recovers fully from her third surgery on her right leg, scheduled for the next week.

Hannah can't believe how stupid she has been, how many mistakes she has made in the past year. Thank god her suicide attempts didn't work. It's like waking up from a fevered dream. Why on earth did she care about what some stupid kids in school thought about her? She realizes now that their opinions don't matter, shouldn't matter.

She wonders how her parents have put up with her for so long; she has put them through so much of her bullshit.

No matter. She's stopping her self-pitying for good. She'll make full use of her fresh start in this place. Cherish her new friends and make some more.

She has woken up in time, and everything is going to be okay from now on.

———

Hannah's mother drives her to the hospital for her third and final surgery, this time to remove the pins that have been placed in her leg.

"Your dad and I will both be here tomorrow morning to come get you. I'm thinking we can go get waffles and ice cream, instead of whatever horrible breakfast they want to give you," says her mom.

"Waffles and ice cream sound great!"

She's still slightly nervous as they wheel her into the operating room, not as nervous as she was during the second round of operations, but still.

It's a different doctor operating on her this time, not Dr. Singh. This time it's a woman with tight brown curls and deep brown eyes. The light is too bright as usual. Hannah can't feel anything thanks to the regional anesthesia they use to numb her entire leg, but it's still disconcerting to hear all the sounds, feel the weird tugging as they work.

After what seems like an eternity, the doctor comes up by her face and smiles at her. "Everything went smoothly. Your leg has recovered very nicely. Now that the screws are all out, you should regain full use of your leg very soon."

"Thank you, Doctor."

"The nurses will take you back to your room. You should be able to be discharged in the morning as expected."

———————

The next morning, Hannah is sitting in bed in her hospital room, waiting for her parents to arrive, when her cell phone rings.

"Hey, kid," says her mom. "How did the operation go?"

"The doctor said everything went well. Are you and Dad on your way?"

"Yes, we are! Hope you're looking forward to the waffles and ice cream! See you soon."

"Thanks, Mom, see you."

The door opens just as Hannah hangs up, an attendant wheeling the breakfast cart into the room.

"Oh, I don't need breakfast, thanks. I'm going to be discharged soon. My parents and I are going to get breakfast together."

———————

An hour passes, then another.

When the cop comes, Hannah feels a jolt of fear. Is he here because she tried to kill herself? Have the police finally come to arrest her as soon as she was done with her final surgery? Is attempting suicide even a crime? She has no idea. She sits up nervously in the small, hard, plasticky bed as he comes up to stand

CINDY R. X. HE

just beside her. Why are hospital beds always so uncomfortable? Don't they *want* patients to get better?

The cop clears his throat. "Are you Hannah Smith?"

"Yes." She twists the thin hospital blanket in her fingers. "Am I in trouble?"

He blinks at her. "No, you're not in trouble."

Oh thank god. Attempting suicide is probably not a crime after all. Now that she's less tense, Hannah notices that the cop is young and rather cute, in a clean-cut kind of way. She's suddenly aware of how she must look, lying there with her tangled hair in this ugly hospital gown. She hasn't been able to change back into her jeans because her leg is still in a cast. She hopes that her mother has thought of bringing her a dress.

Oh, the cop is saying something to her, but she hasn't been paying attention and only catches the last few words: "…injuries were too extensive."

"I'm sorry, can you repeat that?" she asks.

He blanches, then takes a deep breath. "Your parents were in a car accident."

Hannah stares at him. What is he trying to tell her? Questions form and die in her throat.

The cop continues talking, his words coming out in a rush. "Their injuries were too extensive. They didn't survive the car crash. I'm sorry."

"No." She laughs, a short burst that trails hysterically upward. "You're kidding."

The cop shuffles his feet uneasily but remains silent. Hannah wants to shout at him. Why is he making such a sick joke? Her parents are fine. She's the one who tried to kill herself. Twice. Yet here she is, still alive, one hundred percent not dead. It isn't easy to die at all. Her parents can't be dead. They can't be. It's ridiculous. It's a bad joke.

"Get out." She's gasping, breathing too quickly. She can't breathe.

The cop takes a step backward toward the door. "I'll call for the nurse for you—"

"*Get OUT!*" she screams. She grabs the cup of water beside the bed and hurls it at him, then the TV remote. "*GET OUT! GET OUT!*"

He runs out of the room, almost stumbling over his feet.

In the end they have to sedate her. She sobs as two nurses hold her down while a third one injects something into her IV. When the dark comes to claim her, like an old friend, she's glad to sink into it.

———

The drunk driver, Tanner Wallace—a nineteen-year-old college student—ran a red light and plowed into the side of her parents' car. He and two friends had been drinking all night at a frat party when they decided to grab breakfast at a beachside café.

Neither Tanner nor his friends were wearing their seat belts, and his old car didn't crumple on impact like newer cars are built to do.

Tanner—who was the driver—died instantly when the steering wheel crushed his chest.

Daniel Hernandez—who was in the passenger seat—hurtled forward, his head thrusting through the windshield. If his neck hadn't snapped, killing him instantly, he would have died in another minute or so from the loss of blood due to the glass cutting his throat.

Charles Gallagher—"Chaz" to his frat-mates—who was sitting in the middle of the back seat, flew through the windshield and broke his back, and is now paralyzed for life.

———————

Two days later, Hannah is asked to formally identify her parents' bodies in the hospital morgue. The police liaison officer, the same officer who broke the news to her two days ago, takes her to a little room that looks just like a normal hospital waiting room.

"One side of his face is burnt badly," says the police officer in a low voice. Then he leads Hannah through another door into another room, one that is much colder, that smells like bleach and other chemicals.

Hannah sees them immediately, the two bodies lying face up on mortuary tables, sheets of white cloth covering them up to their necks. The left side of her father's face is a nightmare, the skin gone, nothing left but a mess of dark brown tissue and white bone. But that's nothing compared to the horror of her mother's body. Her face looks fine, but her body ends abruptly at the waist, the sheet draping it falling flat onto the table, showing obviously that the bottom half is missing.

"Can you identify the bodies?" he asks.

"Yes, it's them. My parents," she says calmly before turning and vomiting onto the floor, just missing his shoes.

HANNAH

It's decided that Hannah should live with her mother's sister and her family so she doesn't have to change schools again.

The next few weeks pass in a daze. It's like she's going through motions on autopilot. She doesn't answer any of Chiyo's texts either. Later, she won't be able to remember much of anything from those few weeks. The nights are the worst, when she's staring at the ceiling in the dark, alone with her thoughts.

This night, she has a knife, the sharpest one she could find from the kitchen. It's her fault, it's all her fault. They wouldn't have been in this city, would never have moved here, if she hadn't tried to kill herself. They wouldn't have been in their car at that intersection at that time.

She can't bear all her thoughts anymore. If she plunges this knife into her belly—no more fuckups, just take it with both hands and plunge it in—her thoughts will bleed out with the rest of her, quieted forever. She's the one who should have died, she's useless, and now she's gone and killed her parents—

"That's not true," says her mom. "It wasn't your fault."

Hannah jolts up, falls off her bed, the knife clanging on the floor. Her mom is sitting in a wheelchair beside her bed, looking kindly at her; her dad standing next to her mom, the burned half of his face already starting to heal over.

It can't be them. They're dead. *She saw their bodies*—

Then she understands.

She must have imagined the policeman. Been confused, thought for a moment that they died. But that was just silly, because here they are, obviously not dead. Her mom's lower body was crushed by the impact, so she is never going to walk again, but she's very much alive, and so is her dad. The relief that washes over her is so overwhelming, Hannah starts to laugh.

"It wasn't your fault, what happened," agrees her dad. They're both smiling at her, winking.

"No, it's those girls," says her mom. "Naomi, Lucy, and Ella. Especially Ella. If she hadn't picked on you like that, none of this would have happened."

"Yes," says Hannah. "They started it."

Her dad nods. "Ella was the one who started it all. And Lucy and Naomi are just as bad; they joined in, posted on that horrible Instagram account."

"Yes," says Hannah.

"Look what they did to us," says her mom.

"It's their fault," agrees Hannah.

"They have to pay. If you love us, you'll avenge us," says her dad.

"I'll avenge you," says Hannah.

She doesn't know how yet, but that's okay. She can wait. It'll come to her.

———

Hannah doesn't want to go back to school, but Aunt Vera informs her that while she's sorry such a tragic thing happened, Hannah still has to go back to school at some point. And that she's already registered her for the new school year. And that Hannah had better start studying now if she wants to catch up on everything that she's missed.

When Aunt Vera drops her off at school on her first day of the school year, Hannah contemplates very seriously for a few seconds just walking straight to the bus stop to take a bus back to the house. But Aunt Vera will be there, and she'll just take her back to school again. So Hannah clenches her jaw and walks into the building.

Almost at once, she sees a group of three girls who were in one of her classes last semester, milling in the hallway near the school entrance, and she flinches, anticipating the questions they'll throw at her. *Where have you been? Why haven't you been back in school for so long?*

Hannah flushes as one of them glances at her. To her relief, the other girl just looks away again, continues talking to the others. Hannah is relieved, but also a little puzzled. That girl was quite friendly with her just a few months ago. Oh well, it's for the best. And maybe she can make it through the day if everyone else just ignores her like this.

It isn't until after her first class, when another girl—who she's also been friendly with—asks if Hannah is new there, that she realizes that her schoolmates aren't being unfriendly. *They just don't recognize her*, maybe because of the weight that she's lost.

Apparently, some people look very different when they lose even a bit of weight. Just look at Adele. Or plain old Hannah Smith.

That's when the beginning of the idea comes to her.

———

Even though Hannah's parents didn't actually die, for some reason she inherited their entire estate—the new apartment, their small vacation lake house, an investment portfolio of stocks, and their bank savings. There are even life insurance payouts. Everything goes into an estate in Hannah's name and is overseen by Aunt Vera. Aunt Vera—who has three kids and works twelve-hour days on top of that—is all too happy to let Hannah have direct access to the account. She doesn't have time to manage it, and Hannah is almost eighteen after all.

A few months after she's back at school, Hannah has a rhinoplasty to change the shape of her nose. She tells Aunt Vera that she needs it to improve her breathing. Aunt Vera, who has breast implants, doesn't see why not. It's obvious that her aunt thinks that the poor child needs something to take her mind off things and help her feel better about herself. After all, nobody wants Hannah to try to kill herself a third time.

When Hannah wants to do her chin next, Aunt Vera just shrugs. The recovery time is even less than the rhinoplasty's. All it takes is a small silicone implant.

She's nervous after each procedure, but the majority of her schoolmates are all unfazed. Maybe people on the West Coast are used to little cosmetic improvements, or as they put it, *self-care*. Everybody wants to get better, look better, be better. In the land of extreme makeovers, nobody finds it strange that someone would change the way they look.

Hannah's face is quite transformed by the weight loss and these two small procedures. She looks so different, like a completely different person.

Hannah joins the cheerleading squad in her new school. Not because she cares about being popular—funny how she is now, when she doesn't care about it anymore—but because it's something to do to kill time, and because it helps her look as different from her former self as possible. She even takes up surfing, which gives her a tan (which she maintains with a self-tanner when she isn't surfing in winter).

Aunt Vera—just like everyone else—takes Hannah's changed appearance to mean she must be better inside too. That's good, because she *is* so much better now, better than she ever was before. Her parents understand her now, love her for how she is.

It's a small thing to change to colored contacts from her plain ones, and when she dyes her hair from brown to a honey blond—complete with "natural sun-lightened" highlights—her transformation is complete.

The next part of Hannah's plan takes a bit longer to put in place. First Aunt Vera is surprised, then bewildered, then hurt. Aunt Vera doesn't understand why she wants to go stay with her other aunt instead of her. Has she done something wrong? Hasn't she been a good aunt? Besides, what about all the friends she's made here?

Hannah has to reassure her that no, she hasn't done anything wrong, and yes, she's a good aunt, the *best* aunt. That's why she knows Aunt Vera would understand why Hannah wants to move back to Sierton. Aunt Vera has been so kind to take her in, but she doesn't want to keep sharing cousin Carrie's bedroom anymore. Besides, Santa Cruz is amazing, yes, but she's just so homesick for Sierton.

So the paperwork is done to transfer guardianship of her from Aunt Vera to Aunt Madison.

But before that, she persuades Aunt Vera to do one last thing—to get a court order so that she can change her name legally. She wants a brand-new start, and in order to do that, she needs a new name. Aunt Vera voices her misgivings, but Hannah tells her that if she doesn't let her, she'll do it herself when she turns eighteen in less than a year anyway. So Aunt Vera sighs, helps her change her name legally.

Hannah chooses a new name that signifies a new beginning.

She also changes her last name, of course, choosing one that—she explains to Aunt Vera—allows her to pay homage to this time in her life when her aunt took her in and cared for her, like a foster parent (that explanation works to mollify Aunt Vera somewhat).

The old Hannah Smith is gone. Resurrected into Dawn Foster.

"I don't know if I'll ever be able to get used to calling you that, kid," says Aunt Maddy when Dawn asks to be called by her new name from now on.

"Maybe you can just keep calling me kid like you always do," she suggests, and Maddy nods with relief.

Only the final stage of her plan is left. It will be the hardest to pull off, but she will do it. Her parents deserve to be avenged, for her dad's disfigurement and her mom's disability.

Ella Moore, Naomi Chen, and Lucy Aguilar may seem perfect, but they're monsters. And they will pay for what they started, what they caused to happen. They'll pay for destroying her family. Then, and only then, will they all be at peace.

And Ella, the most horrible one, will pay first.

WHAT HAPPENED AT 9:23 A.M.

At the mini-mart, I buy hot cocoa, milk, and a bottle of bourbon. Next, I stop at the gas station to top up the tank and get one last thing. Then I drive all the way here to the cabin. I haven't been here in a long time, and it's better to make sure that everything is okay, nothing broken, that kind of thing. I had to borrow Maddy's car, not just because I had so many places to go, so many pit stops to make, but most importantly because, while I could have taken an Uber to come up to the cabin, it would be near impossible to get one to drive all the way up here to fetch me back home.

The cabin is exactly as I last remembered it: warm cozy blankets on the couch, wood and newspapers prepared by the fireplace in case someone wants to make a fire, even down to the framed photos of my parents and me on the mantel. One was taken right here in this room—a selfie of the three of us huddled on the rug in front of the fireplace, blankets wrapped around our shoulders. That was one weekend in winter four years ago. We spent all morning outside, playing with our sleds on the little slope behind the cabin. I was a pain at first; I was almost fourteen and didn't want to *do lame stuff* with my parents. But my mom insisted, and in the end, even I had to admit that it was fun.

It's the same photo that I posted on Instagram, the one that they commented so cruelly on.

I take the three framed photos down and put them in my bag. Can't have Lucy and Naomi seeing them as soon as they come in.

Then I go into the kitchen, put what I've bought on the counter, and remove other things. Go upstairs, make sure the latches of all the windows are locked. They're just as I remember, the old-fashioned kind that you have to use an actual key to lock.

It's painful being here; too many memories are resurfacing. Before I leave, I take one last look, make sure everything is ready for what I have planned.

NOW: 4:42 P.M.

Naomi is staring at me, her eyes wide. "It was *you*."

"It was me," I agree.

"I don't understand… How?" asks Lucy. "You left the party early. And I googled strychnine too. Ella would have been convulsing ten minutes after being poisoned!"

"I gave her the drink with the rat poison in it just before leaving. I guess nobody was around to notice when it took effect. That's how I knew you and Scott left to hook up almost as soon as I left the pool area." I shake my head at her. "You didn't waste any time getting your hands on Scott, did you? I'd been counting on you all being too drunk to realize what was happening or to help her. But you exceeded my expectations, so thanks for that."

"You…you mean…"

"While you and Scott were busy getting it on, Ella was dying just outside. I'm sure I don't have to tell you how much she suffered; you must have read it when you googled strychnine poisoning. But maybe she was too drunk to feel all that pain. Just like she was too drunk to even notice that her boyfriend and her friend had snuck off to get it on as she was dying."

"Stop!" Lucy starts crying, her eyes leaking tears that run down her face. If I didn't know what a monster she was, if I didn't know that she was crying for herself and not what happened to Ella, I would feel sorry for her.

"So when we came out, and Scott carried her into the house…"

"She was probably still convulsing. Frankly, I was surprised that he didn't notice. He must have been really drunk," I say.

"We did notice," Lucy says in a horrified whisper. "We thought that she was having a tantrum as usual…fighting him because she didn't want the party to end. But…if it was you all along, why did you ask us so many questions? Why pretend that you wanted to figure it out?" She sinks back down onto the couch, then does another huge yawn.

Naomi stares at the last full mug of cocoa on the coffee table, then at me. Her eyelids droop, and she forces them open. Looks back at the mug of cocoa. Panic flashes on her face as comprehension dawns. "You put something in the drink," she says, her words slurring a little. "You used the bourbon to mask the taste. That's why you kept us talking for so long. *You were waiting for it to take effect*."

Lucy stares at her empty mug too. "Oh my god! What did you put in our drinks? Is it rat poison?"

"No, of course not," I say. "That would be boring, to do the same thing twice. Besides, only Ella deserved the rat poison."

"Then what?" Lucy's voice is high and shrill with panic.

"It's just doxepin. I have a prescription for them. I can't sleep without them. Don't worry; it's quite pleasant. I might have given you two enough to knock you guys out though."

There's a few seconds of silence, then Lucy leans over and sticks the index finger of her right hand into her throat, tries to retch.

"Oh, that's right; you've always been good at that. But that's not going to help you. It should be absorbed into your blood-stream by now," I say.

"What did you mean by *only Ella deserved the rat poison?*" asks Naomi.

I don't reply, only tilt my head at her. Naomi is smart; she'll figure it out. Sure enough, she doesn't disappoint.

"Because Ella told Hannah to kill herself by drinking rat poison," she says in a horrified whisper. Another minute of silence as her eyes get wider and wider. "It can't be. But it's *you.*"

"It's me." I turn my palms up and shrug, grinning. Whoops, you got me.

Lucy isn't as quick. "What? Who?" she asks, head rotating slowly, heavily, to look at first Naomi, then me. "What the hell are you guys talking about? Who the fuck are you?"

"Look carefully at her. Her nose and chin are different, and she's lost weight, but look at her eyes. Imagine if they were brown," Naomi whispers.

Lucy peers at me as I wait patiently. Her eyebrows knit together in frustration. "I still don't know what you're talking about. Who the fuck is she?"

"Christ! It's Hannah, Lucy!" Naomi sounds like she wants to throw something at Lucy's head.

Lucy gives a snort of disbelieving laughter. "Is this a joke?"

"It's not a joke," I say gently.

"But…you can't be her," says Lucy, shaking her head. Her large eyes are glued on my face. Realization and accompanying horror dawn in them, mixed with fascination. "You can't be her. She was such…"

"A loser?" I laugh. "Poor Hannah Smith. All she wanted was to fit in. Have friends. What a fucking idiot." I shrug. "She learned her lesson."

Lucy pulls out her phone from her bag and taps frantically at it.

"That's not going to do you any good. There's never any reception, no matter which network you're on. It's always been that way here."

Her eyes dart around the room, locate the old-fashioned corded phone mounted on the wall near the front door. She stumbles over to it, grabs the receiver, puts it to her ears. Drops it once she realizes there's no dial tone because I've cut the landline.

Naomi stands up. She's panting a little, her pupils dilated with fear. "I don't know what game you think you're playing, *Hannah*, but I'm leaving now."

"No one's leaving," I say, but Naomi goes over to the door and tries the handle anyway. When it won't open, she spins around and hisses at me, "Unlock this door right now."

"The key's in the fire." I shrug. "Go ahead and try to take it out, if you want."

She comes over, stopping as far away from me as possible, but just near enough to peer into the fireplace. Then she backs away quickly again. "There must be a second key!" She's breathing fast, her face red.

"There is! My aunt has it. But she's not here, sorry." I giggle.

I wait patiently as they look around the place, at the windows. They can look all they want. There's no means of escape. The windows are large, but they don't open. It's even foggier outside now, the mist a gray-white wall blotting out everything, including the sun.

"Don't make me break the windows," Naomi hisses. Her eyes are frantic now, darting around like a trapped animal.

"You won't be able to. They're made of polycarbonate. My dad was worried of burglars breaking and entering, so he had them custom-made."

"What do you want?" screams Lucy. Meanwhile, Naomi runs into the kitchen. If she's looking for a back door, she'll be disappointed. The front door is the only exit. Drawers clatter as she pulls them open one by one.

"If you're looking for knives, there aren't any there. I've removed all of them from the house," I say. "Well, almost all of them."

I pull out the long carving knife from under my shirt, where I've had it against my body, tucked inside my waistband.

Lucy gets up, sways a little, falls on her hands and knees on the floor in front of the couch. She gets up again and stumbles away from me, putting the couch between the two of us. I start walking slowly around the couch on the right—she stumbles to her right as well—and we both start circling the couch, like a fun dance. Out of the corner of my eye, I see Naomi creeping toward the stairs. I let her.

"Why are you doing this?" Lucy asks, her lower lip trembling.

"Because the three of you are horrible people." I frown. Surely she must know this already. "Ella was the worst of all, so she had to die first. But you two are just as bad. You torment other people, take delight in their pain. You're beautiful on the surface, but you're monsters inside."

"I'm not a monster!" Lucy cries.

"You start things that end with people being hurt. Me, my parents. Isaac's sister. Raquel. And that's only those that I know of. And now, Isaac too. You need to be stopped before you hurt other people," I explain.

"Don't blame them on me! And I didn't make you try to kill yourself! That was your decision, bitch! I don't even *know* what happened to your parents! And Isaac is in jail and is probably going to hang because *you* killed Ella! You're the real monster here! At least *I* never killed anyone!"

The words she spits out are the same ones that consumed me after the accident, tormenting my every waking hour. It was my fault my parents died. It was all my fault. My fault—

No. *No!* "You shut your fucking mouth!" I say. "The three of you started everything!"

"Do it now," says my mom.

"Shut her mouth forever," says my dad.

"I will," I say, gripping my knife tighter and advancing on Lucy.

"Who the fuck are you talking to?" she screams.

"My mom and dad. It's okay; I know you can't see them. They're dead," I explain.

"Oh my god, you're really crazy!" she says. Then she trips and stumbles on the floor again.

I raise my knife and lunge at her. She tries to roll to the side, but she's too slow—too clumsy—her athlete reflexes dulled by the large amount of doxepin that I've drugged her with. My blade nicks her arm, and she screams. I raise the knife again. It reflects the flame from the fireplace; the light gleams and dances along its blade. I made sure to sharpen it this morning. I advance on her again, and she scrambles backward, just dancing out of reach of my knife.

"Have you just been waiting all along to kill us?" Lucy cries.

Good question. I originally intended to kill the three of them one by one, like Mom and Dad wanted…but then I met Isaac, and doubts started to creep in. Maybe my parents were wrong. Maybe we shouldn't be dwelling on the past. Maybe revenge wasn't worth it. I finally decided not to continue with my plan, and to just throw suspicion off myself onto the rest of them for Ella's murder.

Isaac taking the fall for it changed everything.

It was then that I realized there's no hope for me. No happily ever after. Only revenge and death. But she doesn't need to know all that, so I ignore her question and just keep advancing on her.

"Wait!" she says, sobbing. "You're right. Ella was a bitch. But I'm not like her. I didn't want to pick on you. It was her! She made us do it. Actually I…I told her to stop."

"Did you?"

"Yes! I liked you. I told her to leave you alone."

I laugh. "I find that hard to believe."

"It's true! It was all her; she wouldn't let us stop. She *ordered* us to create those fake profiles, to post on that stupid account. You know what she was like. I wanted to be your friend." Lucy's large eyes, brimming with tears, stare at me. *Believe me!* they cry.

"She's lying!" hisses my mom.

"Don't fall for it!" says my dad.

"I'm sorry, Lucy, but I don't believe you," I say. "And anyway, even if I did, it's too late for all that now."

"Fuck you!" She snarls and lunges at me, tackles me like a goddamn linebacker. Maybe Scott showed her a few moves. I hit the floor hard on my back, dropping the knife. She goes for my face, hands clawing and scratching, sharp manicured nails drawing blood, trying to get my eyes.

I reach up. She's too groggy from the doxepin to realize what I'm trying to do, doesn't pull back or try to avoid my hands, and I manage to grab her neck. I start squeezing. She gasps, grabs at my hands, tries to tear them off. But she can't quite get a firm grasp, her hands are too slick with my blood, and I squeeze and squeeze, my arms and hands strong from all those hundreds of hours of cheerleading practice. She rolls to the side, pushes me, tries to kick me, but her blows are weak, and finally she slumps to the floor, stops moving. My hands are cramping, my muscles scream as I make myself let go.

I look around the floor, locate the knife.

"Now get the other one," says my mom.

MADISON

Madison finishes loading the dishwasher. She washes her hands, then stares out of the kitchen window, biting her right thumbnail. The sun is low in the horizon, the sky a kaleidoscope of orange, pink, and red. Mostly red, a vivid scarlet that reminds her of congealing blood. She shudders. She really needs to stop watching those murder shows on Netflix.

Hannah—she'd never get used to thinking of her by her new name—told her after lunch that she was going over to her friend Raquel's house to study together, that she'd be having dinner there, and that she'd probably be back around nine, but Madison can't shake the feeling that something isn't quite right.

First, her request to use her car this morning was already strange. But with everything that's happened, she didn't have the heart to say no. Even so, she worried the entire time Hannah was gone, her mind conjuring up images of Hannah driving the car on purpose into a tree or into the lake. After Hannah's previous attempts, and especially after her parents died in that horrible accident, Madison knows that this is always a possibility.

She tried talking Hannah into going for therapy, but the girl kept refusing, said she didn't need it. Kept insisting that she was fine, really. And she did seem fine, on the surface.

Only, Madison doesn't really believe her.

Like the way Hannah keeps talking to herself in her room. Madison knows some people do that, talk to themselves to work things out when they're thinking...but the first time she heard Hannah murmuring late at night in her room, it raised goose bumps on her skin. Especially when one time, she could have sworn she heard the girl saying *Mom*.

If that boy Isaac hadn't been arrested, she'd have suspected Hannah of making up today's study session in order to go see him. But he's in police custody, so it can't be that.

Madison sighs as she stares at her hands resting on the sides of the sink. Several times now she has almost started talking to Hannah, but she always stopped, unsure of how to go about it, or even where to start. For some reason, the girl got into her head that there was something wrong with the way she looked and never really seemed to have gotten over it. Madison was particularly worried when her niece lost all that weight and did all that plastic surgery. *Jesus*. She didn't need any of that, she was perfect the way she was, and the fact that she did all of that told Madison that there was something very wrong with Hannah's emotional and mental state.

But how to help her? Madison knows what teenagers can be like, can remember when she herself was that age. She remembers when the boy she had a crush on laughed at her and chased after her friend—the one with the long coltish legs—and how she internalized it, loathing her own body then, which she now knows is a perfectly fine body.

And that cheerleading thing. She should have tried harder to talk Hannah out of joining the squad again. It can't be healthy, being in such proximity every day with those girls. Hannah has never admitted it, but Madison has suspected for a while that those girls must have had something to do with why Hannah started being so depressed in her freshman year. But Hannah insisted that she needed to do this, needed to prove not only to herself, but also to everyone, that she had overcome her past. Hannah begged her to understand how much it meant to her, to see how much she loved cheerleading. So Madison didn't say any more.

But then that girl Ella died. Was *murdered*.

For days, Madison lay awake at night, gripped by the suspicion that Hannah was the one who did it, or that she maybe had something to do with it. *Her own niece.*

So when she had the opportunity to leave work early one day, she rushed home and snuck into Hannah's room before she had to go pick her up from cheer practice. To her relief, she found the notebook where Hannah had pieced together the exact timeline of everything that had happened that night, trying to work out who had done it. Which obviously meant that it hadn't been her. Madison felt a rush of relief, then shame for having suspected that her niece could possibly have anything to do with that girl's death.

So why is she feeling this overwhelming sense of unease now? She can't quite put her finger on it, but…maybe it's the new dark circles under Hannah's eyes after they arrested that boy, despite the girl's usual smiles.

Maybe she's just worrying too much, feeling guilty because she knows she should be keeping a closer eye on her niece or talking to her more. But it's hard to focus on her niece when she has so many problems of her own. She knows she needs to start looking for a new job soon; she won't be able to take her asshole boss's sexist comments very much longer without snapping. She's also pretty sure that she and Liam are heading for a breakup. He's been blowing hot and cold toward her for a few months now, ever since he got that new job. When she paid him a surprise visit at lunchtime two weeks ago, he walked out of his office lobby with a pretty red-haired colleague. He wasn't happy to see her. The saddest part of it was, it didn't surprise her at all. Deep down, she'd known that something was going on.

This guardianship thing isn't easy at all. Madison didn't ask for it, has never wanted children of her own. She can barely figure out this adulting thing herself, let alone be responsible for someone else. But she agreed because Hannah is almost eighteen after all, so very nearly an adult already. And Madison has always been fond of the girl.

She's probably worrying too much about nothing. She'll try harder from now on. Spend more time talking with the girl. Tell her how nothing that happens in high school matters, that all she needs to worry about is keeping her grades up. That ten years from now, what a few teenage girls think or say about her won't matter. That they'll probably be miserable themselves, trapped in loveless marriages with men who don't help out with housework, and who married them only for their looks, fading by the day.

Although, who is she to give any kind of advice anyway? It's not exactly like she's succeeding in life herself.

She picks up her phone, considers it, puts it back down on the kitchen counter. Hannah couldn't be anywhere else other than at Raquel's house, right? Madison doesn't want to call to check on her, to let Hannah think that she doesn't trust her. But...

She picks up her phone again. She could offer to come pick Hannah up, save Raquel's mom the trouble of giving her a ride home. Yes, that's a pretty good reason to call.

She dials Hannah's cell. It goes straight to voice mail. She tries again. Again, it goes straight to voice mail.

Why would Hannah have turned off her phone? Madison would feel irritated if she wasn't so worried.

Something is wrong.

Hannah leaves her no choice but to try calling Raquel. Thank god she insisted that Hannah give her Raquel's number before she left.

"Hello?" There are loud noises in the background...and an explosion?

"Hi, this is Madison, Han—Dawn's aunt. May I speak to her, please?"

"What? Hang on." The girl's voice becomes slightly muffled. "Hey, could we pause the movie? Thanks! Um, I don't know why you think Dawn's here?"

Madison feels cold all over. "She said she was going over to your place, to study together."

"Oh...um...she's not here."

Shit. "I see. Sorry for bothering you, but would you have any idea at all where she might be?"

"I'm sorry, I don't." The girl sounds worried. "Would you like me to call a few other of our friends and ask?"

"Yes, that would be great. Thank you."

Madison is about to end the call, but Raquel continues speaking. "Is everything okay? Is something wrong?"

"I... No. I hope not. Sorry, I have to go." Madison ends the call, resists the urge to slam her phone onto the counter. Starts pacing the kitchen.

Where the hell could Hannah have gone, and why did she have to lie about it? And turn off her phone?

Once again, images of Hannah driving into a tree or into the lake flash across her mind's eye. But her car is here, Hannah hasn't driven it to go out.

Madison runs upstairs to Hannah's room. It looks the same as usual. Nothing is missing. Not knowing what she's looking for, she starts opening everything: the door to the closet, the drawers of her study table, the drawer of her bedside table—which contains an envelope. On the front of the envelope is scrawled *To the Police* in Hannah's loopy handwriting.

Her heart suddenly beating so hard in her chest, she can feel its pulse in her head, Madison tears open the envelope with shaking hands. Reads the contents of the letter inside. Reads it again. Drops it.

Then she runs downstairs again, out of the house, and gets in her car.

DAWN

I saw Naomi sneaking upstairs, but I still check to make sure that she isn't somewhere here or in the kitchen. It's dead quiet in the cabin. She must be hiding, just like when she made us all play that Seek and Kill game on Halloween night.

How apt.

I feel oddly cheerful now that things are coming to an end soon. A tune comes to me, one that my dad used to often whistle when we were here, whenever he built the fire while my mom was busy in the kitchen, or as he waited for a fish to bite when he took me fishing down at the lake. I start whistling it, and my dad grins.

"I love that song," he says.

"I love you, and Mom," I tell him. It's so easy to get along with them now that they're dead. Dead Mom and Dead Dad are so wonderfully supportive.

I head upstairs. Just before I reach the top, I pause a moment to check that she isn't hiding somewhere there, waiting to surprise me, to push me down the stairs or hit me with something. I may be crazy, but I'm not stupid.

But she's nowhere in sight.

"Come out, come out, wherever you are," I sing. Naomi doesn't reply, of course.

I remember the way she hunted down Raquel that night. How she encouraged everyone else to scare the shit out of her with those knives. How they recorded her humiliation. I start whistling again as I walk down the corridor.

There are three rooms here upstairs, three closed doors. My parents' bedroom, which has an en suite bathroom; my bedroom; and another bathroom.

I try the first door, the one for the bathroom. It's empty. I check the bathtub just to make sure she isn't crouching inside.

The next door is the door to my bedroom. I try the doorknob. It's locked.

I smile. I didn't lock any of the rooms. This is almost too easy. I fish out the small set of keys for all the interior doors of the house, unlock the door. Open the door slightly. Step back and nudge it open the rest of the way with my foot.

I don't see Naomi anywhere in the room, so she's either under the bed or in the closet. The curtains have been ripped open; she must have tried the windows. Maybe she thought she could jump out of them to the ground below. Unfortunately for her, they've been locked since the last time my parents and I were here, something that I made sure to confirm this morning.

I can almost smell her fear.

Without being too near the bed, I bend to check under it. Nothing there except for a thick layer of dust. The closet, then.

As I approach the closet, there's the faintest sound of scuffling, like someone is scrambling away from the closet doors. I swing them open with a flourish. Crouched on the closet floor, Naomi stares up at me, her face pale.

"Found you," I say.

She screams. I don't know why, because it's not like anyone else can hear her. Then she holds her hands up. "No! Please. Please don't kill me. I don't want to die." She sucks in a breath, lets it out in a shuddering sob. "I won't say anything to anyone. Please, just let me go."

"Come on, Naomi. You know we're way past that point."

"There must be something you want! Money! I have lots of money!"

I laugh. This girl is funny. "I don't need or want your money."

"What is *wrong* with you? You think you're fucking *Carrie* or something? You'll never get away with this!"

"I don't intend to."

Naomi kicks out with her feet. The soles of her boots connect with my shins, and I fall forward, my face smashing against the floor. Stars burst behind my eyes, and it's a few seconds before I realize that I'm the one moaning. I open my eyes just in time to see Naomi's boot come down on my hand, the one holding the knife. I don't let go of it. She raises her foot again, wobbles slightly, and almost falls, slow and clumsy from the drug. I snatch my hand back and jump up, spit out blood. I must have bitten my tongue when my face hit the floor.

Naomi lunges at me again, but this time I sidestep her attempted punch easily. She's off-balance and bangs her hip against the corner of my old table, falls. She scrambles back up as I advance on her and runs out of the room.

I'm impressed. She's moving fast for someone who has all that doxepin in her system. But I don't have to worry; there's nowhere for her to run to, no way to escape.

As I step back out into the corridor, the door to my parents' room slams shut, and there's a small click as she presses the push lock on the doorknob. That buys her a few seconds at best as I look for the key to open that door. But maybe she's used those few seconds well. Maybe she's found something that she can use to attack me with, and she's waiting on the other side right now for me to open the door.

I unlock it, turn the doorknob. Open the door slightly, then step back. Use the same technique as when I opened my bedroom door, nudging the door open the rest of the way with my foot from a distance.

Once again, the curtains are torn apart, so she's tried the windows. And again, she's nowhere to be seen in the room. But this time, I know immediately where she's gone because the door to my parents' adjoining bathroom is closed, and I left it open this morning.

As I turn the handle of the bathroom door—it's locked of course—muffled snatches of words reach me.

"Help…trying to kill…cabin… I don't know the address…"

The bitch must have had her phone in her jeans pocket, and she's managed to get some reception on it.

There's no time to waste. I find the key and unlock the bathroom door, try to open it. It budges a little, slams shut again. She's leaning on it, preventing me from opening it.

"It's by Lake Michigan! It belongs to—"

I put all my weight into it and force the door open, pushing Naomi aside. Her legs hit the edge of the bathtub, and she falls in, knocking her head on the side of the tub. She stops moving. I look at her crumpled body in the tub warily. A small trickle of blood is starting to seep down the side of her head where she hit it against the tub.

"You know what to do next," says my dad.

I'm tired now, all the adrenaline spent. My limbs feel like they weigh a hundred tons. I want to lie down and sleep, but I can't. Because my dad is right; there's one final thing left to do.

I head back downstairs to the kitchen, find the last item that I bought this morning. I take the small tank of gasoline from under the sink, unscrew the cap, and splash the contents liberally. On the kitchen counters, the curtains, the couch, the blankets, the parquet floor. The gas fumes sting my eyes and make me cough. I head back upstairs, splashing as I go. Pour the gas liberally in every room upstairs.

When the tank is empty, I go back downstairs for the box of matches on the mantel. There's only one match left. My hands are shaking. I try to strike the match, but it breaks in half. No matter. I take a fresh stick from the pile of kindling and stick one end of it in the fireplace. I don't mind that the heat from the fire is too much on my skin. It gives me a teaser of what it's going to be like. The stick starts burning, and I drop it on one of the blankets on the couch. The gasoline-soaked fabric catches fire immediately, with a little audible *poof.*

I head back upstairs to my old room and lie on the bed, on top of the bedcover.

I wonder how long it'll take for Maddy to start worrying when I don't come home tonight. I push away the guilt that rises up. I'll be out of her hair soon enough, then she won't have to worry about me anymore.

My mom and dad lie down beside me, hold my hands.

"You did well," says my dad.

"We're proud of you," says my mom.

A tear leaks out of my eyes, then another. "But…why don't I feel like I've fixed anything?"

If I thought they'd answer me, I'm disappointed, because they're silent this time. In fact, my hands are empty. They're not beside me anymore.

But it's okay. It doesn't matter that they're not here. Because soon, I'll be with them.

TO THE POLICE

I'm Dawn Foster, but before I changed my name, I was Hannah Smith.

I'm the one who put rat poison in Ella Moore's drink and killed her.

She deserved it.

Here are the details so there can be no doubt:

On the 6th of October, I bought a 1 lb bottle of Mart'n's Gopher Bait 50 from Lawn & Pest Solutions, along with a pair of green rubber gloves and a 3M particulate face mask. They cost a total of $22.32, which I paid for in cash. I had my hair up in a ponytail with a cap and my glasses.

I added the pesticide to the last drink that she drank, the vodka cranberry which I mixed for her at 11:34 p.m. Nobody saw me add it, they were all too drunk or self-absorbed.

I buried the bottle of pesticide that night in our backyard. It should still be there if you go look for it.

Nobody else was in on it. You charged an innocent person with first-degree homicide. You should be ashamed.

In case you can't identify the other two bodies in the cabin, they're Luciana Aguilar and Naomi Chen.

They also deserved it.

MADISON

Ten minutes into the drive, Madison realizes she should probably call the police, tell them about the letter she found and the cabin it mentions. It can only be the one by the lake. There's no time to stop to make the call; she puts them on the car speaker.

She babbles, frantic, her words stumbling over themselves. It takes at least a good three or four minutes before she manages to explain enough for the officer to understand what she's saying, to give Luciana's and Naomi's full names so that the police can check on them.

After hanging up, she continues driving as quickly as she can, at moments flooring the accelerator. There's a chance she might get there before the police, might be able to stop whatever Hannah is planning to do. She can only pray that she's not too late.

As she heads into the forest and a maddening fog, however,

Madison is forced to slow down. Then she's forced to slow down even more, practically to a crawl, as the road starts twisting and curving up the hill in the fog. She doesn't dare to go any faster, even though her mind is screaming.

The notebook. Hannah was just trying to figure out who else might have had the opportunity and motive, so she could throw suspicion onto them for that girl's murder. *Jesus Christ.*

The words Hannah wrote in the letter keep replaying in her head. How did she let things get to this point? She has failed Hannah. Failed her brother. She forgot what it was like to be a teenager, how everything that adults, with experience and hindsight, recognize as trivial, can seem insurmountable to a teen. Like the end of the world.

She rubs away the tears blurring her vision with the back of her left hand. If she manages to stop this, she'll tell Hannah that it isn't the end of the world. Hannah is still a minor; surely they won't sentence her to life in prison. They'll find a way to fix things. *Please, God, let me get there in time.*

The fog is starting to thin now, as she climbs the last hill up to the cabin. It comes into view as her car rounds the last bend. There's another car parked out front, a BMW. Madison doesn't recognize it. It must belong to one of the other girls. They are in there for sure.

At first glance the cabin looks fine, nothing out of the ordinary. Then Madison's heart stutters. Something is wrong, but what? At first, she can't figure out what's wrong with what she's seeing...but as she's opening her car door, she realizes what it is. She can't see through the full glass windows into the cabin, because the cabin is full of thick gray smoke.

"No!" Madison runs up to the front door, fumbles for her key. When she manages to unlock the door and throw it open, the heat from the fire almost knocks her off her feet. The acrid stench of smoke assaults her nostrils, her lungs. She didn't know how *loud* a fire could be, how angry it could sound.

Maybe it isn't too late. Maybe Hannah and the other girls are still alive in here, somewhere, somehow. Sirens, the sound of a car engine approaching, as she takes a few steps further in... There! A girl with dark hair is lying on the floor. Madison runs up to her, shakes her, but the girl doesn't wake up.

Then Madison is being pulled away, back to the front door. All around her are firefighters.

"Ma'am, you need to come with me!" He has her by her arms, is pulling her toward the front door. They've got the girl too; someone is shouting, *She's still alive!*

"My niece! My niece is in here! Help her!" she screams, and she sees two firefighters running up the stairs just before the one holding her pulls her out of the creaking, roaring house.

ONE YEAR LATER

It's been ten months since they locked me in here. Ten months of beige walls and furniture, and the ever-present scent of eucalyptus disinfectant is enough to drive anyone crazy. If we weren't already insane, of course. Ha ha.

Because I was close to being eighteen, they decided to try me as an adult for Ella's murder, and the attempted murders of Lucy and Naomi. But in the end, I was found not guilty by reason of insanity. According to my court-ordered psychiatric evaluation, I had a "psychotic break related to an onset of schizophrenia" when my parents died. So instead of a life sentence in prison, I've been committed to a state psychiatric hospital for the foreseeable future, where I can finally "get the psychiatric help that I need," and where I "won't be a danger to anyone anymore." Including myself, I suppose.

Maddy comes to see me sometimes, on the weekend. It's almost an hour's drive from Sierton to Milwaukee County Mental Health, so I get why she doesn't come more often. Also, I think it's difficult for her to look at me, see what I am now.

She tells me that if I try very hard to get better, they might let me out one day. For now, I have all the time in the world to contemplate all the bad decisions I've ever made, which is what they want. The other day, I…

I've lost my train of thought. It's the meds. They make me dizzy and confused. And gain weight. All that hard-earned weight loss, gone to shit. And they made my parents disappear, which was really upsetting. But it's okay. I've figured out how to manage the meds, and I hardly get dizzy anymore.

My individual sessions with Dr. Harper are every Tuesday, after breakfast. We covered the heavy stuff the first few months. Why I did what I did, what I feel about it, if I understood the consequences of my actions, blah blah blah. She told me that the accident and my parents' deaths were nobody's fault. Not Ella's, Lucy's, or Naomi's, not even mine. Now, she mostly just checks in on me. How am I doing? (*Much better, thank you.*) Do I still see or hear things that aren't really there? (*No.*) Do I ever feel like hurting myself? (*Not anymore.*) How do I feel about Naomi and Lucy now? (*I hope they're better and that they forgive me.*) We also talk about my regrets. For example, killing Ella. I tell Dr. Harper that I feel horrible about what I did. That I know now that Ella was a deeply unhappy person too. That I made a terrible mistake.

I tell Dr. Harper everything she wants to hear. It's obvious that she's pleased with my progress.

Today is a special day. Raquel is visiting me for the first time. I'm waiting in the visiting room, sitting at a round table with four chairs, the light streaming in from the large window all along one side of the room.

Here she is. The guard escorts her in. Her head swivels around, eyes wide, taking everything in. She's carrying a bouquet of flowers—cheery yellow sunflowers, orange lilies, and red daisies—which I assume security has already checked.

It takes her a few seconds to recognize me, and she does a double take, which she then immediately tries to hide. I know why. With my hair grown out and brown once again—and my bloated face—the last time I looked in a mirror, it was Hannah Smith who stared back out at me.

Raquel puts the flowers on the table. There are a few seconds of awkward silence, then she's the first to speak. "How are you?"

"Never been better. Thank you for coming to see me."

"I meant to come earlier," she says, "but…I've just been so busy, you know, with everything going on in school, and then graduation, then college, you know." She fidgets in her seat. "Seriously though, how are you?"

"I'm fine. I've made some friends here, in the locked unit." Raquel looks at me doubtfully, but just then a petite girl walks past the window in the corridor outside the visiting room. I catch her eyes and she smiles back at me. "That's Jen; she was the first one to talk to me."

"She looks so nor…like she's our age," says Raquel.

"Yeah, she's twenty."

"Why is she here?"

"She's a diagnosed sociopath. She stabbed a classmate in the eye with her pencil when he tripped her on purpose in class."

Raquel ogles at me. How to explain that Jen is cool? And rosy-cheeked, dimpled Annabelle. Her father started raping her when she was twelve, and it went on until she was fifteen, when her other personality, Ivy, took over and killed him. And Helen, beautiful like the mythological Helen of Troy. And a pathological liar and kleptomaniac. I like them all very much. With them, I feel comfortable in a way that I've never felt before. Like I can finally be myself, instead of pretending to be someone else.

"How are you doing?" I ask her.

"I'm majoring in business at UW-Milwaukee. Um, Isaac is going to UW-Milwaukee too. He works part-time as a bartender at the bar on campus."

I feel a not-small twinge. Everyone is growing up, moving on. Everyone but me.

I wonder if Isaac will ever come and visit me.

The thought makes my chest constrict, and I push it away before it can hurt me further. I grasp for something, anything to change the subject. "How are Naomi and Lucy?" I thought I killed them, but Lucy actually passed out from the lack of oxygen when I was choking her, and Naomi was knocked unconscious when her head hit the side of the tub. Perhaps they slipped into unconsciousness so easily because of all that doxepin. Thanks to Maddy finding my letter, the fire department got to the cabin and got all of us out in time, before we died from smoke inhalation or were consumed by the fire.

"They're fine," says Raquel. "They recovered fully." She squirms a little...and then she spills all. "The school board fired Whitlock after *somebody* sent photos of him in a compromising position to Principal King's email, with the general email of the school board in CC."

I grin. "You did that?"

She grins back. "Last I heard, Whitlock was being questioned by the police for having sex with a minor. And they failed Naomi in Physical Science."

Good old Raquel. "So she didn't get into Harvard like she wanted?"

"Nope, she's at Wisconsin Lutheran College." Raquel shrugs. "Maybe her parents think they can keep a better eye on her there."

Eep. Naomi must be mortified to have ended up at "some community college," as she so derisively called them when she was teasing Lucy.

"Lucy and Scott were luckier," continues Raquel. "They got in trouble for making false statements to the police, but in the end the police just let them off with stern warnings. They broke up shortly after. I heard Lucy didn't go to college. Apparently she's an influencer and engaged to some hedge fund guy now. Anyway, did you hear? Sierton High started implementing antibullying initiatives, including training for staff, programs for students, and counseling services."

"That's great."

"Are you…are you feeling better?" she asks tentatively.

I give her a small smile. "I am. Thanks for coming." *Even though you were probably afraid of me.* "It was really nice to see you. And thanks for the flowers."

After Raquel leaves, I stop by the nurses' station for my meds. The attending nurse gives them to me in a small cup, and another cup of water. I empty the pills in my hand, make a show of putting them in my mouth, hand the empty cup back to the nurse. Then I take a big gulp of water, tilt my head back, swallow. Open my mouth and show her that I've swallowed all my meds.

When I'm in the bathroom stall, I remove the pills that I've stowed between the waistband of my pants and my back while she was watching me drink the water, the ones that I never put in my mouth at all. A sleight of hand that I've been practicing in my room, palming small objects like a magician at a children's party. I pee, then throw the pills in the toilet, wipe, and flush.

I locate Jen and Annabelle in the dayroom. They're watching a rerun of *Buffy the Vampire Slayer*, and I sit down and join them.

They like when we spend our free time getting along with other people in the dayroom instead of withdrawing to our own rooms. It shows that our rehabilitation is going well.

Mom and Dad are watching the show too, but I don't give any indication that I see them of course.

They're always watching me, and I can't have them know that my parents are back.

Once you check in here, it's hard to check out. Hard, but not *impossible.*

Dr. Harper is pleased with my ostensible progress, and she's deeply sympathetic about my parents' deaths. She's shared with me that in her professional opinion, I'm no longer dangerous as a result of my mental illness. My case review is scheduled for next week. Next week, she will be recommending me for discharge.

But even if they don't, there's always next year. And the year after that.

I lock eyes with my mom and dad. They smile at me. They're patient. They know that I won't let them down.

Naomi and Lucy were lucky they didn't die one year ago. But I've got a better plan now. The story will be finished, one way or another.

And everyone will get the ending that they deserve.

AUTHOR'S NOTE

When I was sixteen, after half a year of being bullied in school by a teacher, I attempted to kill myself. Even though the conversation surrounding mental health and suicide has improved, that is still hard to write—even now, I still feel shame—due to the continuing stigma of suicide.

According to the CDC, suicide is the second-leading cause of death for teens and young adults, ages 10–34. More than one in three high school students, and nearly half of female students reported persistent feelings of sadness or hopelessness in 2019.

If you are having suicidal thoughts, your pain will feel overwhelming and permanent. Please know that it is not, and that you are not alone. Your situation may feel hopeless right now, but there are people in your life who care about you and want you to be here. Please reach out for help. For free and confidential emotional support in the U.S., text or call 988 or use the chat function at 988lifeline.org. If there is an immediate danger of harm, call 911 and explain that you need support for a mental health crisis.

ACKNOWLEDGMENTS

This book was a team effort.

Thank you to:

My editor, Annie Berger, whose smart, thoughtful edits shaped this book into the best version that it could be. Your suggestions helped the reveal to hit that much harder. Thank you for loving and championing this story. Huge thanks to the team: Gabbi Calabrese, Aimee Alker, Thea Voutiritsas, Teddy Turner, Deve McLemore, Tara Jaggers, Michelle Lecumberry, Rebecca Atkinson, Stephanie Gafron, Stephanie Rocha, and Karen Masnica for all your hard work. It's been a privilege to know and work with you. Natalie Sousa, for the stunning cover. I can't imagine a more perfect home for this book than Sourcebooks Fire.

Librarians, booksellers, booktokkers, bookstagrammers, and early readers, who have found a place for this book in your hearts. I'm so grateful for your support and enthusiasm for this story.

My CPs and beta readers: DJ John, Eleanor Orebi Gann, and Ambrielle Butler, who read the terrible first draft. Fanny Morraglia, who read it in one day and then asked me what was wrong with me. Daniel Radford, Mary Kate Pagano, and Jaq Evans, who emergency read it in one day. Lauren Brown, who helped me figure out what was (and more importantly, what wasn't) working. Eagle-eyed Monika Kim.

My Discord friends: Christina, Taylor, Paula, Janice, Lex, Colleen, Adrienne, Christina F, Melissa, Jamie, Holly, Jamie F, Svani, Ana, Poppi, Ande, Meg, Laura, Jess, Paul, Marina, Nora, Mary, Sara, Adi, Leilani, Erin, Raidah, CJ, Sher, Keshe, Frances, Jo, Kelly, Sierra, Hien, Penny. Writing is a lonely endeavor; you guys made it less lonely. Bethany, Megan, Faye, Bea, Marley, and Ashley. What a team we make! Tess, Keely, Dahlia, Sophie, Charlee, Rosiee, Emily, Marieke, Gigi, Helen, Nicole, Diana, Lillie, Livia, Becca, Eva, Rebecca, Miel, Ana, Jess. Thank you for all your great advice and support, especially when you-know-what happened. Thank you all so much for being there.

My dad, who passed away two weeks before I got my book deal. Thank you for telling me that you're proud of me.

Amelia, Elizabeth, Beatrix, and Greg. I love you.

ABOUT THE AUTHOR

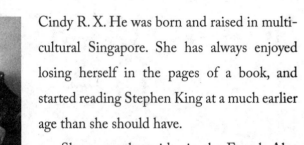 Cindy R. X. He was born and raised in multi-cultural Singapore. She has always enjoyed losing herself in the pages of a book, and started reading Stephen King at a much earlier age than she should have.

She currently resides in the French Alps with her husband, children, and rescue cat. She skis in the winter, gets dragged on hikes in the summer, and hoards books all year round. Her pet peeve is people who borrow but don't return books. You can find her on Instagram @cindyrxhe.

sourcebooks fire

Home of the hottest trends in YA!

Visit us online and
sign up for our newsletter at
FIREreads.com

....

Follow
@sourcebooksfire
online